MERCY

LARA SANTORO was born in Rome and educated in the US and France. A veteran journalist who has worked for the *Christian Science Monitor* and *Newsweek*, Santoro has travelled extensively, covering wars, famines, and the AIDS epidemic. She divides her time between Rancho de Taos, New Mexico, and Boston, Massachusetts. This is her first novel.

From the international reviews of *Mercy*:

'The world is a beautiful and broken place and Lara Santoro is an amazing new voice. *Mercy* is a fabulous novel.' Alice Sebold

'Santoro's experience as a journalist is evident in her straightforward prose and this debut is a notable tale of contemporary forms of suffering and relationships.' *Booklist*

'Santoro's style is laconic and laid-back, but she knows her subject intimately . . . *Mercy* is full of human drama – the very stuff of Hollywood movies. Yet at its heart is a real passion for Africa and its people. It is this passion which makes Lara Santoro's novel so memorable.' *Mslexia*

‘Africa – anguished, impoverished, monstrously beautiful – takes the measure of every novelist daring enough to confront its mysteries. Lara Santoro’s *Mercy* swirls around a self-immolating Italian-born journalist named Anna, the two wildly attractive men she attracts and deflects, and her self-appointed housekeeper, a force of nature named Mercy. The urgent message of this gorgeously written novel, which deals head-on with the ravages of AIDS on a continent of grief: Open your eyes and look hard.’ *Oprah Magazine*

‘*Mercy* is admirably understated, and Santoro keeps the story at a quick clip while allowing Anna to develop convincingly. The writing is exacting and effective.’ *Washington City Paper*

MERCY

A Novel

LARA SANTORO

Portobello
BOOKS

First published by Portobello Books Ltd 2007
This paperback edition published in 2008

Portobello Books Ltd
Twelve Addison Avenue
Holland Park
London W11 4QR, UK

First published in the United States by Other Press in 2007

This is a work of fiction. The characters, incidents, and dialogues are products of the author's imagination and not to be construed as real. The author's use of names of actual persons, living or dead, and actual places is incidental to the purposes of the plot and is not intended to change the entirely fictional character of the work.

A CIP catalogue record is available from the British Library

9 8 7 6 5 4 3 2 1

ISBN 978 1 84627 107 6

www.portobellobooks.com

Designed by Kaoru Tamura

Offset in 11.5pt Sabon by Avon DataSet Ltd, Bidford on Avon, Warwickshire

Printed in the UK by CPI Bookmarque, Croydon, CR0 4TD

FSC
Mixed Sources
Product group from well-managed forests and other controlled sources
www.fsc.org Cert no. TT-COC-002227
© 1996 Forest Stewardship Council

To my mother and father

Show me a place as full of God as this. Show me land gathered at the seams by thorns as thick. Show me rivers as full of light, of tumult. Show me life as cheap, song as full.

*

"*Mini na wewe* ..." Mercy sang in the kitchen, her vast behind keeping stroke.

*

"Why the journalists they come to Africa?" she asks, "To see the people dying?"

"Don't be ridiculous," I mutter, flicking through the daily paper, mentally adding up the dead.

*

"We don't do massacres," my editor warned but what else was there to do? I became a chronicler of pain, the dead stacking up in the mortuary of my mind unburied. "Give us the ray of light in the dark," my editor said but there was no light to speak of. The longer I stayed, the angrier I became, until—with the mute coherence of all seismic events—Africa unshackled itself from my perception and brought me proof of light beyond light.

I

"YOU'LL FIND OUT THE HARD way," people who lived in Africa told me when they heard of my assignment. The truth is that for the first couple of years Africa did not trouble me at all. I spent entire afternoons poring over my Michelin maps, studying the arbitrariness of boundaries, the location of airstrips, the steady course of roads marked in solid red, the tentative meandering of those in somber blue. I traveled without pause.

The heat, the mud, the racket, the heap of bones waiting for me at the end of every story: none of it bothered me. Then, one evening in Nairobi, the monsoon rains came pounding down and a million ant-flies gathered at my doors and windows, desperate for entry. In the morning, the ground outside was thick with insect stumps, gossamer tissue. It was a holocaust. And for the first time I remember thinking: This is how they die. This is how the Africans lose their lives.

What started as a fissure soon became a crack. I lingered in Nairobi, delaying my next assignment by days, weeks. My editor rang. "What's wrong," he asked, his voice inflectionless, cold. I pictured Warren in the newsroom in Boston, the long patrician head frozen in the act of listening, irritation mounting in the cool blue eyes. "Wrong? Nothing's wrong."

"You've been in Nairobi for what? A month?"

"So?"

"So something's wrong."

To my astonishment, I came out with it: "I've started drinking." There was a pause, then Warren's distinctly puzzled voice. "Drinking what?" I bit my lip. "Alcohol? You've started drinking alcohol?"

"Yep."

"How much?"

"Good question."

"Before noon?"

Before dawn at times—to steady the breath, soothe the nerves, ignite a fire whose flames I'd fan all day until I passed out cold at night. "Before noon?" Warren asked again.

"Yep."

"Okay: when did this start?"

I wasn't sure. There had been plenty of drinking in Rome before my assignment to Africa but none of it had seemed so desperate. Maybe Rome itself had exerted a restraining force: a woman drunk, unsteady on her feet was a sight so unusual, so alarming that to run against the grain of that old culture and drink immoderately was to invite scandal and, ultimately, censure.

I'd had a few close brushes: I'd had boyfriends reach resolutely for the bottle and hammer the cork back in as they looked me coldly in the eye; I'd even suffered a long moment of embarrassment at the hands of someone's father one Sunday lunch, when, after refilling everyone's glasses to the rim, he had poured barely a thimbleful into mine. But by and large Rome had kept me honest ... and happy, I suppose, in a way that Africa—burned, bloodied Africa—obviously could not.

Why did I go, then? Why did I leave? It's difficult to say, it happened all so quickly. One minute I was in Rome, badgering Warren, clamoring for new horizons, the next I was in Nairobi brushing my teeth with Coca-Cola. Never use tap water, my guidebook sternly warned, and I remember thinking, as the toothpaste began to sizzle viciously in my mouth, I'm going back to Rome.

It was meant to be an exploratory tour, three weeks maximum, so I'd been taking Lariam against malaria. The drug kept casting me adrift on a sea of paranoia: branches turned into snakes, flowers snapped their mandibles at me, Africa herself seemed to hiss and snarl at my Armani jeans, my Gucci shades.

"So?" Warren asked when I called him.

"Don't think it's a match," I said. "The nature element is slightly overwhelming. Slightly. Overwhelming. Are you typing?"

"Yeah, I'm typing."

"Please stop typing."

Warren reluctantly stopped typing. "So?"

"The nature element."

"What about it?"

"It's overwhelming."

"You won't be covering nature."

I took a nervous look out the window. "Warren, you should see the *size* of these leaves, they're grotesque. And these *roots*, the way they come out of the ground . . ."

"What are you, a botanist? You'll be doing *people*, Anna. People."

"Plenty of those around," I muttered, as Warren resumed typing.

On the flight back to Rome, three weeks later, I began to rehearse my speech, lingering on the more sinister aspects of Africa's abundance—the pap that oozed at the slightest provocation out of things, the statistical improbability of so much vermin life, the stir, the throb, the cackle of night. Yet, when the moment came, I told Warren I would go, and set about packing in a kind of fury, stuffing half my wardrobe into garbage bags I then dumped by the church just across the street. It was August, a week or two before my twenty-ninth birthday, and, although the city was at the peak of its lethargy, I knew I was coming to the end of a long sleep.

Rome can be like that: it can turn time, the essence and mystery of time, into a curious interval between meals. I'd moved there from New York, fresh from graduate school, a black notebook burning in my back pocket. Five years later, the hours stacked like animal pelts on my back, I'd traded in the notebook for designer shoes. Africa would undo all that.

And it did, I suppose, to a great extent. The continent, which had initially kept me at arm's length, reeled me in immediately. In the pain and riot of its villages, under the vastness of its skies, my blood began to simmer, then to boil. I watered it down with drink. More and more and more drink.

When had things spun out of control? I could not tell. All I could offer Warren by way of evidence was a morning in Cyangugu, on the Rwandan–Congolese border, a mere fragment of time, two, three minutes before dawn, during which I lay propped on one elbow looking down at a colonel in full uniform in bed right next to me. His mouth was slightly open, his arms raised overhead, his legs crossed at the ankles. He was beautiful—full lipped, broad-chested, powerfully bound. He had a limp from a bullet in the knee. His wife ran a division of military intelligence.

So I told Warren. I said: "I think I need to leave."

"Leave? You just got there."

I cradled the phone in one shoulder and began picking up odd bits of paper from my desk. "Two years are what? Twenty-four months?"

"Roughly," Warren conceded.

"Thirty days in the month?"

"Roughly."

"How many days is that?"

"Okay," he snapped, "What am I going to do with this?"

We came to an agreement. I was to cover the Ugandan elections, write a Kenyan feature, file a couple of post-genocide stories from Rwanda, and I'd be free to go. It would be a disastrous career move: I would slide to the bottom of the freelancing ladder once again with no one to blame this time except myself.

There were precedents, errors of youth, or so I thought, until I found myself at the age of thirty-one without a proper job. I left the wringing of hands for later and began handing out possessions with the exuberance of the newly freed.

In Rwanda, I went to Chez Tantine in Nyamirambo for a bowl of soup and what I imagined would be a solemn good-bye. "Has Africa been rude to you?" Tantine asked, tucking one breast more firmly into her bra. I told her no, so she went on complaining about her back, her children, and the garbage, which seemed to accumulate with perverse volition in front of her low door. "Don't be forgetting Tantine in Nyamirambo," she said as I got up. "Tantine always needs money."

In Kampala I sat on the patio of the Speke hotel nursing a cold beer, remembering the first time I'd walked into the lobby—lips parched, hair stiff with dust from the drive across the Kenyan–Ugandan border, the whole world in the palm of my hand.

Back in Nairobi I gave away my last two pieces of furniture. My friend Gillian called. "I have nothing to wear," she complained.

"Nothing?"

"Nothing, darling, not a thing, just three closets full of bloody nothing. You? Have you got something?"

I looked down at my jeans. "Well, it'll be nice to get things unpacked."

"Unpacked?"

"Unpacked."

"You forgot my party!" she screamed. I drove to her house under a starless sky and there, in the middle of a rainstorm, under a marquee about to collapse under the rain, I met Nick.

I'd spotted him immediately: sleek, bored as a cat, a flute of champagne held expertly aloft as his eyes roamed the room for a taste of something stronger. Our orbits never met, I made sure of that, slipping beyond his field of gravity every time the gap began to close. My friend Gillian came over and leaned into me with a tipsy smile: "And that, over there, is Nick. Shall we?"

I gave her a black look: "No."

Gillian steadied herself on my arm: "Why on earth not?"

"I don't like him."

"Darling, you haven't met him!"

"Far too pleased with himself."

"Why shouldn't he be?"

I shrugged—a teenage shrug, sharp and tight with contradiction. Gillian staggered off. I went to the bar, procured another drink, and retreated to the farthest corner of the garden. There, sucking guiltily on a cigarette, was a woman I'd met one night in the company of my first lover, Dan, shortly after moving to Nairobi. "Dan is getting married," she told me.

"No."

"Yes."

"No."

"Promise you," the woman said. The sky split open, releasing its catch of rain. The woman stamped her cigarette out and pulled me running toward the marquee. "Tell her!" she gasped when we got there, "She doesn't believe me!"

Nick spun around. "Tell her what?"

His eyes, I wrote spitefully in my journal that night, were way too pale, his nose and mouth too perfect. But when he rang the next morning, a thrill ran down my back and I agreed to lunch straightaway.

He took me to his house, an old colonial building overlooking the Karura forest and served me champagne, marinated ostrich fillet steak, baby greens tossed in the single most successful vinaigrette I have ever tasted: dark, dense, peppery, yet sweet. When lunch was over, he maneuvered his body behind mine and sank his teeth lightly into my neck.

"What do you mean, you're not leaving?" Warren's voice was cold as a coffin lid.

"Staying," I said, suppressing a giggle.

"I thought you had a drinking problem."

"Me too."

The rain kept falling with vandalizing force, the ant-flies kept dying in shocking numbers. Nick slid down banisters like an adolescent and pranced around the house singing: "I feel GOOOD!"

And clearly he did. He felt good. Life, which stabbed people in the gut, which kicked them in the teeth, had only the sweetest notes for Nick. He was a Midas, or so it seemed, minus the curse. The rest of us took up arms daily against a sea of trouble but Nick set about outwitting life and its tedious traps so as to cross the finish line with as much bounce as when he'd set out in swaddling clothes.

It was an uneasy alliance. His joie de vivre thrilled me, it kept the darkness of my moods at bay, but I remember driving into town with him one morning, very early on. We came to a screeching halt at a traffic light and a street child—one of the scarred, scabbed multitude that feeds off the city's waste—came to the window, bony hand extended. "Good morning!" Nick hollered, "Why aren't you in school?" The child pressed his palm flat against the glass. Nick turned to me: "They ought to be in school, you know."

"You're not serious," I said.

"Of course I'm serious! A six-year-old ought to be in school!"

"He's too poor to be in school."

Nick waved a conciliatory hand. "Whatever."

"What do you mean, whatever? That kid ..."

But Nick cut in decisively: "Let's not ruin a perfectly good day, shall we?" And I, who felt like dropping to my knees and crying out to heaven every time I saw one of those children, I who had cursed my way up and down the continent, I bit my lip and didn't say a word.

Love plays crazy tricks, none crazier than the trick it played on us that fall. Nick jumped into the affair with predictable pep while I brooded darkly over my notebook, composing my first poem in a decade. Nick bought flowers and champagne and busied himself in the kitchen. I went in search of a new thesaurus to fix on paper what could not be said—not by me, not out loud, not to him, not to anyone. I wrote seven poems, each conveying deepening degrees of despair as I felt myself begin to slip—and fall. Nick read them with evident delight, barely able to keep himself from clapping. It wasn't lack of depth, it was pure buoyancy, acquired through hardship, no doubt, but alarming all the same.

I knew better than to stand in judgment. I had my own inconsistencies to worry about, the largest of which stood a full six feet, two inches tall. Michael, my boyfriend at the time, was no fool. We'd both been away, now he was back. He drove to my house from the airport at five in the morning; by a minor miracle I was there. He held me at arm's length, his eyes narrowing to pick out the cracks in my unlikely tale of conversion and contrition. "So you're not leaving?"

"No."

We were in my bedroom. He slipped his shirt off, gave me a dark look. "Why not?"

"I changed my mind."

"You changed your mind?"

"I changed my mind."

He sat on the bed, took off one shoe. "Why did you change your mind?"

"Difficult to tell."

He took the other shoe off. "You're hiding something."

"Me?"

"Yes, you."

"I've got nothing to hide."

"Good," Michael growled, leaning back on the pillows and yawning, "Because I'll kick your short Italian ass if you do."

"I'm not short."

"Not suggesting you are. Not suggesting you are."

Was I scared? Yes. All bodies with a degree of mass instigate a curvature in space, but Michael's peculiar density produced a nearly visible effect. No doubt I say this because of what happened later but oftentimes he scared me. Not because his mass intimated violence—I knew Michael would never lift a finger against me—but because he, too, had fallen against his will and now found himself tethered to my black heart like Gulliver on the shores of Lilliput.

By a perverse symmetry he resented me, my levity, the way I resented Nick's. I ran breathlessly from one to the other, stopping only to marvel at how life had conspired to deliver two perfect opposites at my door. Nick with his mocking eyes, his linen shirts, his citrus-based cologne. Michael with his swagger, his scars, the shark tooth he wore over his heart.

I'd met Michael for the first time in a hotel. I'd heard about him, bits and pieces here and there, none of them very flattering because, as it turned out, there was always a trace of jealousy in men when they talked about him. In the hotel, in the immense reception room filled with people, he seemed okay to me. Later, in another hotel, in another city, I realized I would never learn to judge him: I would never find the key to their dislike.

We met at an airstrip in Mogadishu. Michael had a driver, a fixer, and an armed escort; I had nothing. "What do you think this is? Paris?"

I shrugged. Reluctantly, he made room for me in the backseat.

Mogadishu was a shell. Only the outlines remained. The rest had been shot to bits or sold for scrap, packed on containers and shipped off to China. There were metal carcasses everywhere: cars, trucks, buses, tractors, even planes and not a sound between them and ourselves, only the rustle of sand collecting at the foot of things. We drove through a labyrinth of streets, past veiled women emerging barefoot from a private world of smoky courtyards, of pots and pans piled high by an open fire. He did not look at me once.

The hotel was empty, filled with the sound of the wind. The cook spent his days in the kitchen fretting over what he would serve his only two guests for dinner. Late in the afternoons Michael and I sat in armchairs facing one another, the coffee table between us cluttered with pens, notepads, beer cans, cigarettes, and wilting bushels of *miraa*, the bitter drug Somalia thrives on. *Miraa* made my heart flutter like a crazed bird, it made me want to rip it out of my chest and lay it to one side. The muezzin's call to prayer rose over the city, over the corrugated iron rooftops, over the shuffling of the faithful in the hot sand. It filled me with longing: for God, for Africa, for everything we had shut out of that room and now struck me as irretrievable. I walked to the window. "What happens if I lose my place here?"

Michael knew Africa; he had found his spirit in it. Before the bodies got to him, the African sky—immense!—had stirred in him a sense of unimaginable freedom. The *muezzin* cried out: "Allah is great!" and I could see how to the kneeling crowd he must have been truly great, in the cool comfort of the mosque at the end of a day spent milling about in misery, selling something infinitely small, waiting to meet someone for a loan. Michael stripped a tendril of *miraa* with his teeth, said nothing.

We met in the bruised half-light of his room the next day, in the accumulating violence of a thunderstorm. I said: "It's going to be a big one." Michael sniffed the air and nodded. We waited. The wind came tearing in, sending the revolving lid of a trash bin into a mad spin. There was one last pause, a tremor overhead. Then the rain. From the window I saw it hit the ground like a spray of bullets, I saw it fall with appalling force, tumbling down the decayed tarmac road, palpitating wildly at the meeting of different currents until, in the space of a minute, the road had become a river. I turned and found Michael standing behind me. "Don't move," he whispered, his eyes riveted on the mayhem outside, his body pressing slowly into mine.

We were supposed to leave the next day; we didn't. The hotel staff, toothless middle-aged men wizened by the sun, sanctioned the union with deep nods of approval, having for days cast a sorrowful eye on my unattached state. "She make good wife for you!" Ahmed, the one-eyed receptionist, cried as we passed, "Italians, they know how to cook! Spaghetti, *maccheroni* . . ." He waved one hand high in the air, his one eye beaming.

"I had a girlfriend who made me cheese soufflés," Michael whispered in bed that night.

I raised myself on one elbow, struck once more by how much of him there was: how thick his neck was, how broad his shoulders, how muscular his hips. "Cheese soufflés?"

"Mmm, mmm," Michael nodded, his eyes shut, the corners of his mouth raised in a beatific smile. "She made soufflés and she made fresh focaccia and she made the most incredible curries. Oh, and *roast chicken*. She made this roast chicken. . . . But wait . . ." It was his turn to hoist himself up quickly on his elbow: "You know what she did once?" His green eyes were dancing. "I came home after a shitty day, a real bad day, one of those days you wanna fuckin' forget . . ."

"Why?"

His eyes narrowed, became still. "What do you mean, why?"

"Why was it a bad day?"

"What's *that* got to do with anything?" His lips curved around a sneer. I rubbed my eyes, once, twice, not knowing what to do as Michael began to raise his voice: "I'm telling you a story about a girl who can fuckin' cook and you start needling me about the crap I had to go through that day?"

"Needling? Who's needling?"

"You!" he shouted. "You're needling! A story is a story! Listen to the story!"

That was the thing with Michael: rage, arrogance on planetary scale, vague contempt for all but the most unfortunate class of humans. I walked out on him that night, and many others after that. In the end, I suppose, there was his way with children, the pure delight that made its way into his eyes, the depth and breadth of his laughter. Displays of strength brought out his fury, the necessity to crush his opponents, to grind their face into the ground, pulverizing not only their resistance but their ego, was something he was unwilling to discuss, though it must have come from his early days on the rough edges of Brooklyn, where he'd had his first knife fight at the age of twelve, taking on someone twice his age. "It was over in a flash," he told me. "I was lucky he didn't kill me."

So what happened? It's difficult to say. Maybe he lost faith or maybe I did. Everything I did became the object of merciless scrutiny until I felt like a dog on a leash. Then came the cocktail party, the marquee under the rain, Nick's pale, sarcastic stare. I should have left Michael then, but I couldn't. For one, I was afraid of Nick: there was a sterile, cruel streak beneath that fine exterior and I was afraid of what he might say, what he might do. Michael offered paradoxical protection from all that.

And I liked him, I did not want to do without him. We covered the same stories, traveled to the same places, we shared the same blind passion for the continent. His job was more demanding than mine: he was a cameraman and a producer for one of the wires so he worked under the added pressure of time, driven by the need to be the first one in. I came in later, at a comparatively leisurely pace, weighed down by little more than a notepad and a pen, whereas he, poor man, had to carry roughly two hundred pounds of gear everywhere he went.

I loved working with him. Everyone did. He knew where to go, whom to talk to. He didn't waste time. There was a photograph pinned to the door of the news wire's editing room in Nairobi that showed him squatting under a crashing rain in the middle of the Congolese jungle holding an umbrella not over his head but over a generator connected to an editing machine and a dish: he was sending footage to London. Nothing thrilled him more than an assignment: the tougher, the better. Nairobi, with its passable roads and potable water, its generous supply of power, food, and drink, bored him. His demons came clawing to the surface and he went looking for ways to silence them. And I, of course, went right along.

I was lucky that time after Gillian's party: Michael had to leave at midnight for New York to negotiate a new contract. Lucky, I say, but I recall the drive back to town from the airport after dropping him off—the very distinct sense I had of having gambled away what little security, what narrow sanctuary, I had left. You don't make a mockery of Africa in the same way you don't claim your child is ill to get out of an appointment: it's tempting the Fates, possibly exciting their dislike.

I slowed my old Landcruiser down to a crawl. It was close to midnight, the Mombasa road was plunged in darkness but I could make out the gnarled profile of the thorn trees on either side of the road and feel, or so I thought, the full mystery of life rooting down into such inimical soil, winding up—bark thickening, leaves darkening, thorns lengthening into the very things that give the tree its name. Life beats the odds in the savannah. Once victorious, it acquires tenacity unseen in other climates. "That is why," I thought as I drove slowly into town, "you do not fuck with it."

I called Nick the second I got home. "Do you know what time it is?" he moaned.

"It's over," I told him. "I've been a fool."

There was a pause. "I'll take a fool."

"You'll what?"

"I'll take a fool."

"No you won't."

"And a drunk."

I shot to my feet. "I'm not a drunk!"

"Fine, you're not a drunk. What time is it?"

I checked my watch. It was two o'clock. I was totally awake, every fiber, every filament strained by the sorrow of our inevitable parting. "I'm sorry," I said and put the phone down. I waited five minutes, then I went to the freezer and took out the vodka. At four I cracked open a bottle of wine, at five another. At noon I rolled out of bed, picked my jeans off the floor and pulled them on. I tried to cut open a mango but I was still drunk, and the effort was too great, so I walked to the window instead.

The sky was pure ash. The Maribou storks filled the air with their obscene cries: I could see their raw eyes, their beaks like blades. I raised one of the wine bottles listlessly against the light and, finding a good third of it left, raised it to my mouth thinking what the hell. Just then the door swung open and Mercy rolled in—jeans bursting at the seams, breasts popping out of her top, heels painfully curved over a pair of stiletto heels. "You will become a drunk," she said after a long look. "Just like my mother."

I put the bottle down. The last thing I needed was Mercy standing there, yet there she unmistakably stood—big as a mountain, wide as a ship, her feet committed to the ground in a way mine could never hope to be. "I told you my mother is a drunk?" she said, bending over with a sigh and picking my shirt off the floor.

"It's clean," I said, holding out my hand.

"*Ahi*!" she whispered almost to herself. "This is not clean! This is dirty!"

"It's clean," I said between clenched teeth, but she tucked it under one capacious armpit and headed in a clatter of heels to the laundry room. I looked around the room in despair. Why had I hired her? What had come over me?

The truth is nothing had. I'd had no choice. Mercy had walked up to me one morning in the mini-market near my house, a giantess miraculously squeezed into a pink halter-top and fake patent-leather pants. She had crossed her arms over her enormous breasts and bellowed: "You are now living in that place there, the one with the red gate!" I had hesitated. She was a good head taller than me and roughly twice my size, so I'd cleared my throat and asked: "Have we met before?"

"No," was her brusque answer. "But me, I'm a housegirl and they have been telling me. They have been saying there is no one there."

"Who has been telling you?"

"The ones who are staying near there."

"Near where?"

Mercy took a lengthy inhalation: "Are you the one now who is staying in that house where the one from Belgium were now living?"

"Yes!" I told her. "Yes!"

"So I am saying," and here she paused, took a another long, patient breath, "I am saying I am a housegirl."

"Good, I mean, great," but before I could add another word she produced a manila envelope and, after some probing, handed me a crisp C.V. I scanned it briefly: two years with the Austrian high commissioner, one with the Canadian ambassador, six months with the French cultural attaché, who, I was later to learn, tried to feel her up one drunken evening and ended up in the hospital with two broken ribs. "Looks good," I said. "I mean, you're good ... you've got ... experience."

She was at my door at seven the next morning, a look of intense disapproval in her eyes: "In Africa we rise with the sun. Now, you, what time do you rise?" I followed her meekly around the house, eventually taking refuge in my study. When I came out for a bite of something to eat, the house had been transformed: the floors shone, windows and faucets sparkled, the sofa cushions stood preternaturally alert and symmetrically aligned at both ends of the couch, and every single thing—from bits of paper to stray glasses—had been put in its proper place. "You get me a uniform," she instructed that afternoon. "With the apron and the headscarf."

My life changed overnight. My clothes, the greater part of which I could never find, were now arranged by color in my closet, my shirts ironed with such precision I often looked ridiculous. The Tupperware in the fridge was stacked according to size, the eggs removed—and privately consumed, I'm sure—on their expiration date.

I was pleased, of course, but I could not help wondering what sort of opportunity Mercy had sensed with me, how amicable her intentions truly were. I was alone in a deeply alien city, in a house far too big for my needs. I traveled all the time, I was messy, distracted, I lost things. She became indispensable in no time but I never knew where I stood with her. At times she gave the impression she liked me, but once or twice I had caught a flash of something in her eyes. Was it personal animosity? Or was it a fundamental intolerance of her subordination to my calendar, my needs? I had been born white, she'd been born black and poor. Life had been cruel to her that way. But she had—and this is what made her such an enigma—been extremely successful in the past. Before her husband put a gun to her head and made away with all her money, Mercy had supplied the majority of Nairobi's slums with *muratina*.

Money can buy few things worse than *muratina* and from what I gathered Mercy wasn't hugely particular about what she put in it: thinning agents, disinfectant, antifreeze—it made little difference to her. And why should it? She supplied a ragged multitude with the quickest, the most potent medication for its pain. So what if sons killed fathers, husbands axed wives, and people went blind on the moonshine Mercy brewed in industrial vats off River Road? In that first rush of alcohol, in that first blooming of blood, the dead child, the failed scramble for a bag of onions, the sexual favor granted to the unrelenting landlord—the rage, the shame of poverty, were all forgotten.

Mercy didn't touch the stuff. She had a business to run. She coordinated a small army of runners and drivers and was so punctual, so reliable in her deliveries that a rumor spread of a personal connection with the president, Daniel Arap Moi. How else could she elude the tentacles of the police? She paid them, of course. She had an average of fifty officers on her payroll each month. When they got greedy and tried to squeeze her for more, Mercy had drugs planted in their homes and discreetly arranged a bust and had them put away for trafficking.

No, Mercy's story was not one of personal connections and privilege. She had started out as a prostitute in a tiny village near Mount Kenya and moved to Nairobi in her mid-twenties, setting up a bar consisting of a table, a bench, and two large plastic tubs hidden in the back of her mud hut. After years of violent wrangling to obtain payment from her drunken customers—after two broken arms, three cracked ribs, and an inch-long scar across one eyebrow—Mercy had turned her intelligence to the more complex world of wholesalers. Success had come instantly. As her business expanded, so did her fame. She became known as "the woman from River Road," the largest supplier of *muratina* in Kenya.

Her husband came very close to killing her. He didn't just put a gun to her head; he had her deposed in the African equivalent of a boardroom coup. He promised everyone a better deal: cleaner stuff, cheaper rates, higher pay. Of course, without Mercy the business went tits-up in record time and rather than keep paying creditors and employees money he could be spending on himself, Mercy's husband skipped town, the happy owner of a small fortune.

Mercy could have jump-started the business again—her connections were still solid, her reputation unscathed—but a terrible fatigue came over her. "They call it . . . now, what is the word? Depressed! When you are now depressed. Something in the mind that is now affecting the whole body." Barely able to get up in the morning, unwilling to assert herself one more, Mercy decided to direct what little energy she had left to "working for a *mzungu*," a white person. "The work is little, the money good, the housing free," she explained, as if I belonged to a different human category. She befriended a woman who worked for the Austrian high commissioner and on the strength of her persistence and her excellent, if creative, English eventually got a job there. The commissioner left town, and when his successor refused to hire her, Mercy transitioned with little effort to the Canadian embassy, then to the French *cochon*, and finally to me. "Sounds perfect," Nick said when I told him all that. "Let's see how long it takes for her to rob you blind."

I began hiding cash and valuables; my two passports—one Italian, the other American—I kept with me at all times. I knew there was a market for stolen passports in Kenya, and Mercy struck me as the kind of person who would be intimately acquainted with it. One day, barely a month after she had moved in, an airline ticket went missing. "It was here, on the table," I said, crossing my arms. Mercy returned my stare without flinching: "Me, I am not aware."

"What do you mean, you're not aware? It was here! I left it here!" She shook her head: "There has been nothing on this table. I have been cleaning it and there has been nothing." We stared at each other. Mercy was Sphinx-like, her eyes hard and narrow, her pupils anchored to mine without a trace of movement. "So," I said. "What do I do? There was an airline ticket and now it's gone. What do you expect me to do?"

"Maybe you are making your mind to be confused."

"What the fuck does that mean?"

"*Ahi*! Such bad words! I am saying, maybe that ticket is staying somewhere different."

I could tell exactly where she was going. "What are you suggesting, Mercy?"

She shrugged: "Sometimes when people are taking a lot of *pombe* they can be forgetting things in their minds."

"So you're saying I drink too much."

"Me, I am counting the bottles in the morning and, *ahi*! They are many!"

I took a couple of lengthy breaths then said: "Mercy, I did not hire you to count bottles, I hired you to clean the house. And I put the ticket here, on this table, because it's where I *always* put my airline tickets. Ever since I've moved into this house I've been putting them there so, no, I am neither drunk nor confused. And here's what: if by tomorrow the ticket is not *back* on this table, you can pack up and leave."

"*Ahi*!" she whispered, shaking her head. "You are too confused! But we shall try. We shall try." And with that she rolled her sleeves and began searching every corner of the house. I sat at my desk fuming. The woman was *out of a job*, that much was certain! I would write a letter of reference and go back to my chaotic but not altogether unpleasant life without *Herr Commandant* casting a cold eye on me every time I breathed.

Mercy's voice rang from upstairs: "May you please come to the bathroom?" A chill came over me as I began the short climb to the second floor. "Is this the one?" Mercy asked, holding a crumpled airline ticket between forefinger and thumb.

"Where was it?" I whispered.

"In the bin," she said.

She wanted an apology so I gave her one. "Me I am not a thief," she said, raising an admonitory finger. "You can be remembering that, Anna, when you are not finding other things." To test her or, who knows, maybe to tempt her, I began leaving cash around the house—larger and larger sums until the day I woke up in a foul mood and decided to drop the cash for my next assignment, ten thousand dollars, on my unmade bed: with ten thousand dollars Mercy could have reinvented herself ten times over.

I found her sitting on the couch when I got home at two in the morning. "What are you doing?" I shrieked.

"Waiting," she said.

"Waiting for what?"

"For you."

I steadied myself on the back of the couch. "Jesus. Why?"

"Because me, I am wanting us to be straight. Do you want me to go?"

"Go where?"

"Away."

I could barely focus, my head hurt, my mouth was parched from too much drink. "Why?"

"This," she said, rising from the couch, taking my hand and folding it around the cash. I stared at the rolled notes stupidly. "I tell you I was a prostitute?" I nodded. "Me, I was doing such a job for my children. Then I came to make *muratina* and the dirty feeling from the prostitution became little until, one day, it went away. You are now making it to come back."

I stared at her, aghast. "What do you mean?"

"Me, I am needing this job for my children but you are making me to feel dirty because I am accepting things that I should not accept."

"What things," I mumbled, eyes glued to the floor.

"These things," she said, pointing to the money sweating in my hand. "I am not a thief! Why should I be staying in a house where the people are making me to be a thief! It is bad! Bad!" The echo of her voice died down and we stood in silence for what seemed to me an eternity. "Me, I am going," Mercy said.

"No!" I shouted. "Don't go!"

We went through a period of détente after that. I stopped laying traps for her and she stopped showering me with mute disdain. She kept to the kitchen, I kept to the study. When we passed each other in the hallway we jammed our backs against the wall to let the other pass. We then muttered simultaneous apologies and hightailed it. Out of boredom, perhaps, Mercy instituted the tea ceremony. Every day at four she knocked on my office door and made a ceremonious entrance with tea and cookies on a tray as I scrambled to hide my wine glass in a drawer. My messenger of sobriety, I began to privately call her. And why not? Why not delay my fifth or sixth drink of the day by a half hour? Tea never hurt anybody.

It was the cookies, I suppose, that broke the ice. One day Mercy put her hands menacingly on her hips and said: "Now what is the problem you are having with these biscuits?"

"I don't like them," I said defensively.

"What is wrong with them?"

"They taste like cardboard."

"Why are you keeping quiet about them?"

"I don't know."

"Which ones do you like?"

"Ones with chocolate maybe?"

She went to the store and came back with four different types, all chocolate covered. "You can be trying these," she said. "If they are not tasting right we shall be trying some more."

The next day I saw a pair of bright pink rhinestone earrings and bought them on the spot. Mercy's eyes shone as she put them on. A few days later I came home past midnight and found her in the kitchen, sitting morosely at the table. "What's wrong?" I asked.

Mercy shook her head: "Your vehicle is having problems, isn't it?"

"Yes," I admitted.

"It can be breaking down," she said.

"Yes."

"So why are you going around during the nighttime, eh? You know if they catch you sitting in your vehicle, sitting just like that? *Ahi!* Even me, I cannot be going around in the nighttime with a vehicle like that!"

The longer the truce, the bolder Mercy became. "Now your deadline for your boss was yesterday, isn't it? Today is come and gone. This is now two days you have been delaying with your boss. You think your boss cannot find another person? You think he cannot send some other *mzungu* to take care of the job?" And then, of course: "*Ahi*, this *pombe*! This *pombe* is too much! You think you can be taking so much *pombe* and not be damaging your body?"

That day Mercy came back from the laundry room, took off her heels—losing a good four inches but no stature—and bellowed: "I tell you my mother drinks, no?"

I wedged myself deeper into the sofa. "Many times."

"And the people who came to drink *muratina*, they all drink until they are falling like this," and, to great effect, Mercy mimicked a person falling.

I tucked my knees against my chest. "You are the one who made them drunk, Mercy."

She straightened to full height. "Which one can you blame for that now? Was I the one who was putting the liquid down the mouth? No! And you . . ." here she shook her head, "I can see you are heading to be like them."

"Mercy, I never drink in the morning, never," I lied. "The reason I have been drinking is I broke up with Nick." Then, with a painful smile: "That should make you happy."

She didn't answer and, as usual, I could not read her but she had never made any mystery of her feelings for Nick: she hated him. Michael she loved, Michael she adored, because unlike Nick, who bristled at her approach, Michael had courted her shamelessly, breaking down her resistance bit by bit. "Paraffin's the worst shit," he'd informed her on their first meeting, "Kills ya. Your children too," and he had bought her a gas stove. Next he had taken her youngest son to the game park to see the lions and the giraffes. Finally he had come from Frankfurt with a bottle of expensive perfume beautifully wrapped in silver paper: Mercy giggled like a schoolgirl, putting her hand over her mouth to conceal her missing tooth.

But Nick . . . . She never lost any opportunity to pile abuse on him: the way he shed his clothes around the house, the way he put his feet up on furniture, the way he "dirtified" the kitchen, the way he walked around as if he owned the place.

She kept my secret, which, considering her devotion to Michael, was a true test of loyalty. But she was brazen in her displays of animosity whenever Nick came around. "I don't like that *kijana* over there," she growled, pointing her thumb at Nick virtually every time he came through the door.

"So, yeah," I sighed. "No more Nick."

"You have quarreled?"

I tried to read her but she was inscrutable. "Not really," I said, an eye on the wine.

Mercy read my mind and, swooping down on the bottle like a bird of prey, she waddled off with it to the kitchen. "Why you take this *pombe*!" she shouted on the way back, wagging a finger at me. "This *pombe* is bad! Bad for the brain! Bad for the heart! Bad for the ..." but here her English failed her and she began waving one hand through the air, "... the *nini* ... the ... the ... nevermind! It's bad!"

The doorbell startled us both. Mercy raised her eyebrows, a silent accusation in her eyes. "Go!" I hissed.

"Me?"

"Yes! You!"

"It's that *kijana* ..." she muttered sourly as I dashed down the hall. "That one cannot be keeping to himself. He cannot. I am telling you, that one cannot ..."

And sure enough Nick's voice skipped and jumped all the way to the bathroom where I stood gaping at my reflection in the mirror, shocked by what I saw. "Good morning!" he hollered. "You're looking smashing Mercy! A trifle wan, perhaps, but no matter: a bit more *posho* with your beans and you ought to be well on your way to obesity again! Where's Anna?"

Mercy let a full ten seconds pass before announcing with palpable relish that I would not see him "on this day or the ones that will be coming. Your business in this house is finished," she stated. "You may go."

"I'm being dismissed?" Nick asked smoothly.

Mercy thought about it. "You are wanting to know if you are being sacked?"

"No. I am asking you if I am being dismissed from this house." Cursing, I flung the bathroom door open and catapulted myself down the hall and into the living room. Nick's mouth dropped open. "Christ, Anna. Have you been shooting up?"

I did not leave him. I did not even kick him out of the house. To Mercy's visible disgust, I followed him to the kitchen and watched him squeeze half a dozen oranges into three separate glasses. "Here," he said, handing out the first. "See if we can reverse this transmogrification from human to beast."

"Thanks."

"Not at all," and when I looked there was a strange expression in his eyes, as if he were trying to piece me together but couldn't. "Seriously, Anna, what have you been doing?"

I looked away. "Nothing."

"Look at the *state* you're in."

"I was about to have a bath."

"You need plastic surgery, not a bath."

"Maybe you should go," but he didn't go, he waited for me to have a bath and then announced he would take me to the Machakos on a borrowed Cessna.

"Breakfast first," he bellowed, and went to the store.

I bit my nails for a while and then wandered pensively into the kitchen. Mercy was wiping down the counter. "Where is the Machakos?" I asked.

"Why you are asking me?" she snapped. "You ask that *kijana*. He knows everything."

I had to start somewhere, so I told Mercy about Cupid's winged arrows, the unpredictable trajectories they struck, the immeasurable depths to which they could sink. "You try pulling one of those things out," but of course Mercy was not in the least bit amused. I set out to explain: "Have you ever wanted something very badly because you could not have it?"

"Food?" was her arch reply so of course I dropped it right away.

"I'm sorry," I mumbled. She shrugged. "No. Really. I am." It took a while but in the end she softened sufficiently for me to ask again: "The Kerio Valley: is it far?"

She gazed at the ceiling and said musingly: "Now that side . . . that side is Kambaland."

I rolled my eyes. "I'm not asking you which tribe lives there, I'm asking you how far it is."

"Me, I have not been."

"Thanks," I said and headed out of the kitchen but she yelled: "Us, we know them for their witchcraft!"

I turned. "What witchcraft?"

"The one they are now practicing."

I fought the urge to raise my voice. "Who?"

"The Kamba!"

God knows I had no interest in the Kamba, I did not care what laws of nature they could pervert, what spirits they conjured out of the dark ground. But Mercy was dying to tell me and I had a sense she ought to be indulged, particularly since Nick was on his way back and would soon be "dirtifying" the space she had been laboring to clear. "Witchcraft. What kind of witchcraft?"

"*Ahi*!" Mercy said. "Many things. Many, many things!"

"Like what."

She took some time to think. "The snake. You did not heard about the snake?"

"No."

"The one in Kawangware?" I shook my head. "You mean!" she exclaimed, straightening to full height. "And they announced it on the radio!" I gave her an encouraging nod. Assuming the tone and posture of a schoolteacher, she began to tell the story: "Whereby there was a man, a Mluyia, and he married a Mkamba ..."

"Yeah ..."

"... and he got a second wife and when the Mkamba woman found out. ... You did not heard?"

"No."

Mercy broke into a delighted smile. "The Mkamba wife, she turned the man into a snake!"

"The man?"

"The same, same!" Mercy's eyes were sparkling.

"Into a snake," I said.

"A snake!" she confirmed.

I raised a skeptical eyebrow: "Did you see it?"

"Eh?"

"Did you see the man, the snake."

Mercy lifted a wine glass and held it against the light. "Me, I feared to go."

"So you did not see it."

"But many people went! Many!"

"And what did they see?"

"Eh?" she asked again.

"What did they see?"

"The man was screaming," Mercy said, a flash of indignation in her eyes. "The wife had taken him water for the bath. He had just gone like this,"—she threw an imaginary handful of water over one shoulder,—"and the back, the legs, the feet: they become like a snake!"

"So you're saying he was half-man, half-snake."

"Yes!" she thundered.

"All right. Who saw him?"

"Who?"

"The man! The snake!"

"His neighbors!" she cried, and I knew I had her then.

"Do you know them?"

Mercy narrowed her eyes: "Who?"

"The neighbors."

"No."

"So who told you?"

"My neighbors." I burst out laughing. "There were others!" Mercy shouted, "Many others!"

And at that moment, as if dropped from an immeasurable height by the hands of Chaos, Nick appeared. "For God's sake!" he snapped in response to Mercy's withering look. "Could you at least try to be civil?"

Before I could jump to her defense, before I could prevent the inevitable, Mercy took two gigantic steps and brought a finger under Nick's nostrils: "You are the one to be civil, not me! The other one, he comes and makes no trouble. You, you come and make trouble. Noise and trouble! All the time!"

I froze, scarcely able to believe my ears. Nick placed the grocery bag calmly on the counter and, under my hypnotized stare, began extracting from it eggs, bacon, sausages, baked beans, a carton of milk, two mangos, and, disturbingly, a small jar of pickled herrings whose contents he proceeded to drain and consume on the spot. "So," he said to no one in particular, "Who is this *other one*."

I cleared my throat. "It's a ... a figure of speech. The *other* one. Meaning the other *ones*, plural. Right, Mercy?" Mercy shrugged. "Am I right, Mercy?" She didn't even turn around.

"She's not cooperating," Nick said, dry amusement tugging at the corners of his mouth.

"No, she's not," I mumbled.

"Me, I am going," Mercy announced, unfastening her apron as she went.

Alone with me in the kitchen, Nick looked at me as if we had just met, as if I were a stranger in whom he would have to take a fleeting interest before moving on. With him standing there, neutral, discreet, polite, mindful of each passing second yet deferring his attention to the clock just above my head, all I wanted to do was slap my forehead in rapid sequence one thousand times.

How stupid, how foolish, how utterly absurd to lose him in this way! Yet while half of me toyed with the idea of begging for a second chance, the other half relished the prospect of renewed linearity. Honesty saves time. It also lifts the heart. "I'm sorry," I mumbled. "I tried to tell you last night."

Nick gave me a long, bland look, as if I had somehow slipped out of context but, having witnessed far greater incongruities in his time, he was under no particular pressure to do anything about it. "I was looking forward to a nice fry-up," he mumbled to himself. "I think I'll just go ahead and make myself one." And with that, he began to unwrap the bacon.

I phoned Michael in New York. "It's over," I said.

"What's over?"

"You. Me. The relationship."

"Baby, I'm in the middle of some important shit here. Can I call you back?"

"No."

"Call you right back."

I went to the kitchen. Nick was cracking an egg into a pan full of simmering water. "I need a slotted spoon," he said. I looked around, briefly considering the chances of my owning one. "Could I please have a slotted spoon?" Nick asked, his voice tense.

"I haven't got a slotted spoon."

"Have a look, why don't you?"

"Sure," I said, opening the drawer closest to me. "Nothing here. Nothing here. Nothing here."

Nick threw a kitchen towel in the sink shouting: "How the hell am I supposed to get these eggs out?"

For a second I teetered on the edge of appeasement. How, indeed, was he going to get the eggs out? But as I pondered the question I felt myself become almost physically unmoored, swept by a current of pure rage. "Are you out of your fucking mind?" I hissed.

Nick grew rigid. "Pardon me?"

"You want a slotted spoon? Go to the fucking shop and get yourself one!" Nick stared, speechless. "Go!" I shouted, "Go! Get out!"

He got out, of course, and rather than finish cooking what would have been a badly needed breakfast, I drove to the store and purchased four more bottles of wine and one of vodka—Smirnoff, blue label. The day passed in a haze, in a labyrinth of freakish feelings and truncated intentions. The answering machine whirred on and off.

Late that evening I rose from a black sleep, turned on the lights and went to check my messages: three from Michael, one from Warren, and one from Nick, which went: "Anna, perhaps I did overreact in the kitchen with the slotted spoon but nothing, absolutely nothing justifies the way you flew at me, it's just ... not civilized behavior, not ... not the way people behave. ... Incidentally, I don't know who this other fellow is. To tell you the truth I'm not hugely worried. Don't ask me why but I'm not. What I *am* worried about is this temper, this ... this rage ..."

I rewound to the first of Michael's messages. "Baby, baby, baby! What was that all about? Are you home? Pick up the phone!" To his second: "Pick up the phoooone ..." And his third: "Anna, I know you're in Nairobi, I called your editor in Boston ..."

Warren's message was short and not particularly sweet. "Your boyfriend called. He seems to think we're some kind of paging service, which we are not. Please make that clear to him, as well as to any future romantic interest you might have. The AIDS story is four days late, by the way ..."

I went back to the couch and prayed for sleep. It did not come. At three in the morning I went looking for a pill. I moved through the house as if through water, struggling to gain a simple inch. I've thought about that night many times, how difficult it was for me to move, how often I had to stop, collect my breath, organize the next step forward. It wasn't the booze: I'd had far more in a single sitting without flirting with near paralysis before. No, the influence seemed to be external, and although I resisted the impulse for some time, I found myself stepping out onto the terrace and peering up at the moon, waiting for something to make itself seen or heard.

Looking at the sky in Africa brings on an inevitable reduction: you accurately, or more accurately, gauge your size and age against the immensity above your head and feel the irrelevance your small torso, your small arms, the endearing tuft of hair on your head ultimately add up to. The effect can be illuminating or entirely crushing.

That night it was neither. I stood transfixed. Like a child surfacing from a nightmare, I dared not breathe. Africa, the monstrous weight of the continent itself, seemed to be bearing down on me, the air hardening all around me, capturing me, beetle-like, in its contracting core. Had I been able to move I would have let out an animal cry, the feeling of entrapment was so strong.

I'd come so close. Like Lot's wife, I'd nearly gotten out. What had I done to deserve this double slavery? For now there wasn't just Africa with its chronic spasm, there was a man who mocked me in my dreams, who, as the door inched open onto a room of my imagination raised himself languidly on one arm and, with barely a look in my direction, dipped his head between another woman's breasts.

In bed, I fell into a dead sleep.

2

MERCY'S FACE CAME INTO FOCUS with extreme difficulty the following morning. "Get up!" she was shouting, "You will lose your job!"

I peered at her through the fog of my exhaustion and moaned: "I was asleep."

"I can see!" she snorted, hands on hips.

"I need to sleep."

"You can be sleeping later!" Mercy yelled. "The people are waiting!"

"What people?" but suddenly I remembered that I had three interviews lined up in Korogocho, Nairobi's meanest slum, for yet another story on the spread of HIV/AIDS. Mercy had arranged the interviews through a cousin of hers, and I knew, because I'd caught a couple words here and there, that she had already claimed half of whatever I'd agree to pay him. Mercy was far from stupid. She had seen from my expense accounts that a fixer could earn in a single day what she earned in a whole month, so there was no way I would be allowed another minute in bed. "God help me," I whispered.

"God has a funny way with him," was Mercy's tart reply. "He only helps the ones who can be helping themselves. The rest he leaves to rot there on the side."

"Do me a favor," I said. "Spare me. You're only interested in the money you'll be gouging off that poor cousin of yours so don't give me this sanctimonious crap about God and those he helps or doesn't help."

"*Ahi!*" she cried. "Why you are always using such bad words?"

I'd never been to Korogocho but I had heard about it—how foul the air was, how fetid the ground, how extreme the violence, how dark the rage. Back in the old days, Mercy had sold more *muratina* per capita in Korogocho than anywhere else in Nairobi. Drunkenness was endemic there, as was prostitution, child abandonment and abuse. Only the poorest of the city's poor lived there, hemmed in by Nairobi's largest garbage dump on one side and a toxic stream of traffic heading to Thika on the other. "Leave all your preciouses here," Mercy warned.

"Your valuables," I corrected.

"You know what I am meaning."

I gave her a sharp look. "And you? You're going like that?"

Mercy smoothed her top down. "Why? Am I looking bad?"

"No, like you're going clubbing." Aside from the bronzed platform shoes recently purchased and constantly worn, Mercy's outfit featured a jeans skirt a few sizes two small, a bright purple button-down shirt, also too tight, and a pair of gigantic hoops in her ears. "They'll rip those things right off," I said.

"We shall see," Mercy retorted with a little smile.

Once we got past the welcoming committee—Mercy's cousin, his two brothers, four of their friends, and a gaggle of hangers-on hoping to make a buck—Korogocho unfolded before our eyes like an open wound. Red-eyed, raw-boned, clad in noisome rags, people competed for space in a snarl of alleyways to avoid sinking their bare feet in the human excrement floating down open sewers. Scrawny chickens pecked at piles of waste. Smoke—dark, dense, intrusive—rose from puny cooking fires around which people gathered hungrily with tin mugs. The odor of unwashed bodies and the stench from the garbage dump made the air nearly impossible to breathe. Once every so often a half-naked man or woman, sometimes a child, would make a hideous appearance—swaying drunkenly from side to side, shouting curses and obscenities, collapsing in a pathetic heap at people's feet only to scramble up, an extra layer of blood and mud on them, and stagger on.

Mercy surveyed this inferno behind hooded lids, one leg balanced indolently on a platform heel as she harangued each member of the welcoming committee in turn. "Now you!" she barked, singling someone out at random. "How have you been making yourself useful?" No answer proved remotely satisfactory. "African men should just get on a boat and go," she sighed, shaking her head. "They should just go."

Mercy's cousin flashed me a sheepish smile. He had been subject to the longest list of vituperations, alternatively referred to as "that useless one standing there," or "that piece of rubbish." I was later to learn that he had played an utterly marginal role in Mercy's downfall. I was struck, looking at him, by how small a figure he cut next to Mercy, who, although not quite as tall, seemed to tower over him and all his friends. Had I needed confirmation of Mercy's peculiar clout, there would have been no need to go past the gates of Korogocho. I knew that within the walls of our compound Mercy reigned supreme: the gardener, the driver, and both of the *askari* (day and night guards) took turns sucking up to her, complimenting her baroque hairdos and disco-queen attire, bringing in their wives so that Mercy could berate them first, then instruct them with tried patience in the ways of the world.

It was no different in Korogocho. Everywhere we went that day Mercy was presented with ten or fifteen hands to shake. She shook them gladly, flamboyantly, breaking out into peels of thunderous laughter. A permanent entourage, with an inner and outer circle, followed our progress through the slum as Mercy grew more and more demonstrative, cracking jokes, slapping palms, meeting high-fives. Only when we came face to face with Father Anselmo did her demeanor change: she lowered her gaze, offered a two-handed shake, and sank into something resembling a curtsey. "This," she told me, "is Father Anselmo."

Father Anselmo was tall and horrendously thin—collapsed around his midsection as if he'd just taken a punch. His graying hair fell past his shoulders and hung lifelessly down his bony back. His face was deeply wrinkled, his lips cracked, his teeth yellow. Most astonishingly of all, his toenails, left unclipped for years, curved beneath the flesh of his toes. But his eyes ... His eyes were two black furnaces: the light from them blazed and danced and seemed incapable of ever holding still. He held out a calloused hand: "You are the journalist."

"I am."

"Italian."

"Yes."

"Me too. Welcome to my home."

Only then did I remember what Mercy had been telling me for days: that twelve years earlier Father Anselmo had taken the unprecedented step—hotly opposed by those in his Combonian order who dreaded having to follow his example—of taking residence in the slum. His home consisted of two low, dank rooms built out of sticks and mud. There was a rough-hewn table with four chairs in one, an iron bed frame with a lumpy mattress in the other. The only other additions to the household were a countertop stove with two battered burners and a bare wooden crucifix. The bathroom, a hole in the ground behind some corrugated metal sheeting, was outside.

We sat at Father Anselmo's table and talked about the reason for my visit. I was interested in the relatively new phenomenon of AIDS masses: huge, hysterical, day-long affairs in which participants confessed their sickness and placed themselves at the mercy of self-professed healers. Nowhere, I had been told, were the masses as frequent and as extreme as in Korogocho, where poverty and despair had mixed in concentrations high enough to produce a new strain of superstitious belief.

I asked Father Anselmo what he thought of the "healing" practices of the Legio Maria, a Catholic cult popular among the Luos of Kenya. "I hear their masses get quite nasty," I said.

The priest looked me over. "The degree of psychological and physical violence is deeply shocking," he answered slowly. "It is also a very accurate measure of their pain. I understand James, Mercy's cousin, has something planned for you. We'll talk later over a cup of tea."

"For the tea, maybe I think it's better if you can be telling him no," Mercy whispered in my ear as we were leaving.

"Why?"

"Have you seen the place now? You think because Father Anselmo—the Lord bless his soul—you think because is a *mzungu* he cannot give you something bad?"

"So what?" I shrugged. "You think I haven't had the shits before?"

"From Korogocho?"

"Korogocho, Sudan, Congo. They're all the same."

"That is where you can be mistaken," Mercy pronounced. "Diarrhea from this place ... *Ahi*! It can defeat you," and I have to confess that it nearly did defeat me when I got it the next day. But when I emerged triumphant from the struggle nearly two months later, I had a stomach made of steel.

We walked for a good ten minutes and then paused to consider whether we had missed the anonymous entryway into one of Legio Maria's more private places of worship. As we stood there, three hooded figures in bright-purple cassocks slipped past us and disappeared into a passageway. We scurried after them and found ourselves in an unexpectedly large courtyard in which no fewer than five hundred people stood pressed like sardines, waiting for the service to begin. "Let us go to see bishop Daniel," James said loudly to dispel the aura of suspicion that immediately surrounded us.

Bishop Daniel was receiving tribute from two acolytes when we walked in. A man and a girl, both dressed in a white tunic with a purple cross down the back, were pressing his hands ardently against their sunken chests. "They have just joined us," the bishop explained. "They have come to give praise."

"Have they been healed?" I asked.

"Yes," Bishop Daniel said. "They were sick but now they are cured."

"When?" The bishop fixed me with languorous, wildly intoxicated eyes. I asked again, "When were they healed?"

"Yesterday," he said.

The earlier part of the mass is now a blur: except for the selection of twelve people made to stand in a semicircle at the front, I don't remember much. My memory hardens around the slight frame of Clementine, nineteen years of age and the first of the twelve to be surrounded by four deacons and brought firmly to her knees. It's her face I remember as the first shouts rose and the first blows rained down on her, it's her tears I have seared in my memory, her desperate gulping for air as she was forced onto her back, as water was poured into her mouth, her nose, her ears, as a whip was brought out and used viciously against the demons that had possessed her and made her sick. And her smile, I remember her smile when it was all over, the sweet, sweet smile of the truly thankful as she told me, between fits of tubercular coughing, how much better she felt.

Six hours later, with the mass still in full swing, we walked back to Father Anselmo's house. He wasn't there so we dragged the chairs away from the table and sat morosely at opposite corners of the room. Soon it was dark and Mercy began to fret. "I know the man is busy but to be leaving us here like this? It is too much." She was in the middle of organizing a posse for our passage out of the slum when Father Anselmo walked in—tense, gaunt, withdrawn. He was surprised to see us there, having forgotten all about us. "Can you come back tomorrow?" he asked, disappearing into his bedroom and reappearing with a black knapsack into which he was stuffing a candle.

"Where are you going?" I asked.

"Masses. For the terminally ill."

"AIDS?"

"What else?" he snapped.

"Can I come with you?"

"If you wish."

But Mercy stood up. "The place is now too dangerous."

Father Anselmo smiled: "You have become soft, Mercy."

She did her usual straightening-to-full-height, finger-wagging act: "Me, I can just be taking this chair and placing it there where the thugs are moving back and forth but this one cannot. I am fearing for her safety."

"No one will touch her," Father Anselmo said.

And no one did. Three or four times that night we came across ragged gangs of men with knit caps pulled low over their foreheads, fire in their eyes and stomachs. My hair stood on end as I saw the first six appear, shoulders hunched, fists sunk deep in their pockets. They saw me from a distance and could not believe their eyes. Two of them stopped dead in their tracks to make sure I was not a vision, a dream, a spirit come to take revenge. Running into a white woman in the middle of the night in Korogocho was a statistical rarity—better than winning the lottery. There would be tons of cash, maybe some jewelry, and almost certainly a four-wheel drive parked not too far away. There would also be a key to a front door.

I sensed their intent—rapacious, keen. Father Anselmo, on the other hand, showed no sign of having registered their presence, and I remember thinking, in the seconds before our paths crossed, that Africa had taught me nothing, that this suicidal running around in the company of a half-starved priest was the precise sum of my mistakes. Then a miracle happened: the man in the lead recognized Father Anselmo, pulled off his hat and let out a raspy greeting: "*Habari ya usiko, baba?*" How are you this evening, Father?

The priest did not even stop. "What are you doing out so late?" he yelled. "Go home, all of you!"

"*Ahi baba,*" they murmured in turn. "*Tuna rudi sasa.*" Yes, Father, we're going now.

Father Anselmo kept walking. The moon rose over the metal rooftops, casting a harsh light on the strangely deserted alleys, on the grayish ooze festering in puddles and in sluggish streams down the open sewers on either side of us. There were no lights, no sounds except for dry coughing and infant wailing. I was about to switch my torch off when I saw a woman sprawled out on the side of the road, both breasts exposed, one foot turned out at an impossible angle. I grabbed Father Anselmo's arm: "She's dead!"

"She's drunk!" he snapped, pulling his arm away. "Let's go!"

"Shouldn't we ..."

"I don't have time," and he moved on.

I didn't dare say it, but I wondered what sort of priest could walk past a scene of such human degradation without stopping. The answer became clear to me as the evening wore on and what I had imagined to be an exception proved to be the rule. I don't know how many bodies we walked past that night—prone, supine, male, female, fully clothed, almost entirely naked—but it cannot have been less than a dozen, all of them drunk on *muratina*. Eventually we made our first stop, ducking through a low doorway into a frigid room immersed in total darkness. "God be with you," Father Anselmo hollered.

"And also with you," came the tremulous reply.

A match was struck, a candle lit, and in the dim light I saw a woman struggling to get out of a low, dingy bed as a girl cleared a space on a table barely bigger than a stool. Father Anselmo unzipped his sack. Out came a chalice, a gilded plate, a crucifix, a candle, and a small tin box.

Two more women made a timid entrance and lit a candle each. "Good evening, Father," they whispered, but the priest had sunk to his knees and was deep in prayer. By the time he stood up, nearly ten minutes later, twelve more women, holding a candle, each had somehow managed to squeeze into the room and stood with their heads bowed, their lips moving in silent prayer.

Father Anselmo leaned toward the dying woman. "What is your name?" he whispered.

"Jessica."

"Jessica. Where does it hurt?"

"Here," the woman murmured, touching her head.

The priest placed one hand on her forehead, his face filled with pity. "Is this your daughter?" he asked, gesturing toward the girl. The woman nodded. "Other children?"

"No," Jessica whispered. "Husband? Uncles? Cousins?" Jessica shook her head. The priest straightened, took a long, measured breath. Then he began. "We are gathered here today to bring Jessica the love and solace of God our father. May he give her the peace she so deserves and needs."

As if on cue, the women started singing and a low melody of almost intolerable sweetness rose to the highest corners of the room. It rose above the dancing flames, into the grooves of the metal roofing, onto the back of the night. More women came. Unable to get in, they crowded the doorway, bringing in more light, more warmth until the air itself seemed to ignite, atoms flaring wildly to subsume the narrow chemistry of death into the broader flow of life.

"We are here," Father Anselmo began when the singing stopped, "to bring Jessica comfort and light. We are also here to celebrate the night, the sound of a million stars laughing overhead. How can we hear those stars, you ask me, when we have no food to feed our children? How can the beauty of God's creation be seen by us, who have no fire to keep us warm, no medicines to cure us, who spend our days skirting piles of excrement, hiding from thieves, begging corrupt officials? Well, you've heard it a million times: blessed are the poor. It's the oldest trick in a priest's book, right? Well, it's true: the kingdom belongs to you, and I don't mean later, I don't mean tomorrow when you're dead. I mean now, this minute.

"People with cars, bank accounts, family homes, people with pension plans, people with dogs to whom they feed the food they cannot eat themselves, people who don't die of malaria or tuberculosis or dysentery because they can afford the drugs—these people have material comfort but few, very few will enter the Kingdom. God is nothing to them. Listen carefully: He is nothing to them. And so these people, the rich people of the world, are lost and lonely.

"But you ... God is closer to you than your own blood! You listen and so you hear him beating wildly in your veins. You pay attention so you hear him whispering in your ear as you gather water in the morning, firewood in the evening. Because of your faith, he steadies your hand when no one else does. He guides you when no one else can. You know it, I know it, Jessica knows it. And now that she is sick, he never leaves her side. He's waiting to take her in his arms at the end of a long and painful journey: her soul, so pure, so beautiful, is his delight. Trust me: not even the eyes of a child give God as much delight."

I elbowed my way out of the room as soon as the mass was over, but one of the women came after me. "Jessica wants to speak to you," she said. I went back in reluctantly: I did not want to see the woman's eyes, I did not want to tell her that, following Mercy's advice, I had no money on me.

Her face was streaked with tears. Slowly, very slowly she brought one hand to her forehead. "It hurts," she croaked. Tuberculosis, a classic hallmark of AIDS in Africa, had had its way with her, traveling largely unimpeded to her brain. She had three, four days to live. "My daughter," she whispered, her eyes darting in the direction of the young girl.

"I have no money," I said. "I'll come back tomorrow."

"You take her."

"Take your daughter?" She nodded, her eyes wild with hope. "I'm sorry," I whispered.

"You take her!" the woman said.

"I can't."

"She make good housegirl."

"I can't," and this time the woman understood. Turning her face away, she made a weak gesture for me to leave.

"As good as dead," Father Anselmo said of the girl as we walked to our next appointment. "She has no relatives so she'll end up prostituting herself. Eventually she'll catch the virus and die."

I stared at him, shocked not so much by the prediction, which I knew to be true, but the neutrality with which it was delivered. "Is there nothing you can do?"

"Me?"

"You, your organization."

"What organization?"

"The church."

"What church?"

"The Vatican."

"The Vatican?" Father Anselmo looked dead ahead as he spoke.

"They're not helping you?"

"The Vatican gives me enough money to feed, cure, and bury roughly fifty people a month. There are fifty thousand people in Korogocho, one third of whom are dying of AIDS, *all* of whom are starving." We walked in silence after that. Eventually we passed through a doorway as narrow as the first, into a room as cold and dark. "God be with you," Father Anselmo said.

It was past eleven when we finally made our way back to the priest's home. Mercy had left a message saying she would come collect me in the morning. Her cousin James lay curled up on the floor. "Let him sleep," Father Anselmo whispered, placing a tin kettle on the burner.

I looked at him as he fumbled with the matches, trying to get one lit and I realized he was shaking with exhaustion. "Let me do it." His face was ashen when I set a mug of sweet black tea in front of him and, for the first time that day, I felt a rush of sympathy. "You are overextending yourself."

"What a complicated word."

"With simple consequences."

"Could you do me a favor?" I nodded. "There should be some bread somewhere. Could you find it for me?" But he was wrong: there was no bread. "I must have finished it this morning," he murmured. "Sorry to be such a bad host."

"I'm not hungry."

"No," he conceded with a half smile. "You wouldn't be. How was the Legio Maria mass?"

"An orgy of superstition."

"Were they beaten?"

"Yes."

"Badly?"

"Yes."

"Don't judge them. Don't make the mistake of judging them." I sipped my tea in silence, Mercy's dire forecast long forgotten. Father Anselmo rubbed his forehead slowly, methodically, as if trying to remove a stain whose exact location he had forgotten. "I lose my faith, you know. Two, three times a day I lose my faith in God. If it weren't for their faith, the faith I see burning in their eyes, I would have turned into a raving atheist years ago. Their faith keeps mine alive."

"Faith like I saw today at the Legio Maria mass?"

The priest considered the question for a second. "Yes and no. Yes, because the faith we are talking about is, in fact, childlike and will attach itself to someone as ridiculous as this bishop you've mentioned. And no, because, like a compass needle always pointing north, it seems to have a self-adjusting mechanism. These people are desperate. They'll try anything once. But they always go back to what they instinctively know is right. Where will you sleep tonight?"

"On the floor."

"Very well," he said, and went to his room.

I tried to sleep but the sound of coughing kept me up all night: coughing from a million directions, all of it so close, so intrusively, maddeningly close. More than once I had to resist the urge to stand up and scream at everyone to shut up, to leave me alone. It had nothing to do with me: it was a slum, we were practically lying on top of each other. Still, every bout of helpless coughing seemed directed at me with the precise and malicious intent of depriving me of sleep. All that walking around earlier in the day—the bile, the blood, the corpse-strewn pathways, the rigid muteness of people consumed by the virus—all of it had failed to give me the true measure of Korogocho's madness. Beyond the hunger, the filth, the violence, beyond the trauma of constant loss was the insanity of overcrowding.

"People take machetes to each other," Father Anselmo told me in the morning. "They go mad—stark, raving mad. The cumulative effect is almost impossible to fathom. Imagine if you had to share this room with four or five other people every single day of your life. You'd go mad. And people do. They take machetes to each other." He seemed in better spirits, far less prone to snapping. He put Mercy's cousin to work straightaway. "We need eggs, onions, bread, and sugar," he told him.

"Me, I have no money," James said.

"Neither do I. Did I say three eggs or six?" James stared at him mutely. "Make it six."

"But Father, where can I be getting such things?"

"Your problem," the priest answered, nudging the poor man out the door. We sat at the table and talked about Rome—its cumbersome pace, its lack of austerity, the late afternoon light, which sets entire buildings on fire, the soft,

soft night, which makes a carnival out of a maze of cobblestones. "I very nearly made it back," I told him.

"Sorry?'

"I very nearly went back to Rome. Recently. Very recently."

"To do what?"

"What I've always done: journalism."

The priest laughed. "Journalism in Rome? You must be kidding."

"Why?" I asked defensively. "There's plenty to write about in Rome."

"Let's not talk rubbish!" Father Anselmo snapped. "Living life is not a childish task! And we're not children!"

"Who's talking about children?"

The priest spread his arms and shouted: "Rome? You want to go back to Rome? *This* is what the world needs to see! This! Right here! Right now! You should thank the Lord he gave you the opportunity! Everyday! On your knees!"

I stared miserably at my hands. Then I cleared my lungs. "I could not, in theory, agree more. In practice, I'm not sure I have the stomach for it."

"Do some sit ups," the priest said.

"You really have no money?" I asked a minute later, more to lift the pall than to get an answer.

"Not a penny," was his delighted comeback.

"Why?"

"Two reasons. One, I don't want people getting funny ideas and paying me a visit in the middle of the night. Two, it's good to be without money."

"How?"

The priest examined his fingernails, clearly untroubled by the layer of dirt gathered underneath. "Poverty is extremely useful," he said. "It brings you closer to people whose generosity you are often compelled to return, and closer to God, whose munificence you learn to recognize."

"Munificence. There was no bread in this house last night."

"There will be six eggs in this house this morning," and at that very instant Mercy's cousin pushed through the door, the proud carrier of six eggs, two onions, a bag of sugar, and a loaf of sliced bread.

"Look, Father!" he beamed. "The ladies at the market said to wish you good day!"

Father Anselmo took the parcel and placed it in my hands. "Try not to cook it all. It would be nice if there were something left for me this evening."

At home later that day I wrote in fits and starts, between bouts of diarrhea so severe Mercy called a doctor. "What did he give you?" she asked after he left.

"A shot in the ass."

Mercy nodded, pleased: "The injection can do the work now," but I saw no evidence of any work being done by anyone other than myself.

When I filed my story, late that afternoon, I crawled into bed and told Mercy to answer the phone: "I'm not in. I don't care who calls, I'm not in."

Barely five minutes later Mercy was at my door shouting: "Telephone!"

I opened the door, incredulous. "What did I tell you?"

"It's your boss," she said, arching one eyebrow significantly.

"I don't care who it is!"

"You want to be sacked?"

"I'm sick!" I hissed. "I have a right to be sick!"

"Tell that to your boss."

I picked up the phone. "I'm sick."

"Drink lots of fluids," Warren said, "So ... this ... Father Anselmo Morosini ... I presume you haven't made him up."

"You presume wrong. He's a figment of my imagination."

"And he lives *in* the slum."

I looked out the window, past the neat hexagon of my garden table—a gift from Nick—to the great green lawn, suddenly struck dumb by all that space, all that green, by the waves of both light and wind on the grass, by the cool of my hibiscus tree, by the chorus of flowers standing tall and lean against the farthest wall—beyond which, I realized with a start, lay acres and acres of *someone else's garden.* "How big is your garden?" I asked.

"What?"

"How big is your garden?"

"Big."

"How big?"

"Big. What's the problem?"

"Have I ever told you where I live? Have I ever described my house to you?"

"No," Warren said with a sigh.

"I live in a four-bedroom house. Porticos. Terraces. A swimming pool. Two acres of perfectly manicured garden."

"I've got four."

"Four of what?"

"Acres."

"That's good. You'll rot in hell twice as long as I will."

"And I own my property."

The green of the grass had me hypnotized. For a while nothing registered. "Sorry?" I asked.

"I said I own my four acres."

"I'm sure you do. And it's wrong."

"I'm sure it is. We've just sent you a read-back. Let's have the story all wrapped up and ready to go for tomorrow's paper."

"I'm sick," I said.

"Drinks lots of fluids," Warren said.

Warren. I had changed my mind a million times about him. I had thought him harsh, remote, padlocked in that patrician head of his and no more capable of engineering an escape than walking barefoot on wet grass. I was told he lived in a big colonial house somewhere. His wife was a painter. She made no money but she talked a lot. He had three girls, ponytailed wonders between the ages of six and twelve. He said something about a dog once and I bet ten bucks with the Moscow correspondent that it was a golden retriever. I was right.

Then a few things had happened. He had arranged for me to have a leisurely stroll around Africa before deciding to move there or not. He had bullied the library into acquisitions of new material on Africa before I left *and* he had suffered no fewer than five lectures from various relatives on the gross irresponsibility of sending me abroad. "It's the Italian thing," he said. "I saw it coming."

The truth, never confessed of course, was that I had feelings for Warren, that despite my own abruptness on the phone I liked him, I respected him, and I looked forward to hearing from him. His news judgment was infallible, his integrity cold and clean. A cheap story disgusted him, it offended him and while it did not make him mad—nothing made Warren mad—it deepened the chill in his voice to freezing point. A good story had the opposite effect and so that day I dragged myself to the computer and sat down to work on the read-back. "Korogocho," someone had written in CAPS. "Where do you get these population figures? Is the priest your only source?"

"Yep," I wrote on impulse. "How about that?" but then I called Mercy. "Could you get me that Habitat report, the one ..."

She clattered off to the filing cabinet and came back with several pounds of words on paper. "Now, these people," she thundered, slapping the tome with the back of her hand. "Can they be learning to use few words instead of many? Us, when we have something to say, we say it quick, chop-chop! Some few words and we are finished! These people, they can be talking until the morning! Also," and she raised a stern finger, "they can be wasting too much paper!"

"They most certainly can," I muttered.

"That is very bad," Mercy sentenced. "People in China are becoming addicted to the toilet paper so now we are having a problem for the whole planet."

I raised my eyes. "You mean used to."

She shrugged. "You can be getting what I am saying."

"Yes. Trouble for the planet. What do you want me to do? Write to the U.N.?"

"And be wasting more paper?" I smiled. Mercy checked her new watch, a lavish gift from Michael. "It is coming close to four o'clock. Can you see?" and she shoved the watch under my nose.

"I can see."

"Nice, eh?"

"Very."

"Michael is a good man. Isn't it, Anna?"

"It is."

Mercy sighed, a long, high sigh. "Maybe you can be giving him a *toto*."

My head shot up. "A what?"

"A child," but then she cocked her head, gave me a queer look. "Maybe not," she said, walking away.

"Why?" I called out after her.

"Too many *totos* ..."

I wrote like a demon, filed my story, and staggered queasily to the kitchen. "Too many *totos* in the world?"

"In the house," she said.

"Meaning?" Mercy shrugged. "Meaning?"

"Eh!" she snapped. "You can be seeing for yourself."

"Good," I mumbled, staggering back to my study, "Great." I waited half an hour, then called Warren.

"Good story," he said. "We may have to tone it down a bit."

"Tone it down?"

"Just a little."

"Where?"

He drummed his pen loudly on his desk: "I'm not editing your story, Yvonne is. You want to talk to Yvonne?"

"Sure, I'll talk to Yvonne. But this stuff is real and I'm not going to pretend it's not. I can talk to Yvonne all you want but it's not going to change the story."

Warren's voice acquired a very discernible edge. "No one is talking about changing the story. It's not what we do here."

I beat a hasty retreat: "No, of course it's not."

"We're talking about softening some adjectives and verbs, maybe taking out a few overly dramatic quotes. That's all."

"Fine," I said meekly. "I'll wait for the read back."

"And cut it. We're going to have to cut it."

I shot to my feet. "Cut it? What do you mean, cut it?"

Again, the drumming. "Cut," Warren said coldly, "as in: 'to cut.' With or without scissors. Cut. Snip, snip. Four hundred words. Gone."

I felt myself grow dizzy. "Warren ..."

"Anna, I've got the Middle East, I've got the Balkans, I've got a stand-off between India and Pakistan. I know this is terrible and it makes your heart bleed every single goddamn time, but we're not kids, okay?"

"We're not what?"

"Kids! We're not kids!"

"What's the big idea about kids ..." I started to say but the line clicked and Yvonne said: "Hey there, give me a second to pull up the story ..."

A few minutes later, as I sat stone-faced at my desk, the doorbell rang. Mercy came barreling into my office: "It's that *kijana*!" she whispered, her nose an inch away from mine, "He's standing there with some *pombe* and some big ... *nini* ... some flowers!"

Nick's smile vanished the second he saw me. "What in the world ..."

"I've got the shits."

He screwed his face into an expression of disgust. "For God's sake, Anna ..."

"You want to lecture me? Pick up a number. Stand in line."

Nick raised both hands: "Perish the thought! I wouldn't *dream* of lecturing you! No, I'll just tread lightly on eggshells, as has become my custom around you, until your first organ collapse. It shouldn't take long."

"And this is not a lecture."

"Not by any stretch of the imagination. Look at me." I did and found the same queer look Mercy had given me earlier, slow and speculative and ultimately skeptical. "You look terrible," was all he said. I considered making a scene but the frailer part of me clung to him as he took me by the hand, hollered for a vase, laid out two glasses, and popped open the champagne.

The perfect alignment of his teeth, the frivolity of his white linen shirt were obvious antidotes to Korogocho's pain. But there were other mechanisms at work. Apart from the low gravitational pull of physical beauty, Nick was the doorway to a candlelit world whose private, vaguely dissipate vibrations I'd encountered only in passing: the tented luxury of safaris in the bush, the hectic social swirl of the white Kenyan circle, the opulence of lunch parties held in quintessentially colonial fashion—all of it made possible by the smiling solicitude of legions of black Africans whose monthly salary rarely, if ever, made it past the hundred-dollar mark.

"Here's to you," Nick said. I raised my glass and emptied its contents at one go. The alcohol went straight to my head, setting off a buzz, a vibration that drowned out the chill of Jessica's room, the rank odor of the slum, the geographical accumulation of so many deranged souls. "Where were you?" Nick asked.

Despite the cramping in my stomach, I handed him my glass for a top-up. "Korogocho," I said.

"Where's that?"

"Nairoibi."

"Really? Where?"

"Outer Ring road. Next to Kariobangi."

Nick raised his eyes to the ceiling, tabulating the data just received. "Is that a slum?" he asked. I nodded. "Well," he chirped. "I've come just at the right time, then. There's a party on the other side of town this evening. Would you like to come?"

3

THE HOUSE WAS THE ONLY source of light and for miles. A trail of bagged tea-lights led from the parking area to the front door. Nick flung it open and preceded me into a room lit exclusively by candles. A shimmering crowd—women in long evening gowns, men in black tie—swirled in groups of three or fours with none of the stiffness, none of the formality typical of the opening hours of a party. The impression, immediately received and soon confirmed, was one of intense familiarity among the guests—of pranks played and suffered, objects and devotions shared, loves exchanged, and funerals attended over the course of decades rather than years.

My hands began to sweat. It wasn't so much the intimacy as the sensation of having been miscast as an extra on the set of a Hollywood movie. I was by far the least glamorous, no, the least presentable person there, my worn corduroy jacket and jeans absolutely pathetic against the beaded splendor of laced-up bustiers, dark suede skirts, strapless black numbers, and heavy modern jewelry. I rummaged in my bag for a cigarette, already plotting my escape. "Relax," Nick whispered.

"I *am* relaxed."

"No you're not. Let's get you a drink."

We were almost at the bar when a woman detached herself from her group and strode gracefully toward Nick, a smile of delighted recognition on her face. She was tall, blond, slender, her face and shoulders dusted with light freckles. A white sarong clung magically to her body. She was, I discovered up close, barefoot, without a trace of makeup on. "God, how absolutely lovely to see you," she whispered, kissing Nick on both cheeks.

"You look fantastic," Nick whispered back, his eyes dancing. The woman gave me a quick, unfocused smile. "Page, this is Anna." I felt my mouth stretch into a thin smile.

Page nodded vaguely, then leaned into Nick: "Did you hear what your wretched horse did to Justin?" I excused myself. In the bathroom, I leaned into the mirror and grimaced.

My dreams spoke the truth, they spoke the truth: there would be women, always. It wasn't easy to explain, Nick wasn't fickle; he was in essence monogamous but, like Narcissus, he'd been condemned to search endlessly for his reflection in a mirror: not because he was in love with it, but rather because he needed confirmation of a specific density against a stream of conflicting information—and in that way ward off the danger, the very real danger, of dissolution into dust.

I had made several excuses for it during our short time together; I had turned a blind eye, I'd even joked about it ... but God, how bitterly! The truth is that whatever it was, wherever it came from, I was spectacularly unsuited to handle it. My own fears ran deep, jealousy had destroyed my purest loves, casting shadows where there had been none, turning play into brawl, song into hiss. "Shit," I whispered in the bathroom. "Shit. Shit. Shit."

There was nothing I could do but negotiate my frayed, unseemly bulk to where Nick would still be chatting up Page. I hated myself for coming. I hated Nick for taking me. I wanted out. I unlocked the door and stepped out, determined to leave at once when, fingering the hard innards of my handbag for my cigarettes, I came across a blister of pills. I knew, without looking at them, what kind of pills they were and, beating a triumphant retreat to the lavatory, I locked the door, flicked the light on, and smiled. Valium. Twelve pills. Five milligrams each. Two ought to have done the trick. I popped out five for good measure.

Nick, I found, was still with Page; they had retreated to a corner of the room and stood with their foreheads nearly touching, as if in the appreciation of a secret. I got myself a drink and wandered out to the garden on my own—time flying, time shimmering past, not a grudge, not a problem in the world. Nick loved Page, Page loved Nick, and there I stood, on a freshly cut lawn, under a tranquil zodiac of stars.

Time flying, shimmering past. "That's why they're so fucked down there." I nodded, my head flopping back and forth. Who was that? A dark, good-looking boy talking about Southern Sudan. Why? To test me, to annoy me, to shove things in my face. I did not care. I had no issues with him or anyone else: the cosmos and I were at peace. "You see my point," the boy said. I shook my head in vigorous assent.

Another man, tall, balding, with flushed cheeks put one arm around the boy and asked: "Have you seen Marina's photographs of the Nuers?"

"Yeah," the boy answered. "Amazing." An exchange took place between the two as I hazily debated my next move.

I had just decided to meander toward the kitchen when I found the older man glaring at me. I flashed him a conciliatory smile. His expression hardened. "Were you or were you not?"

"What?"

"In southern Sudan!"

"Oh," I said with a start. "Yes."

He let a few seconds pass. "Where, precisely."

"Mostly Bahr El Ghazal." I let my gaze drift. Just speaking the name, just saying the words brought on a sense of distress so acute I pushed my hands in my pockets and lowered my eyes to the glistening grass.

"Where's that?" the older man asked.

I looked up at his face, suddenly struck by the odd unreflective quality of his eyes. "The Arabs in the north call it Bahr El Arab," I said.

"Pardon me?"

"The Arabs in the north call it Bahr El Arab."

Somewhere I have a photograph of a boy between the ages of ten and fourteen. He's on his hands and knees, covered by a layer of dust so thick his black skin has gone chalk-white. Against all that whiteness, the boy's red gums and tongue provide the only reminder of a once distinct humanity. Were it not for the vermillion of the mouth, the spidery frame advancing across the Sudanese desert could pass for a giant insect, the by-product of some insane experiment. He is advancing at roughly half an inch per second—hand first, knee second, other hand, other knee, and so on—in painful, infinitesimal progress past the grounds of the food distribution toward ... nothing. In front of the boy, acres and acres of fissured ground lead absolutely nowhere.

It was April and a quarter million Dinka were starving. We'd seen dead babies held by dying mothers, old people laid out in rows on the hot sand, foam bubbling weakly at the corner of their mouths. The sights and sounds of mass starvation were all too easy to capture, but for some reason we had to keep going back in: there seemed to be a critical mass of words and images that the "international community" had to consume before it could spring into action. Again and again we went.

Each time we built a camp and fenced it off with thorns. At nightfall we pulled out nuts, crackers, canned sardines, and tuna. We pulled out water and juice. We pulled out wine and whiskey. We ate and drank. Beyond our circle of light, behind our barricade, slat-ribbed children pressed their bodies against the thorns, watching us eat. At dawn, we cleared camp and followed the thin, high wails of infants to yet another scene of human suffering.

The boy is inching forward in the dust and this time I can't help myself. I kneel in front of him and put a small carton of juice to his lips. Gerard, my photographer on this trip, catches me just in time. "Are you crazy?" he yells, galloping toward me. "Give him all that sugar and he will die!" I stand back, horrified. The boy lets out an animal wail, his eyes fill with tears.

Back in Nairobi, Gerard finds he has the boy on film. He puts the photograph in an envelope and slips it under my office door.

"The Arabs do what?" the older man asked, his voice garrulous, mean.

I raised my empty wine glass. "Anyone for a drink?" But my head was throbbing and a low, red tide had already lifted me, silently screaming, off the ground. So much for twenty-five milligrams of Valium. When the old man let out a contemptuous snort, I grabbed him by the ears and hissed into his mouth: "You fool! You fucking fool!"

He screamed, of course, as did the boy. There was great commotion and suddenly Nick was by my side. I looked him in the eye and walked away. "Anna, what in the world ..." but I kept walking until I reached the gate. Only then, away from the crowd, did I stop and turn:

"You piece of shit. Don't *ever* come near me again!"

"Anna! For God's sake!"

"For God's sake what?" and, before I knew it, I had slapped him in the face.

He brought a slow hand to his cheek. "You're crazy," he whispered.

"You ain't seen shit," I whispered back. Then I set out on foot alone into the night.

It was a two-mile walk to the corner shop. There, by an exceptional twist of luck, I found a lone taxi. I climbed in, gave the driver directions and passed out cold in the back seat. "I'm sorry, Madam," I remember the driver saying when he dropped me off. "Me, I cannot be beating my customers to be waking them up, but you ... *Ahi! Nili kua nina chapa wewe!*"

The following morning, head pulsing, stomach churning, clad in the clothes from the day before, I made my way to the kitchen. The sight of Mercy nearly gave me a heart attack. "What are you doing?" I yelled.

She stared at me, eyes as hard as flint. "Me, I am washing the dirty clothes. You?"

Reeling in confusion, I looked at my watch. "Isn't it Sunday?"

"No."

"What day is it?"

"Friday."

"No!"

"Yes." We looked at each other as if through binoculars. "Now," she said with a loud sigh, "Michael called. He says you call him back."

"Where?" Mercy raised both eyebrows. "Where should I call him?" Up went the eyebrows again. I considered saying something about the advantages of the spoken word but the truth is that I could barely believe my luck: Mercy was there—solidly, unassailably there. The world could snarl and bite all it wanted: the woman from River Road stood nearly six feet tall, had the arms and legs of a boxer and the face of an angel.

"Nice hairdo," I murmured as I reached for the coffee.

Mercy lifted her lacquered fingertips to the vast pyramidal structure perched on her head. With infinite delicacy, she began to prod its contours as if for structural flaws. "It's not too big?" she asked.

"Too big for what?"

"For my head."

"No," I lied, turning on the coffee grinder and grimacing at the merciless eruption of sound.

"It's somehow heavy," Mercy confessed, still gently prodding. "It's making my neck to hurt a little."

"Get rid of it then."

"Eh?" she cried, indignant. "It was just placed there!" I poured the ground coffee in the machine and switched it on.

Did I really slap Nick in the face? Did I grab that man by the ears? Did I really hiss like a snake into his open mouth? Yes, and more than that. I laughed: a high, shrill laugh with the ring of madness in it. Mercy began detailing the cost of her hairdo while I began wondering when it had all started, when I had crossed that first line and why.

Was it at nineteen, when, drunk for the first time, I uprooted a flower bed and smashed the windows of three cars? At twenty, when, in a fit of jealous rage, I destroyed a stove with a frying pan? Twenty-one, when, in response to a mild episode of sexual harassment, after waiting weeks for the right moment, I slashed the tires of a Frenchman's Porsche? Twenty-two, when, at a student demonstration, I charged a policeman with a broken beer bottle, nearly taking out one eye? That night, in jail, I asked myself what madness was rising to the surface. Where did it live? Where was it nestled? Would it grow cold, malevolent, altering the DNA of every cell, severing every human bond, leaving me at age fifty on a cold landing wondering if those were the footsteps of someone I knew? Then nearly a decade has slipped past with barely an incident. Why the sudden surge? I knew the answer. Despite all Father Anselmo had said, I knew the answer.

"I told her. I said this one seems like it's growing too much but she just kept adding the hair. So me, I just kept quiet and now you can see for yourself what has come."

I did see for myself, it was impossible not to. And once again I asked myself why Mercy, who was capable of exerting enormous force on everyone around her, had allowed a hairdresser to gain the upper hand. But then again, so much of Mercy's obsession with her looks—the purple nails, the fluorescent eye shadow, the punitive heels—had been a mystery from the start. There were no men in her life, she seemed to harbor nothing but contempt for the opposite sex, so it was never clear to me why she strapped, pinched, squeezed, leveraged herself into her disco outfits every morning. I didn't dare ask. I poured myself a cup of coffee, muttered an apology on behalf of the hairdresser, and headed for the bathroom.

I felt remarkably clear-headed when I stepped out of the shower, so much so that I decided to make three phone calls. The first was to Father Anselmo, who could be reached at the Kariobangi parish office on Fridays only, between eight and ten. He seemed to have forgotten who I was. "Who?"

"The journalist."

"Oh," he said after a pause. "What can I do for you?"

Clearly he was in a rush. I felt my face grow hot as I began to stammer. "I wanted to tell you ... no, to thank you. I wanted to thank you."

"For what?"

"For the work you are doing entirely on your own."

"Come visit me from time to time."

"I will," I said with feeling. "I will."

"And bring a baguette from that French bakery in town. Is it still open?"

"Still open."

"A baguette would be nice."

Next I called Kez. Friend. Colleague. Accomplice. Best thing in the world after Mercy. We'd met in room 312 of the Serena Hotel in Nairobi. I had knocked at the door, Michael had opened it, and pulled me violently in. "A kiss," he had whispered urgently, then, smooth as glass: "Guys, this is Anna." In front of the television—tall, hawkish, fiercely elegant—was Derek, a freelance producer from Australia. Lying on the bed was Kez, Michael's cameraman when Michael was too busy with production to shoot his own footage. He had dark, smoky eyes, a sharp beak of a nose, and, when he finally rose, a fluidity of movement that made me—and everyone else—feel hopelessly mired, bound at the wrists and knees.

We'd spent the afternoon together, curtains drawn, television blaring, a bottle of Absolut on the coffee table amid much dispersed white powder. "Kez can't cut for shit," had been Michael's terse and rather accurate assessment.

Kez, of course, had taken great offense: "Okay, Mister-fuckin'-perfect, give us a demonstration," and in a second flat Michael had turned out a thing of such elegance and beauty that we'd shot to our feet and given him a standing ovation.

It pains me to admit it but it had been a great afternoon. At one point Michael had raised his glass and shouted: "To Africa! May it continue to bite us in the ass!"

Kez had slapped his forehead twice, erupting instantly into Arabic, his native tongue, then switching to English: "You want a bullet in the head, eh? Is that what you want? A bullet in the head?"

Michael had gone rigid. The two had locked stares. Then Michael had turned a finger in a lazy circle over the coffee table: "Want to do a voodoo dance for us, Kez?" Kez had spat on the floor.

"Oh, *come* on!" had cut in Derek. "We're just a bunch of blokes, sorry, a bunch of blokes and a gal, sorry, a bunch of blokes and a very lovely gal, trying to have a good time. Okay? All right? Turn out another line, why don't you Michael?"

But Michael had kept his eyes on Kez: "Come on. Do a dance. Wiggle your ass for us."

It was then, looking at Kez, seeing the way he pulled his shirt over his back, the way he balled it in his hands and threw it to one side, the way he raised his fists and lowered his head without *so much as a prayer* that I knew that we were made of the same stuff. The exact same stuff.

It's hard to talk about Kez, hard to explain. We shared the Mediterranean, identical memories of summer on its shores: the blinding light of noon, the pall of silence between two and five as the adult world slumbered, the endless late- night meals in the barely controlled chaos of restaurants featuring three, maybe four dishes and waiters who rolled their eyes at the approach of customers. His past was murkier than mine, his eyes identical—long, brown, flecked with blood from too little sleep. There had never been a physical attraction, I was not his type, he was not mine, and rather than twist this fundamental fact we'd settled immediately into a quiet, often dangerous, camaraderie. The more Michael and I drifted apart, the closer Kez and I became. He'd introduce me to his girlfriends and I would shrug: "She doesn't eat! When was the last time you saw her eat?" Or: "She's a drug addict! You want to marry a drug addict!"

To me he would say: "You're killing yourself, Anna. You're killing yourself."

That day, Kez answered on the first ring: "What."

"Kez!" I hissed.

A pause. "What?"

"You can't answer the phone like that!"

"Why not?"

"It's not polite!"

"*Polite*? What are you, on drugs?"

The door to my study blasted open and Mercy waddled in. "Have you called him?" she boomed. I signaled to her that I hadn't. She clacked her tongue: "Now, you, why are you delaying with him?"

I covered the receiver with one hand: "I'm on the phone!" but I heard Kez say: "Yeah, call Michael." I shooed Mercy out of the room but only after shutting the door and peering into the peephole did I dare tell Kez what had happened the night before.

"You're crazy," he said.

"So are you. Shall I send him around to your place?"

"Who?"

"Michael!"

"Are you crazy?"

"Kez, I'm a mess."

He groaned. "Hold on . . ." and I heard him rummage for a cigarette. I heard him light it and take a deep drag. "Okay," he exhaled. "Here's what you're going to do. You're ready?"

"Yes."

"Get out."

"Where?"

"Don't ask *me*, man. Just get out."

I called Michael. He answered on the first ring. "Don't move, you hear me? Don't move."

Mercy's face lit up like a pinball machine when I told her. "We must make some *chapatti*," she said, wiping her hands on her apron, "*Chapatti* with some *kuku* and some chips. He will be hungry. Make me to run to the store."

I trotted after her to the door. "Not a word about Nick." Her eyes refused to meet mine, so I walked her to the gate. "Understand? Not a word." Again, she refused to look at me. "Okay, you mention Nick and you're fired. I swear to you, you're fired."

"Me, I cannot be talking of such things," she said.

My eyes nearly popped out. "You cannot be talking about such things? The other day in the kitchen did you not talk about such things?"

"Eh!" she exclaimed, pulling her arm away, "You want to talk or you want to eat?"

He busied himself with drinks the second he walked in. "No thanks," I said, when he handed me a gin and tonic. Shrugging, Michael took both glasses to the patio and collapsed into a plantation chair, his eyes narrowing against the light. He took a long sip, closed his eyes, and let his head drop slightly to one side. A line of sweat snaked down one cheek, dipping into the curls of his closely cropped beard. He ran one hand, scarred at the knuckles, brown from the sun, along the back of his neck. "Where's Mercy?"

"At the store. Buying your lunch."

"I'm not hungry."

"Feel free to tell her when she comes back."

He let out a controlled sigh. "Where were you last night?"

"Me?"

"Yes, you."

I opted unhesitatingly for the path of greatest dishonesty. "Home."

"You were not. I drove by. Your *askari* said you were out."

"That's what I told him to say. I did not want to be woken up."

"Is that right?"

"Ask him. He comes on duty at six." Again, he closed his eyes and let his head dip slightly to one side. For two or three minutes no one spoke. Michael kept his eyes closed, his breathing regular, and suddenly I was overcome by guilt. "I'm sorry," I said. He didn't move. "I'm sorry," I said again.

He wiped the sweat off his forehead. "What are you sorry about." It wasn't even a question.

"I've been ... preoccupied."

"With what?"

"Myself mostly."

He sat up, flung his legs around, rested his elbows on his knees, hunched his shoulders, and bore his pupils into mine. His green eyes, fringed with thick brown lashes, were dark with suspicion—not to mention the usual low-grade, combustible rage. "So, Miss Anna. Is it over?"

I wondered fleetingly why neither Nick nor Michael seemed to take anything I said literally. "Well. There is ... there was ..."

I was cut short by a roar: "Don't talk shit with me! Do not talk shit with me!"

"Aaaaahh, no!" a voice boomed. We both turned and, the Lord be praised, there was Mercy—arms crossed, brow knit over burning eyes. "This shouting is too much for me, please. Let us leave the shouting to the children. Let us be like the big people of the world."

A slow smile spread across Michael's face. Mercy tried to keep the fire in her eyes but the corners of her mouth turned up against her will. Soon the two of them were looking at each other like lovers finally reunited. "Great," I snapped. "The mutual admiration society reconvenes on this joyful day."

Ignoring me, Michael went up to Mercy and folded her in his arms. She broke into a girlish giggle. "Got something for you," he whispered and disappeared into the living room, coming back with a cream-colored bag whose waxed handles were tied together by an elegant black ribbon. Bergdorf Goodman, the bag said. My jaw dropped. Without the slightest protestation of unworthiness, Mercy loosened the ribbon and took out a box embossed with the entwined C's of Coco Chanel. Out came a full makeup kit: a compartmentalized *trousse* with gold, silver, and bronze for the eyes, reds and mauves for the mouth and cheeks. Mercy stood transfixed until, having caught a glimpse of herself in the mirror, she raised one hand to her head and, with the same infinite delicacy of before, began prodding the cone-shaped structure there.

I witnessed the entire scene in silence, bile burning from stomach to heart. What about me, I wanted to shout, nothing for me? But I didn't say a word and soon Mercy was going on about lunch. "*Chapatti* and *kuku* and we can be having some rice or some potatoes with some little sauce ..."

"He's not hungry," I snapped.

Mercy gave Michael an astonished look. "Sure I'm hungry," he reassured her.

She giggled, that harebrained twitter she reserved for him, then, placing her hands on her hips, she thundered: "These bad places you are always coming from now! You are chewing on some little piece of goat but it's hard, no? They are too busy fighting each other to grow food, isn't it?"

"He was in New York," I said dryly.

"Eh?" went Mercy.

"He was in New York: capital of modern cuisine, restaurants at every corner, food coming out of everyone's ears." Mercy eyed me with suspicion but Michael put one arm around her.

"Ignore her," he whispered. "She's got something up her ass. Are you really making *chapatti*?" and together they went to the kitchen.

She never fussed over me like that. I paid her salary, her children's school fees, I gave her money for her clothes, for her hair attachments. That ridiculous thing she had on her head? *I* had paid for it. Not once had she offered to make *chapatti* for me.

I sank into the plantation chair, battling the urge to throw them both out at once. Who were they to conspire so openly against me? And at what point in our common history had I become a guest in my own house? Michael had been shrewd about Mercy: I doubted very much that he had been drawn to her naturally. No, he had seen her tender exposed flank, her desperate need for flattery, and had set about driving his hooks in as far as they would go. Now he had an ally. He could stroll into my house and exile me to the patio. Retire to the kitchen and learn to make *chapatti*. And Mercy. Was she *in love* with Michael? Did she not know how absurd, how preposterous her fantasy was, the power it had to crush her?

I rose to my feet and, catching a glimpse of the gin and tonics, proceeded to drain half of each. Next, I began to pace. My life was in shambles. I had lost Nick, I would lose Michael and Mercy in rapid succession and my fall from grace would be complete. Kez was right: I had to get out. I ran to my office and slammed the door shut. Breathing heavily, I dialed Warren's number. "Nigeria," I said.

"Pardon me?"

"Time to go back to Nigeria."

"You're starting to sound like my mother-in-law. She's got Alzheimer's. What's your excuse?"

"Professional fervor. Everyone's going."

"Who's everyone?"

"The agencies. *New York Times. Washington Post. Time. Newsweek*. You name it."

"So?" but I could sense alarm creeping into his voice.

I steadied myself on the desk and said: "Rumors of a coup."

"A coup? From who?"

"The usual suspects."

"No: your source. Who's your source?"

After fabricating the identity of a lawyer in Lagos and a businessman in Abuja with unique access to the corridors of power, I was good to go. "Shit, shit, shit!" I whispered, hanging up the phone. "Shit!" Biting the nails on one hand, I rummaged for my cigarettes in my bag with the other. I took a long drag, grabbed a hold of my Rolodex, scrolled to a page and quickly dialed a number in Lagos, Nigeria.

"Reuters," a voice chirped.

"Hi, Reuters," I said, "Could I have a word with Peter?"

"May I ask who's calling?"

"Anna, from Nairobi."

Peter's thin, high voice had to battle with the static to make itself heard. "How are you, Anna?"

"Not so good, Peter, not so good. I think I may have ... aaah ... overstated the significance of a rumor I heard the other day about a coup."

There was a long, painful pause. "A what?"

I cradled my forehead. "A coup."

"Where?"

"Nigeria?"

"Nigeria?"

"Yeah."

Peter laughed. "You know how it is: rumors of a coup are chronic here."

My spirits soared: "They are, aren't they?"

But Peter was not done. "Except right at this minute."

"No?"

"No."

"Why not?"

"The army simply cannot afford to stick its neck out."

"No?"

"No."

"Not even a little?"

"Not even a little."

"Jesus. Why not?"

"Well, let me put it this way: in the thirty-six years of Nigeria's history, this is probably the single most unfavorable moment for a coup. The generals know it and, more importantly, the colonels know it. Why? Who's your source?"

It was too late. I called the airline and miraculously found a seat on the three o'clock flight to Lagos. The traffic to the airport was vicious but eventually the city began to fade behind me and the first thorn trees began to dot the line of the horizon. The sky became immense and—as always on the road of the airport—I grew giddy at the prospect of landing somewhere utterly foreign and setting out alone, quiet, keen, small as a fly, stubborn as glue: a stranger in a strange land.

4

THE AIRPORT WAS CRAZY BUT David was there—head shaved, toothpick wedged between upper canine and molar, flip-flops held together by the invisible glue of God's grace. "How yo' body?" he asked with a grin. I answered as I'd been taught: "Body dey inside clothes," and pressed his palm against mine.

Put clothes on a naked body and you're in business: this is the essence of the greeting, and the spirit of a nation crammed entirely into the present. The yogis of India have nothing on Lagos, city of fifteen million, Babel of tongues and tastes, of cons and scams, capital of the *here* and *now*. This is where the past is kept constantly at bay, where memory hangs bound and gagged off a tree at the periphery of things. No time for yesterday's grief: *chop-chop*, things move far too quickly for that here. You leap from moment to moment, praying no one grabs you by the heels in mid-flight. And if your prayer goes unanswered, no problem: the present has a million ways of redeeming itself.

I'd left Michael on the plantation chair, replete with *chapatti* and drink, no longer so hostile to my presence in this world. Mercy kept hovering over him. "The *kuku*, it was tough, eh? That *muhindi* butcher is a bad man! I said please, something fresh this time and he just make a sign for me to go! *Ahi!* Bad man!"

My bag was packed. "You're going?" Michael asked, incredulous but in keeping with my new policy of maximum dishonesty, I had no trouble making up a story about being ordered to Nigeria without a minute's delay. Michael narrowed his eyes: "What's going on in Nigeria that I don't know about?"

"Nothing, believe me. Place is dead. We're ... just doing a series about oil."

"Oil?"

"Oil. And its derivatives."

"How come you didn't you tell me this before?"

"You were too busy making *chapatti*."

Mercy had yanked me to one side. "Why you leave him like this?" she had whispered hotly. "There is nothing happening in that place now! There is no job for you to do there!"

I pulled back, surprised. "How do you know?"

"Me, I am reading the *Daily Nation* every day and I am seeing nothing that is unfolding in Nigeria! Nothing!"

"Unfolding?"

"Unfolding. Now you. Why are you running?" and she started flapping her elbows in a perfect rendition of a panic-stricken chicken.

It was all so unexpected that I had to take a moment to think. In the end I raised my arms in an admission of helplessness. "I have to get out. I can't handle this situation a second longer."

"So you lift the legs and run?"

"So I lift the legs and run."

"And what shall be waiting for you when you return?"

"The exact same thing."

Tightening her lips, Mercy held out one arm. "Let's see what you have placed in the bag."

"It's okay, it's done now. I used to pack my bags before you came along, you know."

"You have taken the torch?"

"Yes."

"The radio?"

"Yes."

"The medicines?"

"Yes."

"The *dawa* against the mosquitoes?"

"Mercy! I know how to pack my bag, okay?"

"You know, eh? Like the last time you were going to that place!"

"I don't have time ..." but she was already on her way to the kitchen. She came back with a warm parcel neatly wrapped in aluminum foil.

"*Chapatti*," she said, "for when you are feeling hungry."

I'd gone to Michael for a kiss and he'd pulled me gently onto his lap. "You got Valerie's number?"

I slapped my head. "No!"

He took out a worn notebook and read me the number. "Call her the *second* you get in. Tell her I said hello. Make an appointment and, when you get there, give her a bottle of the most expensive perfume you find at the duty free. Okay?

She'll get you your press card by the end of the day. Don't do shit without a press card."

"I won't, thanks. Thanks very much."

"No problem. It's what I'm here for. Where are you staying?"

"I was thinking the Sheraton ..."

Michael waved the notion aside. "Forget Ikeja. You want to be on Victoria's Island. Go to Marisa's Guesthouse: it's small without the moldy carpeting. Write down the number. And get one of the rooms facing the pool; you'll get perfect sat-phone reception that way." I nodded. He smiled. "Got a driver?"

"Yes."

"Fixer?"

"Same guy."

"Good. If for some reason he doesn't work out call James. He kicks ass. Here's the number. Now, down in the delta the human rights people are not easy to get a hold of. They have an office space but no phone. The only way is to go there. Physically go there. Write down the address. If no one's there, leave a note with your contacts with the hairdresser on the ground floor along with a twenty." I nodded as my ears began to burn. "Where are you staying?"

"I don't know," I whispered.

"In Port Harcourt go to The Rooftop. Here's the number. You're going to Warri, right?"

"Maybe."

"You've got to if you're doing oil. Call this guy. He's a lawyer. He knows everybody. Ask nicely and he'll let you stay at his house. It's a dump but it's a lot better than any of the so-called hotels. Fucking dives, man." By then I felt like crying. "You okay, baby?" he whispered.

Mercy rolled in. "The airplane is at three?" I nodded. She tapped her watch. I gave Michael a kiss.

"Call me when you get there," he said.

"I will."

"Oh," he called. "And don't let Valerie screw you into having a minder. All she wants is a fifty. Slip her a hundred."

I called him from the airport. "I don't deserve you."

"No, you don't, but don't sweat it. You're going to Lagos! Go to the Shrine! Smoke the ganja! Have fun!"

Africa is a place of remorseless realities. The filoviruses that periodically rise out of its dark marrow don't claim a handful of lives: they claim legions. The death toll from floods and famine is never in the hundreds. Droughts breathe fire across the continent, erasing whole villages in lightning displays of sound and fury. But Africa is also the world's last cup of laughter. Laughter surges, eddies, ripples here; it flows so freely and so wildly that you cannot resist it; it tumbles past you like water in a stream, leaving you no choice but to jump in.

David and I took our places at a dingy table with plastic plates and mugs and ordered two pepper soups. Next to us, a woman burst out laughing, spraying her immediate surroundings with specks of food as her companion tucked his hands in his armpits and touched his forehead to the table, shaking with laughter.

The waiter came around with two cold beers. I tossed a handful of peanuts in my mouth and began to giggle. David joined me, shaking his head to signal his reluctance. The more they laughed, the more we laughed until all four of us were howling. David kept shaking his head, steady in his resistance to full-throated laughter.

For reasons never debated and so never fully understood, David preferred a dignified smile to the immoderate contortions of full laughter. As I wiped tears from my eyes, I could not help notice how different things were this second time around.

The hotel had sent him to the airport on my first visit three months earlier, claiming no first-timer in Nigeria could reasonably expect to make it downtown alive. The woman at the hotel reception—an Italian long transplanted in Lagos—had gone to great lengths to assure me of my inadequacy when I called to book a room. "Chris Rupert. He is from Kenya, no?" The name rang a bell and I told her so. "Very good," she said. "First he had his bags stolen, then he was stabbed."

"Jesus."

"Precisely. First they took the bags, then they stabbed him."

"Why?"

"They were after his wallet, although they did not take it, not at the airport anyway. No, this poor Chris Rupert gets stabbed and gives a taxi man at the airport three hundred U.S. dollars to rush him to the hospital. They are driving on the highway and what happens? The taxi driver runs out of petrol. This is Nigeria's national sport, by the way, running out of petrol in the middle of the highway. Anyway. The taxi driver leaves Chris Rupert bleeding in the backseat and goes with a jerry can to fetch some petrol. A car thief comes along, pours petrol into the tank as Chris Rupert is watching, you can imagine the poor man, watching from the back seat as he is bleeding to death. And then the thief does what? He hot-wires the car, rolls Chris Rupert out like a sack of potatoes, and drives off. Are you with me?"

"Yes."

"So now the taxi driver returns and what does he find? Chris Rupert and no car. So what does he do?"

"I don't know."

"He takes Chris Rupert's wallet, credit cards, picture of wife and children et cetera and leaves him there, bleeding on the side of the road." I tried to cut in but the woman barely noticed. "Very good then. As soon as your deposit arrives, we'll arrange for a driver. His name is David. He is a good man."

David was indeed a good man but his car kept breaking down. "Di carburetor," he said the first time. "Di plugs," he prophesized the next. Whatever the malfunction, the result was that I kept finding myself on the side of the road watching David and a dozen improvised mechanics all yelling at each other. Finally I gave up. "I fix di car tomorrow," David swore.

"You will not fix the car tomorrow! Look at it! It's a piece of junk!"

"I fix di car tomorrow," he swore. I told him to forget it but the following morning there he was, in the lobby of the hotel, sitting placidly next to the driver I had hired for the day. "Forget it."

David blocked my exit. "Make we go test di car for one hour. If di car break down again, make you no pay me." And so we drove off.

The car was the same piece of junk as before but by then a bond of sorts had formed between us and I was reluctant to sever it. In the first of many incautious moves, I asked David to drive me down to the delta of the Niger river for a series of stories on Nigeria's oil-producing region. The journey ought to have taken a day and a half: it took us four. "Dey gone get dis one in di dump," David sighed when the car gave out for the fifth time. I sat under a tree and waited for the fireworks to start.

David, I belatedly realized, couldn't tell a cylinder from a piston, but neither could he tolerate anyone pointing that out to him. The sequence of events remained thus unchanged: the car sputtered into lifelessness, someone stopped by to help, an argument started, a minimum of ten to twelve people ambled over to see what the noise was about, the same ten to twelve people began poking their heads under the hood until all hell broke loose. So I finally told David: "You don't know how an engine works. Why do you pretend?"

"I don't know how di engine works? Who gone say that to you?"

It did not matter much in the end. David had proven invaluable on every other front, saving me from a million scams but also laying Nigeria out before me like an X-ray, white on black. When we got to the delta of the Niger, I knew everything there was to know. Our friendship was sealed in Enugu, after an overnight stay with one of David's childhood friends, a priest rising fast in the ranks of the Catholic Church. He wasn't at the Parish office. He wasn't at church. We found Father Edward at the head of his dining room table berating his staff for stealing his beer. "What is an honest man to do?" he asked us, outraged. "Do I lock the cool box? Do I set up a barrier in front of my house and have them searched on the way out?"

It's hard to see what David and he had in common, what qualities had drawn them to each other even as children. The priest was quick, shrewd, with an insatiable appetite for politics. He talked of the late General Abacha's dictatorship as of a personal insult, regretting bitterly that the general's end had come so quickly. "In jail!" he raged. "In the same stinking jails he was putting the rest of the people in! That's where he should have ended up! For the people to try him! To condemn him! To execute him!"

"Will you pray for him now that he's dead?" I asked.

The priest's eyes nearly popped out: "Pray for him? You have had too much to drink, my friend!" But then he softened some. "These things take time. Maybe in a few weeks we shall all go to Lagos to pray for his rotting soul." David chewed on his toothpick and sipped his beer, saying nothing. Father Edward gestured sharply to one of his servants. "Beer! Chop-chop!" Then turning to me he asked: "You are living in Nairobi?"

"Yes."

"A continental disgrace, the Kenyans! They are all stooped at the waist from bowing to the white man! In Nigeria we get a white man at the airport and we tell him: 'First you slip me one hundred dollars U.S., then I see whether I give you permission to enter my country!'"

"Yes," I said with a tight smile. "I am aware of the custom."

His eyes brightened. "Why? They shake you down?"

"No."

"Next time," Father Edward assured me with a nod. "Next time."

He carried on for hours. Like all Nigerians, he was convinced that his country lay at the center of every African hope and policy; unlike most Nigerians, he never tired of producing arguments to prove it. "Nigeria is the biggest country in Africa. It has oil. It has natural gas. It has educated people. It has the largest, no, the only middle class in the continent . . ." Without Nigeria, Africa was doomed. The Kenyans had no self-respect, the Ugandans zero natural resources and not much brain. The Tanzanians had lost their chutzpah with Nyerere. The Sudanese were all crazy, unable to extricate themselves from the world's longest running conflict. The Angolans were steeped in too much poverty. The Rwandans were all genocidal freaks, the Congolese fat and undisciplined. The Ethiopians still hadn't figured out that Egypt was screwing them out of their God-given water rights, the Eritreans too few to matter, and frankly far too quick to take offense. The Zimbabweans? "Please! They are squatting on five percent of their land!" Botswana had diamonds but was destined to lose its population to HIV/AIDS, Namibia was nothing but an inconsequential patch of desert. Despite the black facade, South Africa was still run by whites and so did not weigh into the larger African equation. Of the countries in West Africa, Cote D'Ivoire was the only vaguely promising one, but far too self-indulgent by half. No. There was only one country worth placing any hope on, and it was no coincidence that that country, one hundred million strong, lay on top of endless reserves of liquid gold.

I kept looking to David for help but he just shifted his toothpick dexterously from front to back and back to front, either unwilling or unable to take part in the conversation. As the evening wore on, he indulged the priest in the craziest conspiracy theories—one of which, I still remember, had the CIA detonating a soundless nuclear bomb to end the war in Biafra. "Are you okay, David?" I asked at one point. He gave me a slow nod and a smile. The priest yammered on and I began to suspect that David, who had never had any trouble asserting his views with me, was struggling with a horrible sense of inadequacy. He had not seen the priest in eight years, a decisive span of time during which, I suddenly recalled, David had produced seven offspring, the youngest barely a month old, while the priest had joined the church and devoted himself to "spiritual matters." The result was that David lived in a hole in the wall in Lagos while Father Edward had recently taken possession of a six-bedroom house in the lush center of the city he was born and raised in.

At six o'clock sharp, dinner was served. Out came a platter of goat meat with sides of *posho*, green beans, and shredded cabbage. Father Edward dug right in. David aligned his toothpick with his plate, served himself a modest portion and let a sardonic eye rest on his friend. "Dis a Catholic goat?" he asked, his first words in more than two hours. The priest doubled over laughing. David let the spasm subside. "More Catholic than you," he said, lifting a morsel to his lips.

The priest stiffened. David kept eating. I watched in silence as the balance of force shifted from one to the other. There were no more pronouncements from the priest, only questions, all directed at David. David answered in monosyllables.

When we met the next morning for breakfast, I noticed that David's eyes were bloodshot. "You look terrible," I said.

"I slept only a little."

"Why?"

"Edward. He needed some advice." In the car, I asked him why he had been so quiet for so long. It took him a while to answer. "The man is a cheat."

"And?" I said.

"And he was my friend."

When we finally got to the river, I asked David to come with me but he said no. He was an Ibo man, he told me. He lived in Lagos because that's where the money was. He had driven me to Warri because that was our agreement. But go further on in a motorboat? That was too much to ask. "I stay in di hotel," he said. "I wait for you there. You go."

"What if we raise your daily rate?"

"How much?"

"Double."

"Triple." And down we went.

From village to village. Fish heads, fish bones scattered everywhere, the smell of paraffin and poverty at times too strong to take. Half-naked old men propped against mud walls, women chewing lethargically on sticks, children with bloated stomachs scampering in the mud. The midday sun like an axe, the air so dense you never felt dry. Above all, beyond all, the Niger: immense, godlike, reducing everything to a tiny speck—the villages with their pontoons, the spidery fleet of barges and dugouts, the cracked spirals of ancient roots reaching down for more water. And a presence, a definite presence in the river, which, if given a voice, would tell you to get out of the way—or to come closer. "Na here Jesus stay," David said one morning after we turned off the engine and began floating soundlessly downstream.

"Why Jesus?" I countered. "Why not God?"

"Same thing."

"We could argue about that."

"I don't discuss matters of faith."

The sentence was so clipped, so chiseled and so forcefully put that I raised myself on my elbows to take a look at him. "You don't discuss matters of faith?"

"No."

"Why not?"

"Make us no discuss."

"You can have faith and reason things out a little."

"No, with faith you accept. You just accept."

We stayed three days, motoring up the creeks during the day and finding our way back to the river before dark, as a string of bonfires began to flare along the banks. At dawn, we woke to the rhythmic drumming of boats signaling their positions in the mist and set out again. On the fourth day, with great reluctance, we began to make our way back to Warri.

I think by then we had fallen into a sort of trance, lulled by the lack of any discernible tempo into a curious acceptance of all things—from the revolting fish stew we consumed three times a day to the unmitigated harshness of our sleeping conditions on the boat. The river flowed on, violent and wise, with us in it.

It wasn't long, however, before David formed the delusional belief that his car had been stolen. I, in turn, began to think that I had caught malaria, so numerous were the punctures on my arms and legs. The truth was that I had forgotten to bring mosquito repellant. Mercy and I were at that stage locked in the first of many battles over who should pack *my* bag. Her argument was that I always forgot something. My argument was that I was old enough to pack my own bag. In this first trip to Nigeria, I had prevailed by packing a day in advance with the result that I had over two hundred bites on my arms and legs. "What else could these be?" I asked David as we began our journey back.

"Those bites?" he said, squinting.

"Yeah."

"Mosquito bites."

"I know they *look* like mosquito bites but could they be something else?" He screwed his eyes at me. "Forget it," I sighed. No sooner had the words left my mouth that I was struck by sudden inspiration. "A plant!" I said. "I'll tell her it was a plant! I'll tell her it is an allergic reaction to a plant!"

"Who?" asked David.

"None of your business who."

"But if a doctor …"

"Yeah, yeah, yeah," I interrupted. "If a doctor asks, I'll tell."

The sun began its steep descent. David and I had agreed to spend the night in one of the larger settlements on the off-chance of scoring something other than fish stew, but as darkness approached, we found ourselves by an average-sized village of maybe fifty households and no choice but to pull in. We were still securing the boat to the pontoon when we were told a woman had just given birth to a fish.

The village was electrified. The woman had by all accounts gone into labor early, and pushed out a dark, slimy creature with gills and a tail. The creature lay at the mother's feet as the council of elders debated whether to allow it breast milk or not. The council was also to determine who among the villagers had practiced unlicensed witchcraft and what punishment they would receive. "Must be a badly deformed child," I told David. He shrugged, suggesting it was all below him, but after dinner I returned to the boat and he went looking for more gossip. He kept bringing me unwelcome updates:

"Di child is a fish, no joke."

"Di fish has a tail and makes a sound like crying."

"Di fish cannot breathe this air. They are putting it in the river."

"Di fish is breathing. He is sucking at the breast," and so on, until the blighted household closed its shutters for the night.

We woke the next morning to find a wizened old woman standing by the bow of our boat, trying to peer in. Age had shrunk her to the size of a five-year-old; she had a single tuft of white hair rising Mohawk-fashion out of her shriveled scalp. "Who is she?" I whispered.

David addressed her brusquely and listened to her long, shrill answer with a deep crease in his forehead. "A relative of di fish," he told me when she was done.

"What does she want?" David fixed his gaze on the woman but said nothing. "What does she want?" David barked out a question and the woman let out a cascade of words. By then I had an idea. "She'll take us to see the fish if we pay her, right?"

"Na so," David said, never taking his eyes off her.

I shook my head in disbelief. "Poverty is one thing," I said—not knowing yet that poverty is everything—"but this . . ." David pulled out a couple notes and, crumpling them into a ball, threw them at the woman's feet. "David!" I shouted but the old woman bent over, pocketed the money as if no insult had been intended or, indeed, taken and hobbled off.

David jumped off the boat, stretched both arms above his head and sauntered out of sight. He came back with a brand new toothpick and the latest news. "Di fish is dead."

"Great," I said. "We're off."

David did a minute or so of teeth picking before saying: "Make you give something for di family."

I fished out some notes and handed them over. "Hurry up," I called after him. "I'm starving." He showed up one hour later, surrounded by an odd group of people. They reached the pontoon and stopped, as if debating whether to climb into the boat or not. "What's going on?" I hissed.

"Make we take dis child to di hospital in Warri," David whispered back.

"What child?" David gestured to one of the women. She stepped forward and I saw a small child cradled to her breast. "What's wrong with her?"

"Dis the mother of di fish. Dis dey eldest child."

She was nineteen. Her oldest child, a girl, had just turned two. A week before she had come home with a slightly swollen eye. The next morning, the infected eye was shut and the other had begun to redden. Twenty-four hours later, with both eyes shut, the little girl complained of a sore throat. Her mother found an abscess growing right where the lower mandible softened into the throat. The abscess grew, the girl began to have difficulty swallowing. Next, her breathing slowed. Now she lay unconscious in her mother's arms.

She was unconscious most of the way, her tiny hand moving in search of her mother's only once. We tried to spoon some water into her mouth but she sucked it weakly into her lungs and convulsed. Her breath came out in shorter and shorter rasps. A tiny vein began to throb wildly by her temple, bringing to mind the heart of a bird trapped in human hands. The mother sat motionless, a stone pietà filling the boat with her inaudible cry. When we got to Warri, she rose unsteadily to her feet, clutching her daughter to her chest. "Pass di child," David said. The woman did as she was told and we saw then the girl had died.

That night in Warri, David and I got viciously drunk. David began to ramble. "Di Lord, he di one with di plan."

"Please."

"Di Lord knows. Di Lord decides."

"The lord does not know and the lord does not decide! The girl is dead because there were no doctors, no hospitals, no medicines, nothing!"

"That too," David agreed. "That too."

"In a place that's floating on the best oil the world has to offer a child dies because there isn't a medical facility for miles. There isn't a doctor! There isn't a goddamn pill! So much for Nigeria's manifest destiny! I wish your priest friend were here. Man! I wish he were sitting right here ..." David wedged his toothpick in the furthest recess of his mouth, nodding gravely.

In the morning we started for Lagos. When we pulled into the parking lot of the hotel, covered in sweat and dust, David handed me a scrap of paper with his fee on it. My eyes popped out: "This is double what we had agreed on!"

"No."

"Yes!" David stared obstinately ahead. I counted silently to ten then said: "Okay. Break it down for me," and it turned out that he had slapped on the cost of fuel. "We agreed at the beginning that fuel would be included in your daily rate," I said.

He turned around to face me. "But I gone take di car all di way down! It went far, far! And who is going to fix it for me now? You?"

"Fix it? That car was never fixed!" David dug his heels in. In the end I paid the full sum. "I never want to see you again," were my last words to him.

Nairobi's rarefied air cleaned out my lungs and got rid of some of the sluggishness I had been feeling. Mercy zeroed in on my mosquito bites the instant I walked through the door. "You did not pack the *dawa*!"

"I did too!"

"Then what are you having there on the hand?"

"An allergic reaction."

"Eh?"

"An allergic reaction to a plant." Mercy raised my hand: "Me, I have yet to see such a plant."

"Well," came my smooth reply. "You haven't been to the Niger delta."

That afternoon, my head started to pound, my limbs to shake. My joints were on fire, my bones felt as if someone had taken a hammer to them. In the middle of the night, as I resolved for the tenth time to call a cab and get myself over to the hospital, the phone rang. Two. Three. Four times. Then it went silent. "They've given up," I thought listlessly, as I tried to remember where I had put my jeans. I had to find them. I had to put them on. I had to go to the hospital. Where were they? On the chair by the bed? In the hamper by the bath tub? "Oh God," I pleaded silently. "Not the bathroom. The bathroom is too far." And then, as in a dream, I heard someone booming: "Anna! Anna!"

With an enormous effort I pulled myself up on both elbows. Mercy was standing by the side of the bed, glaring down at me. Astonishingly, her eyes filled with tears. "What's wrong?" I asked, alarmed, but she moved like a whirlwind past me to the closet, pulling out a duffel bag and stuffing it full of things. T-shirts, shorts, a *kikoy*, a pashmina, underwear, two sweaters. Toothbrush, toothpaste, shampoo, face cream. Hairbrush. Towel. I let the darkness draw me under.

It was cerebral malaria. At the emergency room I was put on intravenous quinine and after a few hours of close monitoring I was rolled up to the malaria ward on the third floor of Nairobi Hospital. "What happened?" I asked Mercy when she came to visit.

I could tell she was battling the urge to whack me over the head with her handbag but then she said: "Your driver called from Lagos. He asked me how you were. I said I did not know. I said you were staying the whole time upstairs. He said for me to go check on you. He said you had received many, many bites and he was thinking you were having malaria. He said you were talking such nonsense as being bitten by a plant but I should not believe you."

"You're joking."

"Me, I'm telling the truth."

"David called?"

"Yes."

"All the way from Lagos?"

"Yes." A few moments passed. Mercy took a long breath. "Now me, I am demanding to know why you have been lying, but we are not children, Anna. Malaria is serious. You have to fear it."

"I'm a fool," I murmured. Mercy nodded vigorously. Then, as if the sight of me filled her with a sudden sadness, she turned her face to the window. Keeping her eyes closed, she lowered her voice to a whisper: "Me, I am not your mother, Anna. There are just some few years between us but many times, many, many times I am having to think of you as a child who is trying to do bad things so that the big people can see something is wrong. I come to the door with my key sometimes and I think: no, today I am going back to my place. Because me, I am fearing one of these days I am going to come inside and find you lying dead on the floor."

"Jesus," I said impulsively, but then fell silent.

Mercy took this as an opportunity to enumerate my vices: "You don't eat, you don't sleep, you drink *pombe ninghi sana*, you take cocaine . . ."

"What?" I cried.

Mercy pierced me with a stare so resolute, so final I clamped down on my lips immediately. ". . . you delay with your job. Your boss calls and you don't have the work ready for him, you are always making some excuse, telling him some lie. Your boss is not a fool, Anna." I readily agreed but she was not finished, she was saving the coup de grace for last. "And now," she announced, "you are playing games with that *kijana*, that Nick. You think he can be looking after you? You should be fooling yourself. That one can play games, bring the expensive *pombe* you drink together, but that *kijana* cannot be looking after you. He cannot. It is not in his ... *nini* ... his nature."

I looked down at my hands, fighting the urge to cry. "Will you please call David when you get home? His number is in my black book. Under N, for Nigeria."

For someone so contemptible, I recovered beautifully. Even Mercy was impressed. David and I talked on the phone a couple times and, a few months later, here we were, in Yaba, perversely bent over two steaming bowls of fish soup. "So," David asked. "Where we go tomorrow?"

All good humor drained out of me at once. "God knows," I mumbled. I told David what I had done.

"Confess," he said. "Just confess."

It never came to that. In a staggering twist of good fortune, Kaduna—a furnace of sand and silence in the north of Nigeria—went up in flames that same night. Muslims and Christians were murdering each other at the rate of three hundred a day when David and I got there at noon the following day. People were killed quickly. They were dragged out of their homes kicking and screaming and hacked or bludgeoned to death in the middle of the street. The women, Africa's pallbearers, emerged from their narrow doorways when it was over. Sobbing, shrieking, raking their faces with their fingers, they lifted the body and brought it back inside.

One Christian life for every Muslim life. It went on like that for three days until the cartel of interests that ran Nigeria—the caliphate, it was called—decided that too much blood had been shed. The Nigerian army was resuscitated from the dead and put an end to the commotion in a couple hours. The population of Kaduna disappeared behind closed doors and windows, the local emir made his first public appearance to bemoan the shedding of so much innocent blood.

Just as I was getting ready to fly back to Lagos—leaving David behind to sort out pierced radiators, worn-out clutches, snapped belts—I heard violent pounding on my hotel door. "I'll be out in a second!" I yelled, thinking it was room service.

"Open the fucking door!" It was Kez. He was leaning against the wall, stoned out of his mind, implausibly elegant in his worn jeans and T-shirt. I gave him my hand. He raised it theatrically to his lips. "I was hoping they'd send you," I said, "When did you get here?"

"Yesterday."

"Where's Michael?"

"In Nairobi."

"Why?"

"Said he needed a break."

"A break?"

"That's what he told London. I think he wanted me to produce."

"Shoot *and* produce?" Kez could not repress a smile.

"Yep."

"He's doing this for you."

Kez indulged in a satisfied yawn. "Too bad the story is over," I said.

Kez ran a hand over his shaved scalp and neat goatee and looked at me critically, as if unsure whether to let me in on the secret or not. I waited, knowing he'd come around.

Stretching his back he said: "We sent the stringer to Kano. He just called."

"And?"

Kez curled his lips into a devious little smile. Wagging one finger under my nose he said: "They're being naughty down there …"

I ran downstairs to catch David before he vanished but he'd been last seen pushing the car to the nearest garage. So I got in a car with Kez and drove to Kano, another city in the bone-dry north.

That night, Kez and I sat at his editing machine, the table behind us crammed with ashtrays and empty beer bottles. Kez was cutting footage from the hospital. "Who's this?" I asked, pointing at the screen with my pen.

He gave me a look of mild annoyance. "Mohammed Ahmed Mohammed, twenty-eight."

Mohammed Ahmed Mohammed was laid out on the floor, a gash the color of rust down the length of his forehead. His skull had been fractured and the subsequent swelling concealed his eyes entirely. He looked grotesque, inhuman. Remarkably, he was still alive when Kez caught up with him outside the hospital, surrounded by wailing relatives. One of the women was shouting something into the camera. I stole a glance at Kez. His chin was propped on one hand, his eyes were darting all over the screen.

"What is she saying?"

"I don't know," said Kez.

"Please?" He threw his notes over at me. "*They came from Marakwet. There were five of them. One was commanding the others, he was telling them what to do. They were looking for the father but the father was not there. They kept calling for him, looking everywhere and when they did not find him they took my son. Look what they have done. Look what they have done.*

"What did he do?" I asked.

"Who?" Kez snapped, his eyes glued to the screen.

"Mohammed Ah . . ." but before I could finish Kez got up and started shouting: "I'm on fucking deadline here! I've got forty-two fucking minutes! Michael stayed in fucking Nairobi so I could get the fucking chance and you're fucking ruining it! What the fuck is wrong with you?"

"Okay, okay," I said, raising both hands.

But Kez wasn't satisfied. "Why weren't you at the hospital? Huh?" It was true; I should have made the obligatory stop at the hospital if only to get a reliable tally of the dead and wounded, but I'd chosen to spend the day maneuvering unsuccessfully for access to the local emir. I started to tell Kez but he wouldn't have it. "You never make it to the hospital!" he shouted. "Where do you think the fucking story is? In the park? In the fucking *sandpit*?"

It was my turn to jump up: "I never make it to the hospital? I'm always at the hospital! Always! You want to talk about the times *you* didn't make it to the hospital? About the times I had to hand Michael pages and pages of notes *about* the hospital?"

Kez screamed: a howl, a call to heaven. Then he grabbed his notepad and screamed: "Car mechanic! He's a fucking car mechanic!"

I wrote down "car mechanic," slid my notepad in my pocket, and brought my face within an inch of Kez's. "Don't ever ask me for a favor again."

He was at my door almost exactly an hour later. "I've got something for you."

"Fuck off!"

"I'll leave it right here, okay? Right by your door." I waited twenty minutes before opening the door. There, copied in meticulous handwriting from the original, were three pages of notes from the hospital, at the bottom of which Kez had added: "Contrite as always. Devoted as always. Filed on time."

At the airport in Lagos, waiting for our flight to Nairobi, Kez began to swear. He had woken up with a hangover and had two hundred pounds worth of gear to take to Nairobi. The airline wanted six thousand dollars, Kez claimed he could only pay three. In the end he paid four and a half, all of it in cash. "Fuckin' people," he kept muttering, "fuckin' people don't know fuckin' shit," until I lost my temper.

"If this were Delta Airways in New York you wouldn't be exactly haggling, would you?"

He fixed me with a pair of smoldering eyes: "I don't live in New York, do I?"

"What do you care? It's not your money."

"Ooohhh," he crooned. "It's not your money.... What about this morning? Was *that* your money?"

It was true: he had waited in the parking lot of a hotel for nearly one hour while I tried to get a decent exchange rate. "That's a question of respect," I said. "I'm not paying eighty-three nairas to the dollar when I know the exchange rate is ninety."

"What do you care?" he mimicked, hands on hips. "It's not your money!"

"The guy was trying to screw me!"

"Oh yeah? Well, these guys are trying to screw *me*."

"Kez," I said, lowering my voice, "we're talking about a guy who changes money on the street versus an airline with a fixed policy on excess baggage."

"Fixed?" he sneered. "Fixed? I wouldn't be sitting on fifteen hundred bucks if it were fixed! Wake up, sweetheart, you're . . ." and he looked over both shoulders and lowered his voice to a conspiratorial whisper: "In Africa!"

We took off that night under a full moon, Africa spread like a giant below us.

Why this land should be so full of God, I do not know. Maybe because there is so much poverty, such need of grace, of mercy. The Enlightenment—the cleaving of reason from emotion, of body from soul, of the visible from the invisible—never took place here. And so thunder issues from the lungs of God, fire carries the disembodied longings of relatives long dead, a broken cup delivers the curse of infertility. But that's not all. There is a *kyrie* over the land. It lifts like loosened dust at the passage of animals and people, gathering again at the foot of trees, on the surface of still water, along the blade of the horizon. It hums as it steals on the air, a hairswidth above the ground: a timeless exhalation.

Kez, who was a Muslim of deep but unorthodox belief, claimed the desert of Arabia had the same *kyrie*. It, too, he claimed, made a sound like a low exhalation. "The breath of Allah," Kez said, in a flight of lyricism. He was, I had discovered early on, a man of numerous addictions and strange, at times visceral, faith. He went through phases where he stopped whatever he was doing, took out his compass, rolled out his lavishly embroidered rug—a gift from his father—and prayed five times a day. At those junctures we had argued like cats and dogs. Drunk, I slipped notes under his hotel door: "Predator, victim! Parasite, host! Canine distemper! Surely there could be finer mechanisms than these! Surely God can do better than this!"

"What do you know of the life of the neutron?" he wrote once in reply. "What do you know of the circuitry of the brain? What can you tell me of the balance struck between electricity and magnetism? Which insights can you provide into the event horizon of a black hole? Tell me: what do you know of music of numbers, the clarity of water, the human eye? You know nothing. You sin through pride, my sweet friend. You sin through pride: the deepest, the darkest, the Original sin." He was far less castigatory in person. "Allah is great. You're not. End of story." These pronouncements gave Kez an improbable moral edge over the rest of us. He had his superstitions, like reciting the same six verses of the Koran en route to a scene of mayhem and carnage (he whispered the words fiercely under his breath, making everyone in the car jumpy as hell) but he also had such a finely tuned sense of right and wrong, of pretense and authenticity, that people actually went to him for advice.

His own life was a study in chaos. It was a miracle he was even around. Arrested, beaten, held at gunpoint more times than he could count, the victim of not one, not two, but *three* mock executions, Kez's streak of bad luck had proved so obstinate that his editors in London kept begging him to leave. Yet there he implausibly was, in the row in front of me, lost in a deeply stoned appreciation of Africa's mass, having just been yanked out of the lavatory, joint still in hand, by an enraged stewardess. ("It's okay," he kept telling her. "I'll put it out.") "Ever heard of Mal de la Russie?" he had asked me earlier on at the airport. "It's Afrique, baby. Afreeeeque!"

In Nairobi he did his usual vanishing act, having collected his one hundred and fifty kilos worth of gear well ahead of my single bag. "Tell Michael to call me," were his parting words. "And don't make him suffer too much. You'll regret it."

Don't make him suffer too much. You'll regret it. Words like fruit gone sere: you can't eat it, you can't return it, you can do nothing with it. All you can do is toss it out.

5

"HE IS DEPARTING THIS EVENING for Guinea Bissau," Mercy announced as I walked through the door.

"Are those real?"

Mercy stretched one arm out to better examine her scarlet talons: "Why? They are looking bad?" Trying to suppress a smile, I began climbing the stairs to my room. "Where are you going?" Mercy shouted, her voice a few octaves higher than usual.

"To have a bath."

She checked her watch. "There is no time for a bath!"

"What do you mean there is no time for a bath?"

Mercy eyed me as a teacher eyes a dim child. "He will be going! To the airport!"

"So?"

"So you go! Now! Chop-chop!"

"Mercy, I'm filthy."

"He will not mind so much."

"Forget it."

What came next caught me completely by surprise: in a single leap, Mercy propelled herself up three stairs, snatched my bag and ran—no—sprinted out the door. I caught up with her by the car. "You've gone mad!" I shouted. "Give me back my bag!" But she opened the door and threw the bag on the passenger's seat.

"Now you become responsible!" she yelled. "You go to his house! You look him level and you tell him you are through! You become responsible! Like the big people in this world!"

I sensed the change in Michael immediately. "Hey," he said casually. "Come on in. I leave in exactly ten minutes." He looked good, in fact, better than good: his eyes were bright and he had obviously been spending time in the sun.

"Nice tan," I said. "Did you go to the coast?"

"Nah. I hung out by the pool."

"Really. I didn't know this place had a pool."

"It doesn't."

"No? So whose pool was it?"

"Yours."

"Mine?"

"Yep."

I must have given him a nasty look because he said: "I'll tell you what, Anna. I'm going to be real friendly about this. I'm going to offer you a drink before I go. Would you like a drink?"

"Sure," I said, relieved by the offer, and the time I presumed it would buy me. I had, of course, presumed wrong. He came back with my drink—I honestly can't remember what it was—but rather than hand it over, he held it aloft, forcing me to meet his eyes.

"The series you were going to do on oil? Bullshit."

I took a step back. "You know what happened ..."

"Of course I know, it's my fucking job to know, right?"

"So?"

His eyes narrowed. "So there *never was* a series on oil. I called your editor."

I looked at him in horror. "You did not!"

He nodded deeply, a ghost of a smile on his lips. "Drink up," he said. "You'll need it."

"You have to stop calling my editor!"

"Nah, I'll tell you what I have to do. I have to stop wasting my time on you."

I should have danced the rumba on the corpse of the relationship, so frequent and so obstinate had been my attempts to kill it. Yet all I felt, looking at the tone and depth of his tan, was a flash of pure indignation. "So you spend two weeks sunning yourself by my pool and *then* decide it's over?"

"Yep," he chirped, but his eyes were darkening. "And feel free to let me know if that's a problem with you." I shrugged. He nodded, as if to say: Good, no need to push it further. "And by the way," he announced as he flung his duffel bag over one shoulder, "I wasn't just chilling by your precious pool. I was teaching Mercy how to drive."

It took a while to register. "You were what?" but he was already halfway out the door. "Hey!" I called but he kept bounding down the stairs.

"Shut the door behind you!" Michael yelled. And he was gone.

There wasn't a trace of apology in Mercy's eyes. "We were not going far with it," she said.

"I don't care how far you were going!" I shouted. "It's my car! Who gave you permission to drive my car?"

She gave me an icy stare, behind which, however, I could detect the cogs and wheels of her brain spinning madly. Her answer, when it came, consisted of one name and no teeth to speak of. "Michael," she announced with false solemnity.

"Sorry," I retorted. "Does Michael own my car or do I own my car?" She averted her eyes. "Sorry, Mercy, let's see if we can get this straight: who owns the car that is parked outside?"

"You," she conceded.

"So?"

She pondered the inconsistency. "Maybe he was confused." I began to answer but she cut right in: "Now. Let us hear the truth. Is it finished between you?"

"Yes," I said. "And if it's any consolation I didn't end it. He did."

She broke into a slow tentative smile. "You mean!"

"I mean."

She produced a sharp clap. "So he has been listening!"

"To what?"

"To me!" she cried. "I have been telling him: walk! Just walk! You will see! She will come running: like this," and she began to hop airily from one foot to the other.

"Thanks," I said.

"Fine," she said.

But that was not all. Minutes before noon, as I was putting together my last story from Nigeria, Mercy burst into my office in a chatter of heels and laid a thick document on my desk. "What's this?" I asked.

"Now this one," she breathed, "This one is the exam."

"What exam?"

"The exam for the Ministry of Motor Vehicles."

I scanned it briefly. "What am I supposed to do with it?" She tapped a flaming talon on a cluster of fine print. I leaned over and read: "*The applicant shall complete examination procedures within five weeks of payment, the above procedures inclusive of both written and manual examinations.*" I looked up. "So?"

"So I'm having a small problem."

"What."

"Next week is five weeks." I leaned back in my chair. Mercy crossed her arms. Neither of us spoke. Then Mercy said: "Me, I am getting my permit!"

I raised my arms: "Great! Get your permit! And now I have to work."

Mercy filled her lungs to capacity—a truly awesome sight: "I am needing more practice with the vehicle," she said.

"No." She let her eyes wander to the window and I could tell perfectly well that she wasn't even dwelling on my refusal: she was calculating how long it would take her to make me change my mind. Fifteen minutes is the answer. Just as sun climbed to its zenith, I sat beside Mercy in my Land Cruiser and began to sweat profusely. Mercy turned the ignition and revved up the engine. "Not so hard," I said.

"Eh?" she shouted.

"Not so hard!" Taking no notice, Mercy shot the car forward, nearly taking out the *askari*, and careened out of the compound and into the road without stopping to check for approaching traffic. "Mercy!" I shouted. She brought the car to a violent stop. "Mercy!" I shouted again as a *matatu*—one of a fleet of aggressively driven minivans used for public transportation—swerved onto the opposite lane to avoid a collision and streaked past us, horn blaring.

Mercy shot me a murderous stare. "Now," she said, tightening her grip on the wheel. "This shouting is making me to be nervous."

"You nearly killed us!"

"Me I did no such thing."

"You pulled out without looking! There were cars coming! That *matatu* nearly crashed into us!"

"There were no vehicles," she said.

"No? That *matatu* was not a vehicle?"

"That *matatu* was far."

I wiped the sweat off my face. "I haven't got the stomach for this. Let's go back."

Mercy put the car into first gear. "Let us go to the end of the road," she said, turning the engine back on. "Then we take Gigiri Road and we come back."

"Gigiri Road?" I shouted. "No way!" But there was such fierce determination in her eyes that I grabbed a hold of the hand brake and began moving my lips in silent prayer. The car began to gain momentum. "Slow down," I said, to no discernible effect. "Step on the brake!" I shouted. Mercy stepped on the accelerator. "The brake!" Down went Mercy's foot on the accelerator. "In the middle! The pedal in the middle!"

"I am pushing on it!"

"No!" I shrieked, yanking the hand brake. "Noooo!" There was no answer, only the belated identification of the brake pedal seconds before crashing into the mother of all *matatus*. Mercy stared dead ahead, her body rigid, her knuckles white. "Are you okay?" I asked. She looked at me as if she had not heard, as if she were not sure who I was, where we were. "Are you okay?" I asked again. Before she could answer, a tall, wiry man covered in sweat and driven by pure adrenaline materialized by her window and began beating his fist violently on the roof of the car. Mercy gave him the same disassembled look she'd given me. "I think he's the driver," I whispered.

"The driver," Mercy repeated and then something in her brain clearly snapped because she swung the door open and stepped out. "You have a problem?" she roared in Swahili. The man took a step back. Again, Mercy shouted. A crowd began to assemble. For the third time Mercy bellowed: "Do you have a problem?"

The voice of a teenage boy rose from the crowd: "You're the one with the problem, not him!" A murmur of approval rippled back and forth.

The driver began to shout: "You come crashing into me and you ask me if I have a problem? Yes, I have a problem! We could have been killed!"

But he stood no chance against the woman from River Road. "Was anyone hurt?" Mercy asked calmly. No one was.

"Then why do you beat your fist on the roof of my car? Mistakes can be made by people but violence is not a mistake! Violence is just violence and, me, I don't accept violence! So I ask you: do you have a problem?"

The teenage boy shouted: "Yes, the same one! You!" and this time the crowd broke into open laughter.

Mercy opened her arms wide, as if on stage. Softly, almost apologetically, she began: "What is happening to us that can be allowing the youth of this country to insult us? What happens when the children stop showing respect, when the five-year-old laughs at the fifty-year-old? You!" she said, pointing to a primly dressed woman in her fifties, "Were you laughing at the elders?" The woman shook her head. "And you? Were you answering back to your elders?"

An old man in torn clothes grabbed the opportunity with both hands and began: "Now me, when I was a small boy in K., not too far from Nyeri, maybe two, two and half hour on foot, and there were no vehicles then, it was all done on the strength of the legs and the hardness of the feet. Now, in those times I was not allowed to speak unless I was spoken to first! Never! That was the way then! And then some few years later, at the time of independence, when the young men were coming ..."

"*Ahi, asante baba*," Mercy said, sweetly cutting the old man off and turning with dangerously hooded eyes to the teenage boy. "Where is your mother?" The boy shrugged. Mercy roared: "I'll tell you where your mother is! Your mother is working her fingers to the bone so that you can eat, so that you can ride this *matatu* instead of walking for miles. Is this how you respect her? By insulting a woman her age? A mother like her?" The boy lowered his gaze. Finally it was the driver's turn. Offering him her hand, she said: "Let us be dealing with each other civilly, my friend. Let us be using our words, not our hands."

The man plunged both fists in his pockets. "It's all fine and well with you!" he cried. "You're driving around with a *mzungu*! Me, I am going to get sacked!"

Mercy kept her hand extended. "Stop blubbering like a two-year-old! It's just a small thing. I will tell the police it was my fault." And twenty minutes later, when the police arrived, that was exactly what Mercy did. Asked for her driver's license, she smiled: "Please, officer, I have left it at the house."

"Go and bring it!" the officer barked.

Mercy gave him a bashful smile. Lowering her voice, she said: "I was just thinking because it is approaching lunch hour that maybe we could offer you some small thing to eat." And so we piled in the car and drove home. Two hours later, pockets lined and stomach full, the police officer waddled out of the house, the picture of dissipated satiety.

"Not even a ticket?" I asked.

"Not even a ticket," Mercy confirmed, shaking her head in disgust. "These are the police these days. Now, me I want to say something. With Michael there was no shouting and no accidents. With you, there was shouting *kabisa* and the accident."

"I said step on the brake and you stepped on the accelerator; of course there was shouting!"

"Then me, I prefer to be going alone. I can be fixing the bumper and going alone."

"Go!" I said, tossing her the keys. "Go and get yourself killed."

But she didn't get herself killed. She got her driver's license and decided that her days as a house girl were over. "Me, I am wishing to drive the car. I can be assisting you in such a job after you have raised my salary." We haggled for days. She wanted twice her salary for a position I was in no need of, plus the honorary title of household supervisor with powers of life and death over the new maid, who turned out to be her niece, Felicity.

Sweet and dim, Felicity waited on Mercy hand and foot, making her breakfast, mid-morning tea, lunch, late afternoon snack, and, on the occasions Mercy decided to spend the night, dinner. Mercy ordered her around with almost farcical brutishness; she was quick to point out her flaws and slow to compliment her for a job well done.

"Poor girl," I could not help saying. "I feel sorry for her."

"Sorry?" Mercy bellowed. "I have employed her!" I began to suspect that Mercy was taking a cut out of Felicity's wages, but no amount of persuasion could convince the girl to cough up the truth.

"No, madam," she whispered, looking down at her feet. "I am the one taking the salary home."

From poor, sweet Felicity I began to piece together bits of Mercy's past, how her husband had been a regular *tombeur des femmes* and how his escapades in the early years of their marriage had hurt Mercy deeply, and injured her pride. How, as

Mercy's fortunes began to rise, he had sired an unknown number of children from a large pool of second wives, demanding that Mercy put food on their tables and a roof over their heads. How he had taken to drinking the *muratina* Mercy produced and gone on rampages with crippling financial consequences. And how throughout all of this Mercy had remained faithful, how she had stood humbly a step or two behind him at public events, how when his mother died she had fed a famished crowd the best *nyama choma* and the most copious drink ever seen at a funeral in Kawangware. And then he had put a gun to her head. "*Ahi!* He was a bad man!" was Felicity's near constant refrain when forced into a recollection of Mercy's past.

Felicity's arrival marked a strange transition—an excellent time, really. The rains stopped, the ground hardened, the air cleared. We bought a book on East African birds and took turns finding out which types visited us most often (this became a real passion for Mercy, who haggled viciously for a birdhouse, acquiring it at half price and securing it with a gaggle of granny knots to the lowest branch of the acacia tree). We cleaned the pool and arranged the outdoors furniture rather flamboyantly around it. We even scrubbed down the grill and made plans for a barbeque.

Delighted with her new, lavishly salaried position, Mercy laughed often and recklessly. Felicity lost the haunted look she seemed to have been born with. Nick called once while I was by the pool but Mercy swore Felicity to silence. Michael preserved his dignified silence from the jungle of Guinea Bissau in the middle of what turned out to be a very nasty little war and so life flowed on—predictable, impartial, sweet. I sat in the garden, drinking gin and tonics, marveling at the dancing prisms of lights overhead, at the humble pliancy of leaves, at the awesome gathering and fraying of the wind.

Early one afternoon I stopped by the French bakery at the Yaya center and bought a baguette. Mercy drove me to the church in Kariobangi, on the outskirts of Korogocho, and insisted on walking with me all the way to Father Anselmo's house. Once again, I witnessed the rise of a magnetic field around her: the punks, the drunks, the deranged, all stayed away, taking the widest possible detour, while the women rolling *chapatti* on the side of the road rushed over to greet her. "Remember the bad diarrhea you were now having," were her parting words.

He came late, at nearly seven o'clock, flashed me a cursory look, and went about the same backpack stuffing routine as the last time—retrieving a worn sac from his bedroom and pushing into it a gilded chalice, a thin silver dish, a tablecloth woven in bright African patterns, two candles, and a tin box full of unconsecrated hosts. "You look like a thief," I said and, to my delight, he teetered on the verge of laughter.

"Coming?" he asked, already at the door.

The slum stretched out before us like the ruins of a gutted city, still and silent under a layer of dried and drying mud. The smell of rot, of putrefaction seemed twice as strong this time. Father Anselmo took a deep breath. "It's nice to be out in the open air, isn't it?"

I stole a glance at him. "You're kidding."

"Why?"

"Because it stinks."

"Does it?"

"Yes!"

He looked up at the stars. "You know, I think God has given me the grace of not being able to smell anymore. Recently. Last couple weeks or so."

"You can't smell this?" The priest shook his head. "Really?" Again he shook his head, and there was something in his eyes, a well of awe and wonder and sheer gratitude whose depths he had yet to sound. "Isn't that something," I murmured.

The priest looked at me, clasped his hands behind his back and said: "You know, I am starting to see that everything moves *through* the grace of God. By everything I'm not referring to some abstract cosmology whose invisible laws occasionally become visible to the human eye. By everything I mean everything: the dog emerging from the doorway seconds before the screaming baby goes to sleep, the layer of cement laid down at the corner of Moi and Mama Ngina streets as a Toyota Land Cruiser carrying Mr. So and So parks on the opposite side. The butterfly flittering erratically across a field, the mushroom sprouting blindly by the root of a tree." Waving one hand in the air to encompass the immensity at work, Father Anselmo took another long, appreciative breath and fell silent.

Our footsteps reverberated in the night. "I don't know," I said after some time. "HIV/AIDS. Death by undeserved contagion. One third of Africa out the fucking window because of a virus that mutates so quickly the immune system fails to detect it. It's a hard sale."

"I don't have to sell it."

"You do," I said. "You do have to sell it."

Father Anselmo stopped dead in his track. "Why?" he asked, mirth dancing in his eyes. "I may be poor but I'm free!"

"To me," I said. "You have to sell it to me."

His eyes were like the bonfires along the banks of the Niger: flaring, barely restrained, in total darkness. "Very well," he said. "Try to imagine that death is a problem *only* from where you are standing. That what truly pains and troubles you about people dying is *your own* mortality, your own eventual and certain death, that in some mysterious way beyond your comprehension, death presents no fundamental discrepancy, no inconsistency, *no problem at all*. Let me say that again: no problem at all. That when it comes right down to it, *you* are the problem, not *it*."

I chewed on this for a while. "I don't know. A creature of God dying in agony in their own excrement strikes me as a problem."

Father Anselmo started swinging his arms in such a peculiarly childlike fashion that I half expected him to skip around a bit, perhaps put in a cartwheel or two. "So," he chirped, "have you ever had an experience where your perception of a specific event, object, person or reality was proven wrong?"

The memory of a morning in Somalia came rushing in. I was on the road to J., miles away from civilization but more importantly, miles away from any source of water. As I squatted under the puny shade of a tree, waiting for the members of our convoy to finish stretching their legs, I heard the sound of coffee bubbling up an Italian espresso machine. It was a sound from my childhood, the deeply familiar conclusion to every lunch and dinner. I sprung to my feet and turned my head in every direction: nothing. I ventured forward, then back, then forward again in a wide circle roughly fifty yards in diameter. Nothing. No stream bubbling nearby, no bird with espresso-machine vocalization abilities (no birds in that heat, period), and, barring some undetected fission below ground, not a single explanation for the sound.

"You seem disturbed," one of the gunmen traveling with me noted.

"I've just heard the sound of an espresso machine." He smiled a perfectly toothless smile and pointed to the sun, as if to say: worse things have happened. But I was clearer and sharper in my thinking than I had been for weeks—booze had been nearly impossible to come by on that particular trip—and I knew I had not imagined the sound: I simply had been unable to explain it. My perception, on whose accuracy I routinely staked my life, had tricked me shamelessly.

I started to tell Father Anselmo the story but he stopped me in mid-sentence. "We're here," and he ducked through a doorway into a narrow corridor dimly and erratically lit by a sputtering generator. "This is the only AIDS hospice in Korogocho," he whispered. "It has three rooms. We hope to add more." As we waited, a short, round woman with a large wooden crucifix dangling off her neck emerged from the middle room and, seeing us there, motioned us in. "How is she?" Father Anselmo asked.

"*Ana enda*," the nun whispered. *She's going.*

I don't know the woman's name. For some reason she's always been Margaret to me. Margaret, mother of four, all snatched away by the virus. The youngest one had died that morning but no one—not the nuns, not her surviving relatives—had had the courage to tell her. She lay on clean white sheets, a mere skeleton, convinced her baby was still alive.

Father Anselmo sat on the bed and closed his eyes. "The Lord is my shepherd," he recited from memory "I shall not want ..."

"*The Lord is my shepherd*?" I hissed the second we stepped outside. "The Lord is my shepherd? The woman's dead! Her children are dead! And the Lord is their shepherd?"

Father Anselmo laid a heavy hand on me and when I met his eyes I found that they were filled with tears. "God's ways are not our ways, Anna. Understand that and you won't need to understand anything else in your entire life." I stood like granite, unable to move. "Let's go," he said. "We're late."

I could not sleep that night, not just because of the coughing, which seemed to have gotten worse, but because of what I had seen in Father Anselmo's eyes: an inhuman acceptance of human pain.

I had told no one, but by then I saw God in the frayed edge of leaves, in the beetle's slow unenlightened crawl. I saw God in pasteurized milk, in the swift latching onto of penicillin, in the laser that cut the human eye: the priest himself—sharp-boned, long-toothed, horribly stooped—was the sensational culmination of all of that but every time I heard a child's tenacious wail grow weak, every time I saw the last residue of life seep out along with tears, I felt only rage—impotence and rage.

That night I abandoned the cot—Father Anselmo's unspoken recognition of our friendship—for the harshness of a chair. The priest tore past me when he woke up. "I'm late," he said, heading for the outdoor latrine. Mercy came to pick me up at dawn and drove me home.

"There are new chocolate biscuits," she said. "From Holland."

"Where is the gin?" I asked, my voice cold, mean.

Mercy shrugged. "It is not my place to be moving the *pombe* in this house."

I snorted. "Who are you trying to kid? Tell me where you've put the gin."

She sighed. "Under the sink."

"Which one?"

"Kitchen."

I took a shower, put on my bathing suit, fixed up a gin and tonic, and went to lie by the pool. I fell almost immediately into a strange sleep, from which I kept waking with the same dread of a tightrope walker falling to his death, until my name rang out and I shot up to see Mercy bursting out into the garden, waving both arms as if to signal the advance of an enemy army. Behind her, clad in spotless white linen—skin gleaming, teeth shining, blue eyes blazing—was Nick. "Too late," I heard him say as he elbowed Mercy to one side. With enviable energy, as if fed on pure ambrosia, Nick lifted one of the plantation chairs and brought it over to my side. "You look like an African," he said. "Black and ropey. How long have you been roasting in the sun?"

"I don't remember inviting you," I said, struggling to keep calm.

"I know, terribly rude of you. Are you going to offer me a drink or am I going to have to battle the fearsome Mercy for one?"

"You are going to have to get up and leave."

"I can't," he said, suddenly somber.

"You will."

"I can't. I'm in love with you."

I flung my legs around the plantation chair, dimly aware that Michael had completed the same rotation a few weeks earlier. "Love! You know nothing about love! You left me standing on my own in a house full of people I didn't know! For hours! Like a fool!"

Nick gave me a bitter smile: "Twenty minutes. *If* that."

"Twenty minutes my ass!"

"Give or take five minutes." I felt the urge to slap him again and, sensing that, he closed his hands around my wrists. "Don't hit me." I tried to wrest my hands free. "Don't hit me, Anna. You'll never see me again."

"What do you want?" I shouted. "What do you want from me?"

He tightened his grip: "I want you. And me. Together."

Incredibly, I thought of Mercy. What would she say, what would she *do* if Nick and I resumed our little dance? Would she quit? Would she pack up her bags and slam the door on the way out? And so, while every molecule in my body longed to make contact with Nick's pellucid skin, I cleared my throat and said: "I've got to run this past Mercy."

Nick blinked. "Mercy?"

"Mercy."

He shook his head, the sort of slow fluctuation of the neck that generally follows a fall or an unexpected blow. "I don't think you heard me," he said. "I just told you I'm in love with you."

"You come and go, Nick. You're a ... seasonal occurrence. Mercy is solid, she's here, now, always. I can't afford to watch her go."

Nick propped his elbows on his knees: "Anna, she's your *maid*."

"Wrong," I said, prey to sudden emotion. "Very wrong."

"Then what is she?"

I did not hesitate: "She is the rock on which my present circumstances rest."

Nick rose to his feet: "You've lost it. You've really lost it. Are you on drugs?"

I smiled brightly. "Gin and tonics. If you're good, I'll make you one."

"So what are you saying? That you need her permission to see me?"

"Be right back."

Mercy gave me a perfectly inscrutable look. Gaze fixed, pupils mildly unfocused, she asked: "He will be staying here in the house?"

We were in the kitchen. "No," I said.

Mercy picked up a dishrag and began to wipe her hands. "Is he forbidding me to drive the car?"

"Of course not."

Her expression softened and she let out some air. "So am I understanding correctly that he is *not* coming to stay in the house and that he is *not* making problems for me with the car?"

"Yes, you are understanding correctly."

She shrugged: "Then why are you making me to be informed?"

We looked at each other as if from across a desert. "I thought you hated him."

She clapped her hands—a sharp clap like the bite of a whip. "Me?" she smiled. "To hate that man? Aaah, no!"

I grabbed the gin, another tonic, and walked outside. "She's delighted," I said, but Nick was sunk deep in his chair, arms crossed, eyes fixed obstinately ahead.

I lowered myself next to him, silence settling over us like dust. Eventually he spoke. "You're unstable."

"Me?"

"Yes, you. If something were to happen to this country—an army coup, generalized unrest, whatever—that woman will dance on your dead body. She will dance on your dead body."

I sprung to my feet. "What do you know about 'that woman'? What? Do you know how many children she has? Where she was born? How old she is? What her current predicament is? Do you know where she lives? What school her children go to? Do you know what her favorite food is? What her ..."

But Nick stopped me in mid-sentence. "Funny enough, I do. Meat. Grilled. With plenty of fat on it." We stared at each other. He was right, of course: few things made Mercy happier than a plate of sizzling beef. "She's an African," Nick whispered, reaching for my hand, "a poor African who happens to work for you. Don't make her into something she's not. You'll regret it."

The truth, of course, is that Mercy wasn't poor; her new salary had propelled her safely into Kenya's middle class (as negligible as that category was): her three children attended private boarding schools, she cooked with gas rather than paraffin, the range of her disco-queen wardrobe was nothing short of symphonic. Finally and perhaps most importantly, she was on the verge of purchasing her own vehicle. No, she wasn't poor, and that—I confusedly sensed—was the sine qua non of our relationship. I said nothing to Nick. We sipped our gin and tonics in silence, fanned by a gentle breeze, until Nick jumped up and held out a hand. "Let's go," he said.

I peered up sleepily at him. "Where?"

"To the farm."

The shock registered immediately. Nick's farm had been shrouded in secrecy, its location, output, and profit kept offensively vague from the very beginning. I'd wrested two pieces of information only: coffee was the crop, Thika the nearest town. All attempts to find out more had been so obstinately and skillfully deflected that I suspected an arms-smuggling operation beneath it all. Then once, at a dinner party, someone had asked Nick a question about coffee and the reply had come so quickly and been so precise that I had revised my suspicions on the spot. Still, nothing had changed. Despite my pleading, "the farm" had remained an unapproachable reality, a fragile and, who knows, perhaps purely imaginary construct. I stopped reading up on the earthly eminence of the Arabica bean, with time I stopped asking questions altogether. "Is it far?" I mumbled, hoisting myself up on an elbow.

"Just over one hour," Nick said.

Two hours later, covered in thin red dust, we pulled up to a tall iron gate. Nick hooted, and an *askari* came running to the gate. He greeted us with a broad smile and a fine piece of gossip: the farm manager had gone to town to woo the young and beautiful daughter of a local kiosk owner. "How many does that make?" Nick asked, "Three, four?"

The askari began counting on his fingers. "Now this one," he said. "This one is number five."

Nick laughed: "Five wives! Can he afford them?"

The *askari* nodded gravely: "I think he can."

"What about you?" Nick prodded. "How many have you got?"

The *askari* shook his head: "Me, I cannot be having more than one."

"Why not? Don't I pay you enough?" The man looked down at his shoes. "You people!" Nick hollered, still full of good cheer. "Always more! More! More!" Eyes screwed to the ground, the *askari* smiled—a tense, labored smile that vanished as quickly as it came. Nick lowered his sunglasses and stepped on the gas. The car shot up a gravel driveway impressively flanked by Thika's famous flaming trees—tall, grooved things with flowers like torches. I closed my eyes, filled my lungs. The air was full of scent, of languor, with notes of compressed longing in the whisper of leaves. We came to a stop in front of a large colonial house ablaze with white bougainvillea. "Excellent!" Nick said, checking his watch, "Just in time for tea."

Under the portico, in front of a sloping lawn, between fragrant mouthfuls of black tea served by a silent woman in an immaculate white uniform, we watched the sun's descent toward the horizon. Then, for the second time in one day, Nick stood up and offered me his hand. "Now's the time," and we began our tour. We walked up a small hill, shoulder high in coffee, against a human tide of laborers retiring for the day. The workers walked in pairs, sometimes in threes, all clad in the same dark-blue overalls and gumboots. They nodded shyly at our approach, moving aside to let us pass as they whispered their low greetings. "Look," Nick said, coming to a sudden stop and pointing somewhere in the distance. "You see that windsock?"

I squinted. "What windsock?"

"To the right, over there," but I could detect no hint of a windsock anywhere. "Why don't you wear your glasses?"

"I forget."

"You forget?"

"Just tell me where it is."

"Up there," Nick said, pointing. "It's white and it marks

the northeast corner of the farm. And the end of the airstrip, of course."

Again, I reduced my eyes to slits. "You know Nick, I'm not *that* blind. How big is this place?"

"Twenty-two thousand acres," he said.

We walked back, the sun bleeding hard and fast into the sky. A hawk circled overhead and Nick stood for a full minute watching the creature's consummate ascent. "Isn't that something?" he whispered.

"How about a gin and tonic?" I shot back.

He gave me a long, cold look. "You really have no sense of beauty. Or romance, for that matter."

My face grew hot. "I see a lot of shit, Nick."

He shook his head. "There's nothing soft about you, not one thing. You make it very difficult to love you."

"What's this?"

"A thought," he said. "Just a thought."

But now I was angry. "What's this? Tell me. You want me to feel worse than I already do?"

Nick glared at me: "Why are you *so* aggressive? I didn't know you felt bad to begin with."

"Bad doesn't begin to describe it, Nick. I feel awful. I need a liter of booze in me before I can get anything done. Or haven't you noticed?"

Our eyes locked. He put a hand on my shoulder: "Why, Anna? Why?"

I shook my shoulder free. "Fucked if I know."

Nick plunged both hands into his pockets: "There's something I want to say." My back began to ache and I had a strong urge to run but I did not move. "The reason I never took you here, the reason I didn't want to take you here is because I was afraid you'd piss on this place the way you piss on everything."

I took a step back. "Of course I see the beauty. And I don't piss on everything."

Nick shook his head slowly, as if genuinely sorry, for the first time, to contradict me. "You piss on everything." The wind wrapped a strand of hair over my mouth. "Dinner will be ready soon," Nick said. Clasping my elbows, I followed him to the house.

Under the portico, the light of a dozen candles dancing between us, Nick and I toasted my first visit to the farm. I drained my glass in two long gulps and set it down without a word. A tall, thin man in full livery brought out a steaming terrine. "Madame?" he asked. I nodded. He ladled out some soup then noiselessly moved to Nick's side of the table.

"We need more wine," Nick said, snapping his napkin open and laying it on his knees. For an intemperate second I considered putting out a noble hand and releasing the servant from the tiresome obligation of slaking the drunkard's thirst. I said nothing of course, and the servant vanished, returning with a bottle of claret. "The lady first," Nick said.

"*Ndiyo*," the servant whispered.

I have heard it said that red wine has the same consistency of blood and that, like blood, it goes straight to the heart. That night, by a near-forgotten alchemy, black bile turned into blood, suffusing me with warmth. I leaned across the table and took Nick's hand. "I'm sorry," I said. He looked away, but later, when I went to move my hand away, he kept it anchored to the table below his.

We were woken at six o'clock by two discrete taps on the door. "*Chai, bwana*," a servant announced, setting down a large silver tray with tea and shortbread biscuits. After a mid-morning meal under the portico served with the same silent reverence as the night before, we drove back to Nairobi and settled by the pool.

"Do you ever put in an honest day of work?" asked Nick.

"No, not of late."

"How do you get away with it?"

"There's no story. I work when there's a story."

"So we could go somewhere."

And so at noon the following day I found myself climbing self-consciously aboard a flight to Zanzibar. "You're going to the beach?" Warren had asked me the previous evening at the end of a long and drunken preamble.

"No, not *to* the beach per se, no."

"Didn't you say Zanzibar?"

"I did."

"That's what I thought: you're going to the beach."

"Okay, I'm going to the beach. But I plan to file three perfectly good stories."

"What stories?"

"I told you: the spice story, the separatist story, and an analysis of Tanzanian identity. Quasi-national rather than exclusively tribal."

"Stick to the spice story. How many days are we talking about?"

"Two, three at the most."

We stayed one week. Zanzibar was a marvel of taste and scent. Nick and I had the roof of an old Swahili house to ourselves. Breakfast came at eight: fruit salad, pancakes and sweet rolls, and pot after pot of light, pungent coffee. By lunchtime we were at the beach, sipping our first cold beer of the day. In the afternoon we looked for sand dollars in the wet sand and slept in the jagged shade of palm trees. In the evening, dinner came to us on the roof. Ginger crab. Prawns masala. Bottle after bottle of chilled white wine. Nick's eyes, always so pale, acquired a hint of indigo; his mouth lost all trace of cruelty.

The next morning, fresh from the shower, he brought me coffee in bed. I lifted myself on my elbows. The air was soft and full of promise, a lazy breeze lifting the corners of the mosquito net. I let my eyes wander around the room and it seemed to me as if that scene, that arc of time—so finely, so intensely modulated—would never become the past.

At sunset on the sixth day I sat on a white cushion on the roof like a grand vizier in the hours before a palace coup, planning a monument to folly so grand, so over the top that the entire sum of my past mistakes would seem trivial by comparison. I would ask Nick to marry me. We would have a child. I would stop drinking. I would stop running like a madwoman around Africa. I'd be a mother and a wife.

Twelve hours later, undeterred by a million warning signals, I grabbed Nick's hand and asked him to marry me. "Let's get married," I said. We were in the spice market, sacks of ground saffron, cinnamon, cardamom, and cumin stretching in wild chromatic lines on both sides of us. The swirl of smells was intoxicating.

"Let's get married," I said. Nick shot forward, leaping over a legless beggar. I remained rooted to the spot, receptor after receptor clicking shut in my brain. For a few seconds I felt nothing. Then only the blinding certainty that the island was too small for the both of us. Having trampled over the same beggar, Nick was now standing in front of me, peering anxiously into my eyes.

"Let's leave this for some other time, shall we?"

You spend years out in the cold—larva, tabula rasa—then something draws you from under the rock you picked for yourself. You feel the sun on your back, the wind in your hair. Your nerves start to tingle, your skin to glow and you ask yourself why you spent so much time in the shadow of a rock, sucking in the wet air, tonguing granules of dirt. You forget. You forget there was a reason, a sound logic to the pallor of that concentrated life: enemies breed in open spaces, they germinate in wide expanses. Once you're out there, they'll take your life, your scalp.

I didn't need Nick to know that. It was ancestral knowledge, passed down the generations from my grandmother to my mother to me. So why did I give him my days, my nights?

Why did I wrap my leg around him as he slept? I asked him to marry me, and he said no.

Nick was saying something but I wasn't listening. My mind was already fixed on the complexities of my departure. I had to call Air Kenya and find out when the next flight to Nairobi was. I had to settle my half of the hotel bill. I had to change some money for the cab ride to the airport. Above all, I had to slip away without Nick realizing it. I knew nothing would stop me. I would negotiate every obstacle, crush every resistance and find myself in Nairobi at the end of the day. In Nairobi I'd be in a position to recover. Mercy would make *chapatti* for me. Friends would come around. Kosovo was simmering on the front page of every newspaper—a potential war in the heart of Europe bound to dwarf the sum of Africa's conflicts. A couple of friends had already left. Warren would surely send me.

Nick was talking and, as I raised my eyes to his, I was struck by how two-dimensional he had become, compressed into near inexistence by my need to get away. "Sorry," I said. "I need to find a restroom." I walked—a slow, measured walk—until I was out of the spice market. Then I broke into a wild run, knocking into half a dozen people until I turned a corner and found myself standing in front of a small hotel. Barely visible in the darkness, a tall slim man hovered ghost-like over the reception desk, his hands folded primly in front of him. "Do you happen to have the number for Air Kenya?" I asked. He recited it from memory then, with great ceremony, asked me if he could put the call through himself. I realized I'd been mistaken for a hotel guest. "Please," I said.

There was one last flight to Nairobi and it left at five. I had a little more than one hour. Back in the spice market, Nick had his nose buried in a small satchel of cloves. "Smell this," he said with a bright smile, lifting it to my nostrils. I gave it a perfunctory sniff and said: "I left my cell phone in the hotel."

"You did not."

"I did." He rolled his eyes. "I'll be right back. Ten, fifteen minutes."

"It's okay," he sighed. "I'll come with you."

"No!" I yelled.

Nick came to an abrupt stop. "Why not?"

I lowered my voice to a more conciliatory pitch. "There's no need. Stay, have a look around. Buy something."

"Nah," he said with a shrug. "I have no reason to stay. I'll take a shower and we'll come back together later if we feel like it."

I shot him a look of pure incredulity. "A shower? Another shower? How many showers are you going to take in your life?"

"I'm hot," he complained.

"Of course you're hot!" I snapped. "It's a hundred fucking degrees! That doesn't mean you have to take a shower!"

Nick cocked his head. "You sound a bit manic."

"Manic? You have no smell, Nick. No smell!"

He buried his nose in his armpit. "I do have a smell."

"No, you don't. In fact, you smell of nothing. Nothing. Occasionally there is a vague carbon smell, a mineral smell, nothing human. But that's only occasionally. Why? Because you're always in the goddamn shower, that's why."

Nick picked up another satchel tied with rough, brown string and brought it to his nose, turning his back as he did so. I ran like hell, peeling out of the market, leaping over gutters full of rotting waste, bolting breathlessly into the lobby of our hotel and bounding up three flights of stairs without stopping. I stuffed my belongings in my bag with such violence that I sprained my thumb. As I cradled my injured hand, two curtains lifted by the wind swirled languidly around each other, forming a knot in midair. I stared at the sudden union, then, muttering obscenities, I streaked downstairs, settled my half of the bill, and hailed a cab. I cried a little on the way to the airport but stopped the second I realized I had no Tanzanian currency on me. "Have you got change for a hundred dollars?" I shouted when we pulled up to the curb, zero minutes left to departure.

The driver peered at me in the rearview mirror, screwing his eyes to heaven in the calculation—no, the apprehension—of the sum. One hundred dollars. What was that? He arrived at a vague approximation because his jaw dropped and he swiveled in his seat to face me. "*Mia moja*," he said, lifting a long, wrinkled finger in the air.

"Yeah, *mia moja*!" I snarled.

He was an old man, a poor man. His hands were full of knots and tremors. His neck was a tangle of tendons and nerves. There was a milky circle around the iris of both eyes. I'd watched him pull a half-smoked cigarette out of one pocket and light it with almost palpable regret. I knew he had legions of children clamoring for every coin he brought home. I knew they turned his days and nights into catalogues of denied petitions, unmet needs. Still I snarled: "Yeah, *mia moja*!" And worse than that. I leaned forward and hissed: "You're a taxi driver. You've got customers. Customers require change." He turned and met my eyes in a queasy attempt to decipher my intentions. I crumpled the note and threw it against the windshield. Cursing, I kicked the car door open and ran across the tarmac, waving my passport and ticket in the air.

In Nairobi, I took a taxi straight to Ollie's. "A vodka tonic. Double." A man with graying hair gathered in a rat's tail took a long, leisurely look at me. "Fuck off," I said.

He straightened in his chair, his eyes widening. "What the ..."

"Fuck off!" I said again, my voice gravelly, mean.

He looked around the bar for support. None came. "Crazy bitch," he spat out. There was a long silence, then a lull during which very little happened. I ordered a second drink, then a third, all the while struggling to keep the pain of Zanzibar at bay. Every time I came close, a noise, a word brought me back to the island—to its pale shores, its light untroubled dust, the muezzin's call in the dead of night. I ordered a fourth drink, folding over it like a weeping willow. A heavy hand came down on my shoulder.

It was Kez. Nostrils twitching, pupils drawn, he searched my face for clues. "Have another one," he said. "On me." He asked the person to my right—a serene, pot-bellied aid-worker I'd met at some stage, in some African country knee-deep in shit—to scoot over one. Draping his arm around my shoulders and lowering his head like a priest in the confessional, he sighed: "Okay, tell papa everything."

A knot formed in my throat and I whispered: "Run the marathon, right?"

Kez shot me a quick look: "What marathon?"

"Any marathon."

Kez gazed deep into my drink for a good minute before saying: "Why do you have to run the marathon?"

"I don't know. It's what you told me the last time you scored some coke. You kept saying: 'Run the marathon, run the marathon, none of this shit will matter to you after you run the marathon.'"

"I did?"

"Yeah." He nodded deeply: "A solid piece of advice." We laughed. "So," Kez said, "I hear you dumped Michael."

"Wrong: he dumped me."

Kez examined his fingernails. "You know he went to Freetown." I sobered up instantly. Freetown on that warm day in January was the single most dangerous place in Africa, which is actually saying something. The capital of Sierra Leone had been carved up into warring sections, half of which were in the hands of the RUF, a sinister rabble whose repertoire of terror included amputations.

"He went to Freetown?" Kez nodded deeply. "To Freetown?" And that, incredibly, was when Kate walked in. She saw us, Kez and I, sitting there, and she covered her mouth with her fists, fresh tears pooling in her eyes. I can't say I *knew* because I didn't, but as she approached I felt the muscles in my back contract and lock in a painful spasm. Next to me Kez did an extraordinary thing, which to this day torments me: he thrust both hands forward, palms up, and craned his neck backward in a primitive display of grief. And then he whispered: "Nooo..." until the sound died in his throat and he fell forward like a marionette suddenly unstrung.

6

KATE WAS THE GIRL MICHAEL was seeing when he was shot by an RUF rebel on a cooler day than normal in January that year.

Kate and Nadja and, we later learned, Deirdre.

There must have been at least thirty of us at his funeral in New York: all ex-lovers with a theoretical claim to a tract of his vast heart. We outnumbered his male friends by far, although they, too, covered large distances to be there that evening. Kez staggered in, practically bleeding from his nostrils and unable to stand on his own. Derek arrived at the last minute—raw-eyed, mute, his heart spliced open like a fruit. Michael's mother, Ingrid, greeted each of us at the door, nodding frequently and absently, her eyes two pools of pain.

It was a difficult affair: the minutes, the hours, the speeches, the silences, the collective, futile effort not to cry. I stood against a wall with Deidre, Kate, and Nadja getting slowly, quietly drunk. Kez crossed the room unassisted and hung heavily on my arm. "You carry your guilt," he hissed, "You carry your guilt." On the table by the door, Mercy's flowers towered over the gathering—distant, opulent, cool.

"Who is this Mercy?" Ingrid asked me, and I had trouble answering, torn between the urge to dismiss her as a shit-poor

African to whom Michael had become curiously devoted and the desire to convey the large, riotous presence she truly was. In the end, with Mercy's blistering censure still ringing in my ear, I did neither.

"She was a friend."

"A good friend?"

I shrugged, thinking of how Mercy had straightened her spine and pushed her shoulders down her back—her gaze steady, her hands heavy by her side—when I told her Michael had been mowed down by a single burst of automatic gunfire. She stood by the stove, possessed by the sort of estranged cool that, in my mind at least, heralds outrageous acts of violence. Felicity bumbled in and cheerfully inquired whether it was time for *chai kidogo*, a little tea. "Shut up, you fool!" Mercy barked, looking at me. Felicity let out a whimper and scuttled out of the kitchen sideways like a crab.

I braced myself for the assault, telling myself once more that Michael had been my lover, not hers, and that my grief had as good a reason to exist as hers. Still, nothing could have prepared me for the sound of her voice, the guttural clash of consonants and vowels that spilled violently out of her painted mouth: "You are finished with him now," she said. I pressed my lips together but she went on: "You are finished with him now that he is in the grave."

Blood rushed to my head. "What grave? His body is rotting in Freetown as we speak." Mercy's eyes grew wide. "He was killed in the middle of a war, Mercy. An African war, one of the many you can't seem to stop having. You think they're going to stop butchering each other for him? So his body can be flown out to New York? So he can be *buried*?"

Mercy's face grew pale. "You," she whispered. "You are having no respect."

A second, crasser wave of blood rose along the back of my skull and down my face. "Respect? I'm not the one who cut him down, Mercy, I'm not the one who killed him." She took a step back. "Who do you respect, Mercy? Tell me: do you respect the Kamba? Do you respect the Luos? Do you respect the Maasai? If you could spit in their faces every morning before breakfast you'd be singing the Lord's praises: that's how much you respect them! And *that*, whether you like it or not, is the reason Michael is dead. He went to Sierra Leone because none of you—none of you!—know what respect is! Don't talk to *me* about respect!"

That evening in New York Michael's mother lost interest in Mercy straightaway and if there had been a shred of decency, of sanity left in me I would have taken her by the hand and explained that those flowers were worth two thousand dollars because Mercy had wanted it that way. I would have explained that the car Mercy was on the verge of buying would never be bought, that Mercy's savings would be wiped out in no time at all because the job she so desperately needed had been forsaken in the name of a higher loyalty. I would have taken her to one side and explained that this higher loyalty was Michael, whom Mercy loved and for whom she had walked stiffly to her quarters that morning in January and packed her belongings into a myriad garbage bags lined up like sentinels by the gate when I left for the airport. "You buy some flowers," she instructed brusquely when she finally got a hold of me in New York forty-eight hours later. "You tell his mother they are from Mercy."

"Fine," I snapped, wrapping a towel around my head, my skin still steaming from the shower. "What kind of flowers?"

"Big flowers. Nice flowers. My severance pay."

"That's two thousand dollars, Mercy."

"My severance pay," she repeated.

I let a moment pass. "Two thousand dollars. Two years of school fees for your children."

"Hallo?" she said. "Hallo? You tell his mother they are from Mercy."

I went crazy in New York. So did Kez. He hired a limousine to take him around—a bizarre display of madness that cost him ten thousand dollars and nearly bankrupted him. The limousine driver, a graying whippet of a man called Henry, tried to quit on the legitimate premise that he was "not a porter"—a reference to the number of times he'd had to physically carry Kez to the car. I don't know why he didn't just drive off but I suspect that Kez's pain was of such a stark, desperate nature that leaving him slumped over some bar counter was more than Henry could morally endure. "What happened to him?" he asked me once, bewildered. And because I had just been on the phone with Felicity and learned that Mercy would never see me again, I looked at him from behind a curtain of tears: "What happened to all of us," I whispered.

Kez was finally arrested for disorderly conduct and left to sober up in jail for one night. When he got out, his passport had mysteriously vanished so I left for Nairobi without him. Felicity kept backing herself into corners when I first walked in, terrified by my face, by what I might do.

I asked her where Mercy was but she just stared at her feet and wept. The more I asked, the louder, the shriller her sobs became until I gave up. I tried to bribe both *askari* but, whether out of loyalty or genuine ignorance, they professed themselves unable to lead me to Mercy. I asked the cashiers at the mini-market. I asked the attendants at the fruit and vegetables shop. I talked to the butcher, begging him to throw out a discreet string. "It's impossible to keep a secret in Africa," I said.

"Especially with such a woman," he winked.

I glared at him: "What do you mean?"

He capped and uncapped his pen. "All those colors," he muttered, looking away.

At home, I sat at my desk and gazed at the extravagance of the garden without seeing it. The fevered bark of the acacia tree (Mercy's birdhouse still hanging from it), the immodest concentration of color at the center of the hibiscus flowers, the fluted marvel at my fingertips: ashes in my mouth.

I dismissed the staff and sat alone in the house for three days, waking up and sleeping at four-hour intervals, my dreams snaking out like tentacles in the darkness, dragging me through a labyrinth of streets in search of people who were never there. I sobered up once, drinking cup after cup of coffee so hot and dense my esophagus took days to heal, and called Warren. "Who's in Kosovo?" I asked.

"Plenty of people," he said.

"I want to go."

"Good, I'm glad."

"Can I go?"

"No."

"You'll need people."

"Maybe."

"You always need people."

"Maybe. Out of curiosity, who covers Africa while you horse around the Balkans?"

"No one."

"A vacant bureau, how ingenious. Why did I not think of it before?"

"No one cares, Warren. No one gives a shit."

"That's for me to decide. So. What do you have for me this morning?"

"Nothing."

"Nothing is not good, Anna."

"Warren, I have to go. I *have* to go."

There was a pause, an exasperated sigh. "Why? Why do you *have* to go?"

What could I say? That time had to be reduced, compressed, folded altogether for me to slip undetected through it? That once the bombs started to fall and the adrenaline to flow, Belgrade would be a stab in time, a barely registered twitch at the end of which I would step onto the curb of my new life as if from a Rolls: bright-eyed, smooth-skinned, a swagger in my step.

I gripped the phone, frantically searching for the magic formula. It was past midnight. Except for two cans of chick-peas consumed in a single sitting, I had not eaten in three days. I heard Warren tapping away. "Are you typing?"

"I'm typing."

"I haven't eaten in three days." The typing stopped. "I'll starve myself. I'll go on a hunger strike."

"Good luck."

I squeezed my eyes shut. "You have no heart."

"I have no time."

"I'm in a bad way."

"I'm sorry to hear that."

"You *really* have no heart."

"I have a job, Anna. It's more than you seem to have."

I drew myself up. "Why? You're getting rid of me?"

"If this goes on much longer, yes."

"If what goes on much longer?"

"The drama, the theatrics. We go to press every day at midnight."

"Midnight. How interesting."

"It's the only thing *I'm* interested in," he snapped. "I'm interested in *copy*, filed at regular intervals, and I'm interested in midnight."

Hearing the change in tone, I shot to my feet. "I understand."

"Good."

"Now can I go to Kosovo?"

He did not say yes, he did not say no. He commissioned a

three-part series on the troubling fluidity of borders in Africa. "But Warren," I protested, fighting off tears. "It's going to take weeks."

"Yep," he said. I put the phone down and hit the gin bottle, with the difference this time that I took it over by the pool. The water was green and brackish. Ocher dust had settled over the furniture.

How rapidly ruin sets in. How quickly rot and rust sink their teeth into the heart of things.

The next morning, I set out: first to Rwanda and Congo, then to Ethiopia and Eritrea. Upon my return, two weeks later, I gave Felicity a small duffel bag full of filthy clothes and holed myself in my office to write. Kez came back from New York, his head freshly shaved, a few ounces of flesh hanging pitifully off his bones. At my insistence we met for dinner every night at Mediterraneo.

He told me about his childhood in Egypt, about his famous father, his glamorous mother, the incalculable distance they had placed between themselves over the years—between themselves and him. I watched him eat as only an Italian could: the whole of my intelligence concentrated on every morsel he negotiated past his goatee and into his mouth. If his rate of consumption slackened I found a million ways of bringing it up to speed—a skill clearly passed down the generations but lying dormant in my genes until then. I learned to read his eyes—when to talk, when to remain silent.

Every morning for the next four days I sat at my desk with a cup of black coffee and a *mandazi*, a triangle of fried dough, and wrote as if my life depended on it. I was wrapping up my assignment when Kez walked in and draped himself panther-like over a chair. He lit a cigarette, took a fierce drag. "What," I said after a while.

"Just passing."

"I'm on deadline, Kez."

"They want to get rid of me." His face was barely visible behind a swirl of iridescent smoke but I could tell he was quivering with rage. "They say they can't trust me. They say I'm a loose cannon."

I lowered my eyes. Kez was brazenly suicidal, not a molecule in him in disaccord with his body's ultimate objective. He was alive by a trick of Nemesis, denied what he most wanted by the stubborn fact of his mortality. "You think I can't be trusted?" he asked, a sharp challenge in his voice.

"Of course you can," I said. "You're suicidal but your employers are the last people in the world who can get on your ass about it. They *need* your suicidal drive, they're entirely dependent on it. How else are they going to get their footage? You're the best thing that's ever happened to them, Kez. The best. You're cheap, too."

He looked at me without blinking. "So why are they on my ass?"

"Because you head-butted your editor, Kez."

"That was over a month ago!"

"What happened today is the result of events you set in motion over a month ago when you head-butted your editor in the middle of a meeting and smashed his glasses into a million pieces." He glared at me. "They don't want to get rid of you," I said. "Just show a little humility. Call them.

Tell them you didn't know what you were doing. Tell them you were fucked up by Michael's death."

"No way," he said, rising quickly to his feet.

"You were."

"No way!" he yelled, crossing the room and slamming the door behind him.

I rang Warren. "I'm done. Can I go now?"

"What are you, on speed?"

"No."

"Then what?"

"Nothing."

"You're *on* something: I've never seen so much copy in so little time."

I felt a pinprick of annoyance: "Well, it ain't speed. Can I go now?"

"I'll ignore your last statement. How are you getting there?"

"Nairobi, London. London, Rome. Rome, Bari. There is a ferry service from Bari to Montenegro. It leaves in the evening. I should be there Monday, Tuesday at the latest."

I went home, packed my bag and drove to the church in Kariobangi. Then I walked to Father Anselmo's house. I pushed the door open and to my surprise, there was Father Anselmo sitting quietly at the table with a book.

"Bring a baguette?" he said.

"No."

He nodded, gesturing me toward the only other chair in the room. "You don't look too good."

"No," I said, "Not too good."

He yawned. "Today is my day off. I haven't seen anyone all day. It's been marvelous."

I rose to my feet stammering: "I'm sorry. I'll come back some other time."

"You're here now. May as well get it over and done with." I took a long breath. "I don't remember the last time I went to confession, it must be more than twenty years ago. I was … I was hoping you would hear my confession."

"That's easily taken care of!" Father Anselmo said breezily. "I don't hear confessions."

I stared at him. "You don't hear confessions?"

"I don't hear confessions."

"You're a priest."

"I don't hear confessions."

"Why don't you hear confessions?"

"I don't have time for confessions. Father Malachy does. He comes in on Wednesdays and Fridays." An explosion of childish laughter filtered in from outside, putting a smile on the priest's wrinkled face. I scratched my head. "Why don't you have time for confessions?"

He stood up. "A cup of tea?"

"Why not," I muttered but then remembered. "Actually, no. Thank you very much." He filled the blackened kettle with water from a jerry can and placed it over the single burner of a paraffin stove. He struck a match, turned a knob, and the sickening smell of paraffin spread instantly across the room, making my stomach turn. "What happened to the gas burners?"

"God knows," he shrugged. "I think I may have promised them to the hospice. I came back one evening late and they were gone. They left this."

"I hate paraffin."

"You do?"

"You have no idea how much."

"Really?"

"Really."

"Interesting. How does one get so worked up about paraffin?"

"It's the smell of poverty, of human suffering, of Africa. You've forgotten."

He slapped his thigh: "Damn right! Can't smell a damn thing!"

I smiled, so pleased was he with his novel condition. But I wanted to know. "Why don't you hear confessions?"

"Useless things. Perfectly useless bloody things. And while I don't condemn the sacrament of Confession because it is not my place to condemn the sacraments of the Church, I do not hear them. I heard one, just after I was ordained, and never heard another."

"That bad?"

"On the contrary—paltry stuff, run of the mill stuff: 'I wish my mother-in-law would vanish into thin air' stuff. I absolved her and she went back to wishing her mother-in-law would vanish into thin air. How useless is that?"

"Didn't she receive God's pardon? And through the pardon, experience renewed closeness with the Divine?"

"Baloney. The only pardon she received was her own. So she could carry on exactly as before. She needed to understand: herself, her mother-in-law. Understand, and through the process of understanding, maybe, with some luck, tear down the barrier that divided them. What we need is vision, not repentance. Vision. Understanding. Awareness. I'll help you gain awareness, that I'll do, I'll show you where your fear is, I'll show you where your prejudices are but I won't help you purge yourself, I won't help your bulimia."

"I'm not bulimic," I mumbled mildly. "Raging drunk, but not bulimic."

"Thank God for small mercies. The truth is, I've had enough of people who come to me saying: 'I've been bad, I want to be good!' No, you haven't been bad, you've been blind! You want to see? Open your eyes! Look at your fear! Look at your prejudices! Wake up, for God's sake! Wake up!"

The kettle began to hiss. Father Anselmo got up and, muttering under his breath, began searching every corner of the kitchen until he found a plastic mug and a spoon. "I knew they were here somewhere."

He came back, stirring his black tea and looking very much at ease so I said: "Can I at least tell you what happened?"

"I know what happened."

I pulled back. "Did Mercy come to see you?"

"She did."

"What did she say?"

He made a sharply dismissive gesture, implying that the content of her revelation was of no importance. Under my searching stare, he added, brusquely: "Something about a boyfriend dying and her having to leave your employment."

"What else did she say?"

"She said you had offended her."

I buried my face in my arms and broke into tears. I wept for a long time before I could say: "I did. I offended her. I was out of my head. She ... she packed her stuff into all these garbage bags and I drove right past them."

Father Anselmo fixed me with cold eyes: "Mercy is a woman of quality."

Again, I burst into tears. "She won't see me again. Ever again."

The priest shook his head, a terrible impatience in his eyes. "Do you know why she came to see me?"

I wiped my tears on my sleeve. "No."

"She wanted me to call you, to see how you were. She thought you might try to kill yourself."

Silence filled the room, broken only by the minute eruptions of ordinary life in the slum outside. "She thought I might try to kill myself?"

"She was certain of it."

I raised my eyes accusingly to his. "I guess you were not *overly* concerned."

He shrugged. "I'm not in the business of rescuing people. If you want to rescue yourself, fine, great, I'll be there to help. But not until then. Not until then."

I got home that night, took out the gin, and sat under a swelling moon by the green, foul water of the pool.

I called Kez the next day from the airport. I could tell immediately that he was on a bender—locked in some hotel room with five or ten grams of coke, peering into the peephole every three minutes under the paranoid persuasion the police were about to break down the door. I'd spent long afternoons bent over coffee tables with him; I'd seen how bad he could get. So I said: "I know exactly where you are."

"I'm good," he said.

"As I said, I know exactly where you are so, no, you're not good."

"Fuckin' shit, man," he finally let out. "I'm trying to get out of here but I'm too goddamn twitchy, I'm all over the fucking place. Someone's going to stop me in the lobby on the way out."

"No one is going to stop you in the lobby on the way out."

"Baby, you ain't seen me."

"Put your hands in your pockets and walk out."

"How are you doing?" he said.

"Fine."

"What you said before about Michael? Bullshit." I said nothing. "The truth," he went on, "the truth is I couldn't stand the motherfucker. He kept shitting all over me. When he died, part of me felt great! Great!"

"What about the other part?"

"What other part?"

"The part that was trying to drink and snort itself into oblivion."

I heard him light a cigarette, take a long, shaky drag. "Well, that's what people do when people die. They cry. They drink. And, if they got it, they snort it. Okay?"

"You cried like an infant. You couldn't stop."

"Because of my guilt!" he shouted. "Because he taught me everything I know and his body was rotting in Freetown and I all I kept thinking was how I didn't have to take his shit anymore! How I was free! Free! He treated me like a fucking dog. A fucking dog …"

"Michael loved you."

"Oh yeah? Funny way of showing it. The time he pushed his foot down on my throat? The time he almost killed me? Motherfucker …"

The scene was seared in my memory. Day One. Room 312 of the Serena Hotel. Michael standing over Kez at the end of an all-out dogfight—shirt torn, sweat streaking down his face, one foot and all his weight pressed down on Kez's throat. Shouting: "Have you had enough? Have you had enough?"

"He almost killed me," Kez said and started to cry.

I closed my eyes. "You kept messing with him. Every single story there was something you refused to do. He said, do this, and you said no. He said, go there, and you said fuck you. He was the producer, you were the cameraman. He told you what to do, not the other way around."

"Yeah, move your stupid ass. Move your stupid Arab ass. Fucking dick …"

"If he'd been a dick, he would have gotten rid of you, Kez. Day One he would have gotten rid of you. He would have called London and said: 'I can't work with this asshole, he breaks my balls all the time.' And you would have been history. History."

Kez was sobbing and for a second I felt like crying. I looked around the terminal for something to anchor my mind on. Why did it happen? Why did he die? "Look at the mess you've left behind!" I wanted to shout. "Look at him! Look at me!"

Instead I listened to Kez's convulsed sobbing until it stopped. "Fuck," he said after a long shaky breath.

I cleared my throat: "Too bad you're coked up to your eyeballs: this might have had some meaning."

Kez's voice got sharp: "It's got meaning, it's got meaning. Don't you worry about meaning. And since when do you go around busting people's balls over a gram or two?"

"Your balls, Kez. Only yours. Get out of that filthy little room."

"I'm in a four-star suite."

"Grab a couple shower caps on the way out."

"You wear shower caps?"

"No, Mercy does. In the rain. You know how African women get about their hairdos. Bring them to Felicity. She'll make you a cup of tea and then she'll take the shower caps to Mercy. Mercy will call you. You will offer her a job. If she takes it, you'll be okay."

And she would, I knew she would. Because she had heard Michael say of Kez, once: "I'd do anything for that kid. Anything."

7

DARKO REACHED BEHIND HIM FOR a bottle and a glass and placed them on his desk. He filled the glass with clear, unctuous liquid and handed it to me with a nod. "Drink. Very good for the heart."

Everyone complained about Darko, the way he had of sitting you down and making you drink. Ten in the morning and there you were, face to face with Belgrade's chief of police, head throbbing, innards on fire. I didn't mind the drinking half as much as I minded him—the oversized pipe, the foul smoke he blew right in your face. He had oddly curved teeth; paper-thin, minutely cracked nostrils; wild, yellow eyes. Implausibly, he had the hands of a pianist: long, smooth, exceptionally pale.

I hated the visits to his office, the endless waits on the hard, narrow bench outside his door. I hated his broad face as he watched me with an openly amused smile, waiting for the next installment of sycophantic praise. I hated the building, I hated the street, I hated the city—the square, squat thing laid out in bitumen and concrete without a single concession to beauty, to poetry.

Something happens when you're kept away from the horizon for too long: the gaze drifts downward, obsessively picking up the grime of life. Belgrade got to me in a million ways: the combination, the accumulation of mood, of color: the dark mutterings of people, the chill stare of the lanky men at the hotel reception, the resolute refusal to connect cause and effect: They are bombing us, the pigs.

Belgrade fumed, not so much from the bombs the North Atlantic Alliance randomly and infrequently dropped as from the venomous exhalations of its inhabitants. That morning I had driven under a dour sky to the army press center. I had listened to the ravings of a colonel. I had progressed to my weekly pilgrimages to Darko's smoke-filled office. My car had come to a stop at an intersection and I had noticed a middle-aged man—a short, aging figure clothed in nondescript Balkan gray standing barely three feet away. The man was staring at me, pure loathing in his small hard eyes. I must be imagining things, I thought, and looked again. The little man raised two fingers and sent me straight to hell.

I hated Belgrade, I hated it with a passion bordering on pathological. I'd made my entry illegally from Montenegro in the boot of a car. The driver, a Serb supremacist called Branko, kept threatening me: "You do this, you write this, otherwise ..." And he made a cutting motion across his throat, sticking his tongue out for effect. He delivered me to Belgrade one sodden afternoon, waving a finger out the window of his rattling Skoda as he peeled off shouting: "Tell the truth! Always tell the truth!"

"Yeah," I thought. "The truth of how we Serbs wuz robbed."

Weeks passed and I started dreaming of Africa, angling down in an airplane over ground the color of burnt almond cut by streams of water all the way to the horizon. In my dream my heart contracted with emotion and I composed a prayer of vehement, almost violent thanks. Then something woke me up: the alarm clock, the telephone, the low fever in my brain, and I found myself in Belgrade.

Each morning I swore it would be the last. Each morning I swore I would march on Darko's citadel, demand my passport (confiscated on the grounds that my entry had been illegal), and get on the one o'clock bus to Hungary. Somehow I always found myself in the drinker's seat, a slip of paper awaiting signature sweating in my hands.

Darko played with me, a cat with a mouse. "You come from Montenegro like an outlaw. An outlaw, yes? You say outlaw?" I nodded, drunk. Darko nodded too. "You don't have proper visa. You don't have paper of authorization. You don't have nothing! You come to me with nothing. Crying." He folded his face into a caricature of distress. "Please give me visa! Please give me permit!" Shaking his head, sucking on his pipe: "Now. If Ministry of Foreign Affairs don't want to give visa, how can I give police permit?"

I sang the valor of the Serbs, I raised my glass to his personal pluck. I let my eyes linger a second longer than necessary on his hands, averting my gaze with a jolt of false embarrassment. I poured another shot down my gullet, staggered down three flights of stairs, got a new slip of paper and waited in line again for Darko's signature. By lunchtime, I had my weekly police pass to the city of Belgrade.

That morning I asked Darko for a second shot. "You are nervous?" he asked. "Nervous, yes?"

"No," I breathed, grimacing.

"Yes. Nervous."

"Fine. Nervous. Okay?"

He sat back in his chair. "Everything is okay for Darko. They bomb my city? It's okay. They do not bomb my city? It's okay too! It is all the same for Darko." Then, unexpectedly, he leveraged himself dramatically on his feet and rapped his knuckles hard on his desk: one, two, three times: "You have been conducting journalistic interviews with Rakan!" he shouted. I stared at him, speechless. Back in his chair, after a full minute of silence, Darko said: "It is better for you not to listen to the things that man has to say. He is no one now. No one. We have forgotten about him." He smiled. I smiled. But then he brought his fist down on the desk again: "He's violent man! You know what he has done?"

He'd dragged dying civilians out of hospitals and shot them in the head; his men had raped thousands of women. He was a war criminal. He was wanted at the Hague. And he took his tea at my hotel every day at four.

Rakan was his nom de guerre, the identity giddily assumed when the Balkans caught fire. I remember the strange thrill on seeing him for the first time. Someone pointed him out in the lobby of the hotel and I stood there astonished at the unafflicted physicality of evil: a body, two arms, a great elongated torso, a nose like a scimitar, hands balled by his side as if ready to strike. Fancy suit. Ballooning tie. Fastidiously blow-dried hair. I thought, Christ, here's the real thing, here's the genocidal mind, the genocidal heart at work in a living body; neither dead nor dying, not even behind bars. Fully accessible. Fully recordable.

I got to within five yards of him that day. "What you want?" one of his bodyguards growled.

I pulled out a business card and tapped my chest. "Journalist. Interview?" The goon—thick-necked, slack-cheeked, doused in cheap cologne—shooed me imperiously to one side.

Fifteen minutes later, Rakan took my hand for a split second, his gray eyes wandering in slow motion just above my head. Lazily, as if the answer was of no importance, he asked: "Why you want to interview me?"

I made up some garbage, something about the presumption of innocence forming the bedrock of democracy: "You haven't even been tried yet," I smiled.

He looked at me as if he had not heard, as if my voice had failed to register. Then something in his eyes stirred, something bald, almost metallic: a current of pure violence. "You think you can *fuck* with me?" his eyes whispered, "Do you know who I am? Do you know what I have *done*?" I stood perfectly still, counting the seconds to my release.

"Forget it," Warren told me, "Not worth the trouble."

"Not worth the trouble? Are you typing?"

"Of course I'm typing."

"Please stop typing." Warren stopped typing. "Do you know what he has *done*?"

"Makes no difference. You'll walk away with nothing."

"You don't know that."

"I do. The most you'll get are denials, for which you're going to have to take a lot of shit anyway. *And* he may be dangerous."

"What's he going to do to me?"

"Anna, do as you're told for once. This is costing us enough money as it is."

I let my eyes wander around my room, at once pleased and annoyed by the luxury—the antiqued desk with the Tiffany lamp, the plush, silk-covered sofa, the king-sized bed with its immaculate linen and oversized down pillows, the deep cream carpeting, the chintz on the walls. Beyond my line of vision, the bathroom, nearly as large as the bedroom, was of pure marble. Belgrade wasn't exactly thriving—water and power shortages were chronic, air-raid sirens constant, fresh produce unattainable—but you would have never guessed it from the nearly depraved vantage point of the five-star hotel the press was headquartered at. The breakfast buffet alone was a slap in the face of hardship. "Do as you're told," I muttered lamely. "Since when do I *not* do as I'm told?"

"Your country," Rakan asked when we met again in the tea room of the hotel. "What is your country?"

"Italy," I said, tearing my eyes from his small hands.

"Mafia?" he sneered. Far too used to the insult to take offense, I looked away, my face frozen. Rakan filled his cup. "I drink my tea like the English. Plain. With a drop of milk."

I smiled, obliging. "I hear you don't drink alcohol."

"No."

"Why not?"

He tapped his forehead delicately with his middle finger: "Control. I do not like to lose control." Then, bored with platitudes: "What are you selling? To who? If you are selling Rakan the killer, Rakan the criminal, Rakan the disgusting Serb who rapes poor Muslim women, you can sell your grandmother. Do you have a grandmother?"

"No."

"What *do* you have?" I searched his eyes for the correct answer. He cocked his foot on one knee. "Come tomorrow," he said. "Same time, same place." We do interview. He didn't say it that way, of course. His English was surprisingly polished, surprisingly good. He used words like "unfocused" and, once, to my astonishment, "refractory." "The refractory nature of portrayed reality."

"They say I am war criminal but who are they? Mirrors. Just mirrors. Look at me. Look in my eyes. Are these the eyes of a criminal?"

It became routine, the childish translation of objective into subjective reality. He stood accused of dragging a male civilian out of his hospital bed and through the snow, of forcing him to kneel and shooting him at point blank range in the head. There were two eyewitness accounts, both on file at the Hague. Were they true?

Bug-eyed with fury, he hoisted himself halfway across the coffee table. "Look at me! You think I could do a thing like that? You think I could do that? Look at me! Are these the eyes of man who could *do* that?"

Four women, one of them eight months pregnant, in a church near K. Did he instigate their rape? Again, eyewitness accounts. Quivering with rage, he asked me if I had seen his wife. Yes, I said, lovely woman, very lovely, very shapely (while she, a woman with farcical tits, chatted on her cell phone, turning a diamond the size of a nut around her middle finger). "With a wife like that you think I go looking for Muslim women to put in my bed?"

I kept my eyes peeled to my notepad. "They're not accusing you," I said. "They're accusing your men."

His men were gentlemen! His men did not drink! They did not gamble! They shaved! Every morning they shaved! They observed the highest discipline! They were trained to function on three hours of sleep! But forget his men! Forget them! Did I think he was the kind of man who would stand by and watch a pregnant woman get raped? After all this time? After everything he had told me? About his life? His childhood?

Those were the good moments. For the most part he sat back in his chair pondering how best to silence me, frighten, humiliate me. "History. You don't know history. You don't understand history. That's why you ask such stupid questions.

"You have no children. No husband, no children. Women without children don't know what it is to love. To love your children, your country. What do you love? Hamburger and potato chips. Hollywood movies.

"Your coat is dirty. Do you ever wash your clothes?

"Are you deaf? Do you want one of those things old people wear in the ears?

"You are like a monkey, repeating noises other people make. You want a banana?" And he laughed.

And he succeeded: he frightened me. A jerk of the hand, a sudden fixity in his pupils and I'd go into a spin, coming out of it desperate to appease, to placate. In the beginning, before I learned the script written out in advance for both of us, I bristled at his tenth allusion to my childlessness. "My private life is no concern of yours," I snapped. "Drop it."

He blinked and *something*, a neural malfunction, a short circuit of consciousness seemed to push him to some remote corner of the universe. He propped his elbows on his knees, rested his chin on his hands and asked me my name. I stared at him. "What is your name?" he asked again.

"You know my name. I've given you my card."

He gave a fleeting smile. "Vladimir has your card. Or maybe he doesn't. Maybe he has flushed it down the toilet. Or maybe he had used the corners of it, you know, the ends, to take bits of food out of his mouth," and, looking me in the eye, he bared his teeth all the way to his gums, inserting the nail of his pinky finger between his two incisors.

I got used to it. After the contrived dispersion of rationality, no, of *personality*, came the ostensibly involuntary—but of course entirely deliberate—exposure of a deep, shocking violence. I learned to empty myself in those moments. I carved myself out, ran a quick sponge over the surface of my nonbeing, frantically picking up unseemly droplets of self.

Fatigue kept me longer and longer in bed until I was averaging ten, twelve hours a night. It still wasn't enough. I began napping after lunch, dreading the summons I knew would come at four. At some point—blurred, undetected—I lost track of what I was doing and why. Warren was no help, having divorced himself from the project: "You do it on your own time and at your own risk. Understood?" But do what exactly? I was no longer sure. Three weeks into it, all the lines had blurred. I had three hours of Rakan on tape but every time I tried to flesh him out on paper I never made it past the dateline: Belgrade.

Darko must have seen the helplessness in my face that day in his office, and mistaken it for indecision because he brought his fist down on the desk once more. "Stay away from him! Stay away! Say: 'Thank you very much, now I have finished with such and such an interview. That was very nice, thank you very much.' And you go. You go!" I nodded queasily as he went on. "If you stay it becomes ... it becomes ..." Waving one hand in the air. Grimacing. Looking up at the ceiling, visibly pained, for the first time, by his inability to express himself in better English. Suddenly his eyes lit up and he jabbed his breastbone with his forefinger: "You. You can just be sitting there, doing nothing, just writing in your notebook: 'This and this happened at such and such a time in such and such a place.' Very good. No problem. But to him, now, you are part of the problem. Understand? You are sitting in the same place, writing of such and such a thing but to him, you are part of the problem."

"What problem?" I asked, knowing the answer.

"The problem in his head!"

I stood up, we shook hands. "Thank you," I said.

"Very good," he said, nodding. "Very good."

That afternoon when I met Rakan, I took out my notepad, lifted my eyes to his and found not a single thought, word, or impression to convey. And not a single excuse for my silence either, fear crawling like an ugly insect down my spine. I mumbled an apology and made my way to my room. I sat on the bed and because it was a Friday, I put a call through to Nairobi. "Hello? Hello?" the nun at the Kariobangi parish office shouted. "Hello? Hello?"

"Hello!" I shouted. "Is Father Anselmo there?"

"Yes, but he is in a ... *nini* ... a meeting. You call some few minutes from now." I smiled.

Oh, the longing, the longing to go back! To find Mercy, to find myself! I'd understand the precise weight of things this time. I would open myself up to the reckless abundance of the garden. I would clean the pool myself. I would buy a car for Mercy. I would go back to my Michelin maps, I would travel the continent barefoot if I had to—if that's what it took for me to find my place in it again.

"Are you crazy?" Father Anselmo shouted. "How much is this costing you?"

"Nothing."

"Nothing?"

"Nothing," I repeated. "How are you?"

"Fine. Bosnia, you said?"

"Belgrade."

"Good Lord. When did you go to Belgrade?"

"The day after my failed attempt at confession. Six, seven weeks ago."

Father Anselmo murmured some instruction to someone nearby. "Sorry, clerical business. I thought Belgrade was being bombed."

"Not really."

"You sound as though you were calling from next door."

It was true, it was a remarkably clear connection with none of the static and delay I had come to expect. That, and the priest's voice, had a calming effect on me and I found myself able to focus more clearly than I had for weeks. "You remember the last time we spoke you said that people were not bad but blind?"

The reply came immediately: "Of course, I'm not that old."

A wave of relief washed over me. "So here's my question: I've gotten involved—don't ask me why—with a war criminal. Cruel. Violent. A quality of violence I've never seen before."

"What do you mean, involved?"

"I'm interviewing him."

"Thank God for small mercies. Why are you interviewing him?"

"Because he's a war criminal."

"Is he telling you that?"

"Of course not."

"Then why are you interviewing him?"

I sighed. "I don't know. I suppose at the beginning I had hoped to explain why he did the things he did. Delve into the nature of evil sort of thing. Stupid. Anyway. Here I am. In Belgrade. With a war criminal."

"And?

I got up, lit a cigarette. "And I am alone in this. I can't take it anywhere except maybe in the direction you mentioned. He's violent, aggressive, crass but not psychotic, not delusional, not crazy. He's got a good brain, he's even got a sense of humor. He's got nine children: can you believe that? Nine children. Anyway. You said blind rather than bad. What are we talking about? This guy's raped women he wasn't able to see? He's planted bullets in skulls he couldn't quite make out?"

The priest's voice came through clear as a bell: "I haven't met the man so I cannot comment on the specifics. What I was trying to say is we have come to understand evil in moral terms and violence ... we've come to understand violence as violence against others, and we've attached a moral weight to it. Well, it's the moral weight, the conclusion, the immediacy and finality of judgment that prevents us from understanding it to begin with." I thought about it for some time. "Violence against others. Of course: what else would it be?"

"Blindness. I hate to repeat myself, Anna. I'll make an exception because you're calling from Bosnia, but blindness is what we're talking about here. You raise your hand against your brother, you do not see your brother. More importantly, you do not see yourself. Your vision is clouded: by fear, by prejudice. You steal somebody's property, you seduce somebody's wife: you are blind, you do not see. 'Father, forgive them because they do not know what they are doing.' The people who nailed Christ to the cross: were they evil? Or were they blind?"

"I don't know."

"They were blind! This man you're dealing with: he's blind. If he could see the world, the beauty in the world, it would never occur to him to spoil it with violence. That was what Christ was saying, and by the way, many of the early Christian communities did not define evil in moral terms at all. They did not even call it evil: they called it *aporia*, roadlessness. There is a road, there is a path, but you do not see it. You're neither good nor bad. You're blind."

"Then we're all blind," I snapped, waving my cigarette in the air. "We should all be let off the hook! Free to rape and pillage."

"Don't be ridiculous. If a man kills, you put him in jail. But if a man kills and you want to understand why he has killed, you must ask questions."

"Such as?"

"Who did you kill? Who? Describe him to me. His face. His tastes. You'll find out that he can't. Because he killed the image of the man, the preconceived idea he had of the man based on his prejudice and fear, not the man himself. It's a little tricky, I know, but believe me, he did not kill John Smith: he didn't even *see* John Smith. Had he *seen* John Smith he would have bought him a drink, talked about football, complained about his wife. But he did not see him, so he killed him."

"Meanwhile, back at the ranch, John Smith is dead."

"Let the dead bury the dead. Pay attention to the living instead."

I sat in my room, ignoring the ringing phone, until the sky darkened and a few lights flickered uncertainly here and there.

The city was starved for power, entire sections of Belgrade, dreading the onset of total darkness, were batting down for the night. I'd been out after sunset twice and crossed the entire city in a mere ten minutes. Belgrade seemed uninhabited, charred at the core by a secret explosion. Both times I had driven through a massive intersection, a place ordinarily full of noise and traffic, and found it trapped in such stillness, such quiet that for a moment the cracks in the tarmac had all the pathos of fissures in fossils.

When the last gradation of color drained from the sky and there was nothing more to look at, I made my way down to the lobby. I slipped past the tea room, past a second room in oranges and blues, and was nearly at the restaurant when a rare pinprick of certainty made me turn on my heels and gallop back up to my room.

Darko picked up the phone on the third ring. "What are you doing?" I asked him.

"Watching the television with all the bad news."

"Come to the hotel. I'll buy you a drink."

"I don't drink."

"You don't drink?"

"Never in my life."

He came over anyway in a worn dinner jacket, a tie like a rat's tail. "I told you he's violent man," he said, struggling with a miniature paper umbrella for access to a fantastically colored fruit cocktail. I sipped my gin and tonic, sat back, leveled my eyes to his. "I'm afraid I have become part of the problem."

Darko cocked one eyebrow. "Why? He has said something?"

"Well, he wants to see what I've been writing. He's upset that after all this time nothing has been published. He wants me to publish something."

"That's not so bad," Darko said.

I shook my head. "I'm afraid it is. What I would write, if I were capable of writing anything at all, would send him through the roof."

Darko took out his pipe. "Okay," he said. "There is problem."

I drained the last of my gin and tonic: "And there's more."

The pitch, the intensity of Rakan's abuse had grown not at constant but at exponential rate and he seemed on the verge of physical violence. "He wants to hit me, smack me in the face every time he sees me."

Darko let out a cloud of foul, black smoke through which his yellow eyes shone brightly. Cat's eyes, I thought: cool, removed, yet totally alert. "So," he asked softly. "What game you were playing with this man? You were thinking: 'Ah! Now I have a new toy'?" A full minute passed, him sucking on his pipe, me staring at my hands.

I cleared my throat a little. "I wanted to explain him. The turning points, the progression."

"Progression. What progression?"

"From good to evil. The old question, I suppose, revisited."

Darko broke into a narrow toothed grin. "Rakan is not evil! Rakan is criminal!"

I crossed and uncrossed my legs, trying to find a comfortable position. "Very good, as you would say. What's the difference?"

"Simple. The evil man does not exist, only the criminal. The criminal, he say, I go and take such and such a gun and with this gun I go and kill one million people. Okay, very good. And now I am finished and I go and kill another million people."

"You've lost me," I confessed.

Tipping forward as if he were about to part with the oldest secret in the world, Darko whispered: "Evil is nothing! It doesn't exist! Listen to Darko! He knows! Evil does not exist! Only stupid people exist! Stupid people with stupid problems in their stupid minds!"

That night I could not sleep. Bitter-mouthed, bleary-eyed, I switched my computer on at three in the morning and tried, for the millionth time, to capture the deviation. "Rakan. Picked oranges in Sicily in his early teens. Bucolic setting, his father arranged it. Next thing we know, he's in jail for petty theft. Gets out. Gets thrown in again. Takes part in an armed bank robbery in Belgium. Does time there too. Wanders east, is jailed in Croatia. From jailhouse to jailhouse, violence hardening like a second skin around him. You add the Balkans. You add the hatred, the backlog of injuries. The Muslims impaling the Serbs, the Serbs cutting the throat of the Croats, the Croats doing God knows what to whom, frankly I don't give a shit, I just want to get out of here. The fact is, history matters. Or is it just a pretext?

Just a vortex of violent possibilities taken by some, ignored by others?"

In the morning there was an envelope waiting for me at the front desk. "From Belgrade police," the concierge said with a black smile, his imagination clearly riveted.

I tore the envelope open and found my passport clipped to a note in Cyrillic. "Could you help me?" I asked, handing the man the letter.

Eyes alive with anticipation, he began: "Anna. A., passport number Y. has resided in Belgrade without..." he raised his eyes, smiled, "a proper entry visa but..." here his voice trailed, "... with the full consent of the authorities. She has permission to leave the Yugoslav Federation with the full consent of the authorities not a day sooner nor a day later than June 1st. Safe passage is to be granted to the border."

"What day is it today?" I asked.

The man peered at me from the bottom of his disappointment. "The 31st of May," he said.

I packed my bag, called Warren. "I'm off. Tomorrow at one."

"You got your visa?"

"No, a police pass to the border."

Outside, a pale sun was streaming through the trees, carving delicate arabesques of light and I felt a quickening of blood. Belgrade may have occupied real time, real space, but it belonged in my experience to the discarnate world of ghosts. By a miracle, a sudden twist of fortune, the nightmare was finally coming to an end. In my room at the hotel I stripped and crawled under the bed covers, luxuriating in the feel of the sheets against my skin. Burying my face in the pillow, I let out a long sigh, flipped onto my back, and fell instantly asleep.

The phone woke me at four: I was wanted downstairs. "Why?" I asked, stupidly.

"Now!" a voice barked so I pulled on my jeans, washed my face and rode the elevator down six flights of stairs, gaining clarity with each second of my descent. By the time the doors opened onto the ground floor, I knew exactly what I would do, I knew what I would say.

He was furious. His eyes were like worn plastic. He sat with his massive shoulders hunched, twisting one fist slowly into his hand. "Where's the article?"

"In my computer, ready to go."

"Bring it!"

"Now?"

"Now!"

In my room I made a phone call then I cradled my laptop to my chest and rode the lift downstairs. I laid the computer on the table saying. "It's a long piece, five thousand words. You can read it here or you can take it home. Only don't bang it around, it can break."

"Don't bang it around, it can break," Rakan mimicked and he lifted the laptop in the air and made as if to throw it across the room. My face filled with horror and he laughed.

I laid one hand over my heart: "I thought you were going to throw it."

"You think many stupid things," he snapped. "This is just one example."

I emptied myself out—*whoosh,* the whole of myself—then I said: "You know, one thing I have not been able to understand all this time is how you *see* things."

"See things?"

"That's right."

"What things?"

"Things!" I smiled brightly.

Propping his elbows on his knees, he began to shake his head. "This is the problem with you journalists. You talk as if words did not mean anything. Precision. You don't know what precision is."

"Okay," I said. "How you see *people.*" I looked past him, too scared to meet his eyes. Even so I had the sensation of a separation of consciousness, a pulling of the plug. He's going to slap me, I thought, and once the first blow comes, a thousand more will follow. He will punch and kick me until I am dead.

Rakan's voice was so low when it came that I could tell I hadn't been far from the truth. "What people?" he rasped.

I waved one hand lightly in the air. "Let's take the Croats, why don't we? You were born and raised in an area with particular tensions between Serbs and Croats."

"The Croats," he whispered, running his knuckles along the rim of the coffee table. "Who do you think I am?"

I met his eyes. "Sorry?"

"Who do you think I am?" I offered him a perfectly blank stare. "You think I'm stupid? You think I'm going to tell you I have a problem with the Croats." He leaned back into his chair, crossed his ankle over his knee, brought the tip of his fingers together—all with a knowing smile. "The Croats are good people. Sometimes they make mistakes. We all make mistakes. When I was a child, they burned all the houses in my town, they chased thousands away from their own land. As I said, we all make mistakes. Human beings make mistakes. The Croats have made their mistakes. It would be ..." he paused, resumed with a pale smile, "stupid for them to make the same mistake again."

"So when you see a Croat you see someone who burned down your house?"

He leaned forward, lips drawn: "Who killed my grandmother, who put my father in prison, who put *me* in prison, who strangled children. Do you know they strangled children? Innocent children. You don't have children. You don't know what it is to love a child, to lose a child. You don't know what it does to your heart. They. Strangled. Children."

"So when you see a Croat you see an arsonist and a murderer?"

He emptied his eyes in the customary fashion and I know, I *know* that he opened his mouth to deliver a lofty message of ethnic inclusion but that he failed. "I see no one," he said, "Absolutely no one."

I let out a slow breath. He filled his teacup with a steady hand. Ten seconds later I checked my watch with a sudden jolt: "I must make a phone call."

A gleam came and went from his eyes. "From the front desk," he said.

I went to the front desk but did not stop. Without turning, I walked down the marble staircase and through the revolving doors into the gathering dusk. Then, careful not to run, I made my way down the long ramp to the first taxi in the line. "To M. Street," I told the driver as I climbed in. At M. street I walked back ten blocks, took a right turn down an unlit street and came to a stop in front of a large metal door unevenly coated with gray paint. I stood there for a moment listening to the strains of a Mozart concerto. I pushed the doorbell. "Very good," Darko said, waving me in. "Very good."

8

IT WAS WINTER IN NAIROBI when I got back; the air cold, the ground sodden. People too poor for umbrellas stood with their backs peeled to buildings staring up at the swollen sky, waiting for a reprieve in the rain to make a run for the next building. The Maribou storks—haggard, huge—clustered on the top of thorn trees, dipping their loose gullets into the wet air, their red eyes gleaming. Half buried in the mud, blue and black polythene bags fluttered frantically in the wind as I drove into town from the airport.

Felicity came out to greet me in the rain. "You are having no bag?"

"No. No bag."

It was strange, seeing the house, strange reckoning with its size. Nothing had changed in the three months since Mercy's muted exit, yet the place looked desiccated, dry, as if drained of vital juices and now waiting only for the inevitable dissolution. I went out into the garden. The pool was filled with rotting vegetation so putrid and dense I leapt back, repulsed. From somewhere in the past, a voice rang in my ears.

Michael's voice, hard, tense. "You got a pool, right?"

"I do."

"I'm coming over."

He showed up with a cooler full of beer. I told him I had been in the fridge but he waved my statement aside: "You got the bottled stuff, the good stuff."

"So?"

"So today I'm after the full American experience. I want lousy fuckin' beer in a can."

It was the beginning of our relationship, I had barely seen him, he'd been covering the war in Liberia. "Why do you want lousy fucking beer in a can?"

"Because I want to chill. Pretend like I'm back in high school. Like I never fucking left."

"By drinking beer in a can?"

"You got a better idea?"

We went through his six-pack of Budweiser while Mercy busied herself in the kitchen. Night fell. We lit some candles and sank into a deep silence. I did not know what to say, he was packed so tight with rage I was afraid a single syllable might set him off. He lay on the plantation chair, the air whispering quietly around us. Mercy came out, spectacularly balanced on a pair of green, faux crocodile leather heels. "Quick!" she shouted. "The food is now ready!" I rose to my feet. Michael stood up and after a moment's hesitation, he took my hand.

"There was a boy," he said. "He was two, maybe three years old. He was sitting in the crook of his mother's arm, right here," and he curved his arm. "She was dead but . . . the way she died, with her arm folded around the kid, you could tell she died with the kid staring down at her."

I steeled myself. Michael went on. "Kid wouldn't move. He had his scrawny ass nailed to the ground. You tried moving him, he wouldn't move, he hung onto her arm, her dead arm, with this ... this strength, this incredible will. Anyway. I went to pick him up." He shook his head: "The kid starts yelling his head off. He's holding onto his dead mother's arm and he won't let go and after a while I start yelling, then the guy from the ICRC comes over and starts yelling too ..." Michael rolled his eyes. "Now everyone's yelling and the kid's crying and I'm so fucking angry I'm stiff, you know, my arms are stiff, my neck is stiff, I'm out of control, completely." He paused, ran both hands roughly down his face. "Out of control. You know why? Because London's telling me to pack up and get out: none of the networks are picking up our shit anymore. It's Africa. No one cares. No one gives a shit. I tell Angela: 'Wait a minute: there's no peace agreement, there's practically constant gunfire.' And you know what she says? She says: 'We're short of people for the German elections.'" Our eyes locked. "Shit," he said, lifting his hands to the back of his neck, looking up at the moon, "I need a drink."

"Why does no one ever clear the pool?" I asked Felicity back in the house.

"The pool?"

"The pool."

Felicity considered me with grave eyes. "Now me, I don't know. You were the one who was saying that it should remain like that. With all the bad things inside."

My head shot back: "Me?"

Felicity nodded. "Us, we have been confused. Because the place there is now very bad with many, many animals that have been going inside. Rats and even snakes. The neighbors, they have been complaining too much!"

"Me?" I asked again, staggered by the implications.

Felicity gave me a second, solemn nod. "Yes, Madam. You."

We had to hire a fumigation team. Evacuate the premises, seal the pool with a tarpaulin, insert a tube attached to a pump and smoke half of Nairobi's vermin life out of there. The first thing I did when the pool was full and sparkled like a tear-shaped jewel in the inconstant sun was call Kez. The phone rang half a dozen times then, distinctly, without possibility of error, I heard Mercy's voice: "Hallo? Hallo?"

"Mercy," I said quietly. The line went dead.

Fifteen minutes later I was standing at the gate of Kez's compound under a crashing rain demanding entry. The watchman shook his head. "Mister Kez, *ana enda.*" He left, he's not here.

"No problem," I said, struggling to keep calm. "I'll see whoever is at home."

"Now," the *askari* said, switching back to English. "The house girl is the only one who is staying there. Can you be talking to her?"

"Yes. I can be talking to her." He took out his keys and held them tantalizingly before my eyes as he smiled and pleaded: "And Madam, may you give me something small?"

It was funny, I was unprepared for it. The most common occurrence in Africa had me standing shock-still in the rain, appalled. Yet he was poor, poor as only the Africans can be—shorn of all excess, his bowels hot and loose, his tendons frayed by wear and worry. How many children did he have? How many had he lost? I searched my pockets, extracting first a thousand shillings bill—twenty dollars, his weekly wage—then a single coin of twenty, the average tip. I raised my eyes and found him staring at the money with such intensity, such hunger that I felt my stomach turn.

To have such power is to lose one's soul. Twenty dollars is nothing to us, nothing, yet in my hands that afternoon they made the difference between pain and relief, exposure and shelter. "Here," I said, giving him the bill. He held it between his palms, a slow smile spreading across his face.

The rain had not slackened, if anything it was coming down with greater violence. "*Mzee*," I said, "I am getting wet." His eyes widened in horror and with a gasp he unfurled his raincoat and placed it canopy-like over my head. We ran across the courtyard. He bid me good-bye by joining his palms and raising them to his forehead. I nodded. Then, alone, I began the climb to Mercy's door.

I had a million things to say. I had my grief, still unexpressed; I had my regret, my loss, the silence in my bones; above all, I had my guilt. I had my seriousness, new, shiny, hard-gotten; I would give of it in carefully calibrated doses, in ever-increasing quantity. No use telling Mercy that I would buy the car she wanted; she'd only sneer, she'd call it a blood-gift. No, I would offer to subtract the sum from her salary and then I would put the money aside for when she would be able to accept it. Nor, of course, would I announce that I was having the servant's quarters gutted and renovated; I'd go in one morning and notice the slits that perversely served as windows. "Why would anyone put slits instead of windows?" I'd comment. Then I'd bring in the builders and punch a goddamn hole through the wall the size of a proper goddamn window. I'd have the bathroom tiled. I'd have a new shower put in. But all very gradually, very slowly, so Mercy would not think that I was buying her, massaging her into submission. Because I wasn't. I wasn't.

I rang the bell, the door opened and I caught a glimpse of Mercy shrinking away as if scalded by the light. I closed the door and followed her to the kitchen. She stood by the sink with her back to me. "Mercy," I said gently. She said nothing, she did not even move. Slowly, obtusely, a sense began to form of something terrible, some tragedy whose conclusion would bring me to my knees. Something was wrong. And then it hit me. A shapeless dress the color of mud. Flat, rubber-soled shoes. A red paisley bandanna knotted at the base of the neck in the fashion of a *kikuyu* peasant.

As the silence thickened, her wasted frame came into focus: the gauntness of her shoulders, the dry, flaked skin around her ankles. She had rolled up her sleeves and the sight of her forearm sent a long shiver down my spine: angular, brittle, with none of the dimpled abundance she had gloried in. All that flesh: gone. As she began to wipe the counter down, my eyes came to rest on the ragged profile of her wrist, on the nervous, irregular construction of her fingers and I was pierced by sudden certainty.

AIDS. She's got AIDS.

Mercy had her back to me, she had her elbows tucked by her side, her shoulders crammed by her neck as if she expected the sky to come crashing down on her any minute. She had that flaking skin, that scalloped surface of flesh beneath which she cowered in open-mouthed terror at the advance of death. She had her back to me and I could not breathe. I stood behind her, my muscles stiffening until I noticed the dark glasses: two saucers—huge!—propped loosely on her nose, covering half her face. Just where the bandanna met one eyebrow I saw a patch of gray, translucent flesh and my spirits soared. She's been run over, I thought, she's had her face ground against the tarmac. "Did you have an accident?" I asked. Mercy kept wiping the counter. "Did you go to the police?"

She swung around—a sharp turn that nearly threw her off balance. "The police?" she rasped, steadying her glasses with one hand, "The police can be curing AIDS these days?"

I reached one arm out but she pulled back so vehemently that her glasses, barely balanced, went flying across the kitchen, exposing a web of raw flesh over an unseeing eye.

Gasping, I took a step back. Mercy made no attempt to retrieve her glasses. "My God," I whispered. "What is it?" She headed for the door and I thought she would walk out of the apartment altogether, determined not to spend a second longer in the company of one so bitterly, so consistently disappointing.

But she didn't leave, she came back with a piece of paper held stiffly in one hand. "Take," she said.

It was an article from a medical Web site. The headline ran: "Herpes Zoster Ophthalmicus and HIV-Aids in Sub-Saharan Africa." I looked at her quizzically but she spurred me on with her long, dry hand. Four passages had been underlined. I read the first. "Herpes zoster, also known as shingles, is a common infection brought on by the same virus that causes chickenpox. Herpes zoster ophthalmicus, or herpes zoster of the eye, occurs when the latent chickenpox virus in the trigeminal ganglia of the ophthalmic division of the nerve is activated. Such infection is more likely to occur in HIV-infected patients and often heralds the onset of full-blown AIDS." I skipped to the second underlined passage: "Infection and inflammation secondary to zoster can affect all adnexal, ocular, and orbital tissues resulting in serious and often painful impairment of vision." And the third: "Systemic antivirals and tricyclic depressants have positive effects if applied early on." Finally I read: "In sub-Saharan Africa, the cost of therapy is beyond the reach of ninety-nine percent of the affected population."

Bracing myself, I looked at Mercy again. The infection had devoured the tissue over and around her eye, disfiguring her. Later, I heard of how she had ignored the first pustules, painful as they were, because she believed them to be the physical embodiment of her guilt. "Not the sign of the devil for the punishment of my sins," she said, crossing herself. "They were mine, they had come from inside, from this body, so they could show themselves and show me, myself, for my same self."

"Why?" I asked, incredulous.

Mercy shook her head, her lips compressed around a tiny, wistful smile. "People think such foolish things and me, I was a fool just like them. I was thinking I made Michael to die in that bad place. And you to die by your own hand."

She had ignored the first pustules, the widening lesions until the virus had burned a trail to the center of her eye and the pain had become too much to bear. At the clinic in Kawangware she had been given an aspirin and told to go to Nairobi hospital. There, a young *muhindi* doctor had explained to her that the infection could be stopped, the herpes virus temporarily suppressed with a three-week treatment, available only at select pharmacies, for the sum of three hundred dollars. "These tricyclic depressants?" I asked.

"The very same," Mercy said. "Now me, I thought he was playing jokes because who can be having such money? Maybe when I was a rich woman, on River Road, before my husband took all the things."

"Before he gave you the virus," I spat out, unable to control myself.

Mercy harnessed her emotions the way an expert rider reins in a horse: with little effort and no fanfare. "Yes," she said quietly. "Before he gave me the virus. But now for me, that sum was very great. Very, very great."

"Why didn't you call me? I would have sent you the money."

Mercy looked away. Resumed her tale. "I went back to Kawangware and stayed in bed for some days but the pain was not going; in fact it was getting so much that I sent my sister to take Janet out of school and get the deposit back."

And so the treatment was got. The infection lost ground, the virus retreated from the tip of Mercy's scorched filaments to its secret hiding place. But one morning, barely six weeks later, just back from church, Mercy felt a burning sensation across the same arc of skin and nerves. Two days later, crippled by pain, she rang Kez, who was covering the war in Kosovo from the capital Pristina and begged him to send some money. "And did he?"

"*Chop-chop*," Mercy said with a proud smile. "The very next day. One thousand dollars. I took it from the same Western Union you were using."

I thought of Kez, of what he must have done to get the money out to her so quickly. He'd probably called London and thrown a fit over the phone: "You get that money out to her now!" The thought brought a smile to my lips.

By then, however, Mercy was on her second round of dysentery. She had cured the first with antibiotics but after a week's pause she was down with the shits again. AIDS didn't become "full-blown" with Mercy: it exploded, blasting tsunami-like through her resistence, ravaging her last line of defense in no time at all. The dysentery was followed by stomach cramps, by loss of appetite and finally by revulsion of food so overwhelming Mercy told me: "Grace, you remember Grace. She was hearing that I was sick so she came to visit with some chicken. Nice, you know. Cooked with some little *ugali*. I told her: 'You go with it. You just go with it.'" I shook my head. "Where's Kez?"

"In Egypt. His father has been very sick. He has improved now. I am waiting for him to come back." I stood up. "You're coming home with me."

Mercy began to smooth her dress down against her thighs: "My place is here now," she said.

"Please," I said but she shook her head: "My job is for this house." I took her hand, and although she stiffened, I held it between mine: "Please, Mercy, please."

But she said no, so I left.

At home I rang Philip Leduc at Doctors Without Borders. "Your pilot project with anti-retrovirals in Kibera, is it still on?"

"No," he said. "We finished it in May." I told him I needed help and he gave me the name of Doctor Wasunna at Mbagathi District Hospital, one of maybe three doctors in the whole of Kenya able to administer anti-retrovirals. "He comes in on Tuesday mornings only," Philip warned. "There is a line all the way to the road, *enfin*, all the way to the highway so you must go early. And you must push. It's not nice but it's the only way to get to his door. If you tell him I sent you he'll let you cut the line. He'll do some screen tests—liver, T-cell count—and if your friend is okay, he'll get him started."

"She," I murmured.

"Sorry?"

"My friend is a she."

I went out into the garden. Mercy's birdhouse was no longer there. I realized with a start that she must have come in my absence and taken it down herself: no one else would have dared. When? When had she come? The answer was obvious: when the realization had dawned on her—silent, unsparing, a death sentence consigned to secrecy from the start.

I knew how it went: I'd seen the virus suck the blood out of the continent, I'd seen it make a mockery of weddings: the bride young and plump, the groom a specter; I'd seen births turned into wakes. I'd gone to places and found old bones clinging fearfully to doorways, children squatting in the shadow of their loss, pierced by dreams of impossible reunions. I'd walked through villages and found the riotous pulse of African life reduced to a whisper. I'd seen the hospitals of Africa: part hospitals, part mortuaries, the dead and dying stacked sideways on a bed. I'd seen all that and more.

Mercy would try to keep it a secret. She was probably already meeting people's eyes with a mute admonition—you wag your tongue, I ruin you. But rumors would fly regardless and what was a neighbor's sly comment next to her children's expert assessment of her shrinking frame? "They are not stupid," Mercy told me. "They can see for themselves what is happening."

That night, watching the empty space where the birdhouse had been, I swore I would extract *one* living body out of that orgy of death if it was the last thing I did.

9

DOCTOR WASUNNA WAS AN ANGEL, one of those strange, shimmering creatures occasionally assigned to human affairs. He had a perfectly round head beautifully balanced on a stalk of a neck. "What do you call those sweet things on the stick children like to eat?" Mercy asked.

"Lollipop?"

"Lollipop!" she clapped. "That is the one! Now you have seen! This man is a lollipop!" And for the first time in God knows how long Mercy exploded into laughter.

The doctor's undeniable resemblance to a lollipop had little to do with it; the fact was that after all that pretending, all that fear, he had taken Mercy's face in his hands and told her he was sorry. Sorry for her pain, sorry for her disfigured face, sorry for the circumstances that compelled her to speak of her probable death as of a change in weather patterns. He had said, mostly to me: "These people! They enter this room and they *know*! The end is just some few minutes away! But they say: '*Habari ya asubuhi daktari.*' How is the morning, doctor? A bit cold, eh? Maybe tomorrow it shall be warmer."

"Have you had counseling?" he'd asked Mercy.

"I am not aware," she'd answered, defiant. Dr. Wasunna had cocked his billiard ball of a head to one side as if trying to establish exactly who she was: "Most people I shall see today will not live, they don't have the money. If they are lucky they will be buried in the same place where they were born according to the customs of their people. But that is only if they are lucky. Now, you, it seems you are having greater luck than them and I expect you to live. For that you must talk and you must listen. I can see for myself you can talk. Can you listen?"

"Listen to what?"

"To people who know more than you." They had stared at each other, the plump angel in the immaculate white coat and the woman from River Road.

"I can listen," Mercy said.

I nearly burst into tears then, the morning had been so hard, one minute slamming onto the next without a hint of clemency. Nothing could have prepared me for Mbagathi District Hospital on that ashen morning. "*Ahi*!" Mercy cried as I parked the car. "We shall never get through!"

"We've got to push," I said and push we did, to Mercy's acute embarrassment, through the meek, the silent multitude. I'd been in crowds before but I had never had to plow through one as large, as gaunt, and as desperate as that—my own vitality and strength a mark of shame. "I am sorry," I mumbled over and over as I bulldozed my way to the doctor's door. "I am sorry."

More than once I felt a cold dry hand close around my wrist, trying to hold me back. I turned to face neither anger nor resentment, only a naked plea: *Take me with you*. I tried to smile reassuringly as I wrested my arm free but, in one case, a woman grabbed me with both hands, her eyes smoldering as she whispered: "I have six children. Six children. Six children. I am sick, too sick. Help me to the doctor. They have no food."

"Mercy!" I cried, and Mercy somehow covered the distance between us and wrapped her own weak hands around the woman's wrists. "Let go," she said. "Mama, please let go."

"No!" the woman shouted, tightening her grip, "I have six children! I am sick!" I picked her fingers off one by one as her shouts turned into sobs and Mercy said, in soothing tones, "Mama, let us try not to shame ourselves. Let us try not to shame ourselves."

I tripled, quadrupled my efforts at that point, pushing my way through people as if through mere clutter, my gaze fixed maniacally on the doctor's door. Mercy yanked my sleeve and hissed: "Now me, I don't like to proceed this way!"

I stopped, mindful of the sensation we were creating: the black, imperious woman and her white, agitated counterpart doing battle a few yards from the doctor's door. "We have no choice, Mercy," I said in a whisper, "We have no *time*." She flashed me a scornful look but when I got to Dr. Wasunna's door, she was right behind me. And when the door opened, she tightened her shawl around her shoulders and followed me in.

As I said, he was an angel. He prescribed a battery of tests, all to be done at different hospitals. "We can't even do a test for dysentery here, imagine counting T-cells!"

"How long will it take?"

"A month," was his breezy answer. Mercy and I exchanged queasy looks. "Does she *have* a month?" The doctor smiled. "She has a strong mind. After the counseling it will be even stronger. Now," he said, sitting at his desk and pulling out a pen. "You are prepared for the expense?" I nodded. "The tests alone will cost you twenty to thirty thousand shillings. The anti-retrovirals will be between twelve and fifteen, sometimes twenty thousand shillings a month, depending."

"On what?" I asked. Dr. Wasunna rose to his feet. "Many things. Send my regards to Philip. Tell him we miss him around here."

"Sorry doctor, depending on what?" He looked me over for a second then he said: "There is much you will have to learn. Let us say good-bye for now. As you can see, I have a busy day in front of me."

"Forty five thousand shillings just to start," Mercy murmured as we climbed into the car, "These people are not having a clear mind. How can they be expecting people to pay such money? People who cannot feed their children, who cannot pay school fees: where can they be getting such money?" I nodded, thinking what a ridiculous sum six hundred dollars was for Mercy's life.

I had expected worse, far worse. Things were looking up: Dr. Wasunna clearly knew what he was doing, Mercy seemed to grow less defiant by the minute, Kez would eventually return and agree to release Mercy from her obligations. The anti-retrovirals would kick in, Mercy would gain weight and be herself again. The only bad news, as far as I could tell, was that I had to be back at the hospital in the morning for Mercy's counseling.

I stole a glance at Mercy. Maybe I could drop her off and pick her up after her counseling session. I'd nip around the corner, get myself a coffee and a *mandazi*, read the paper and, I hope, come up with a couple story ideas for Warren. "Listen," I said. "I need to get some work done. Can I drop you off and pick you up after your counseling tomorrow?"

She did not answer so I turned to look at her again. And what I saw astonished me: I saw a woman consumed, devoured by the virus, her lower lip secured against a violent tremor by a spasmodically clenched jaw. And *this*, this specter, this shadow of a human being I was willing to send out on her own so that I could be spared the sight of *thousands exactly like her*. How? How had it happened? The purely imaginary construct of Mercy as a reasonably healthy woman capable of gaining ground in that circus: where had it come from? "I'm sorry," I whispered.

Father Anselmo flashed me a strange smile when I went to see him the next day: "It's what I've been trying to tell you! When you called from Bosnia ..."

"Belgrade."

"Belgrade, Bosnia ... whatever. Your war criminal could not distinguish a human being from a sack of potatoes and that's why he killed them! People in the West cannot see twenty, thirty, forty million Africans dying of AIDS and that's why they are dying! You yourself can become blind to the virus that has reduced Mercy to mere bones. There is a terrible equivalence of guilt, of responsibility except you try to get people to listen. They're too busy eating their organic mushrooms and baby greens!"

"Do I detect a hint of envy?" Father Anselmo tore into the baguette I had brought him with his teeth. "Couldn't digest that fancy stuff after twelve years of raw onions and beans. But look, it's inevitable, at some point people *will* see and the period of great recrimination will begin. Until then, the thing to remember is that while sight is the supreme gift—and the supreme necessity—even the most enlightened beings have gone through spells of embarrassing blindness. It's important not to get too worked up about it. To keep an even keel, if you get my point. Can I offer you some tea?"

"No thanks," I muttered.

"It's good tea, loose tea, not the bagged kind. I think it's from Ceylon. Somebody brought it as a gift. Would you like some?" Again I shook my head. "No one ever wants to drink my tea," he murmured, a note of resentment in his voice. "I guess I make bad tea."

He asked me how Mercy was doing. I told him she'd come out of counseling shaking. In the car, away from a million probing eyes, she had buried her face in her hands. "I shall be dead, *Mungu ani saidie*, I shall be dead. Can you be helping my children, Anna?"

"Don't talk rubbish!" I'd hissed. "Do not talk rubbish!" She'd shrunk away, clamping down on her trembling lips, turning her face away, looking blindly out the car window.

How many times during Mercy's sickness did I fall prey to the power I had? Extreme power. Power of life and death.

Power to stop the virus. Power to send it for a final spin. That morning Mercy pressed her worn handbag to her chest and bit down on her quivering lips. Then she took her glasses off and covered her ulcerating eye with one hand, sighing deeply. "I am fearing the spectacles shall be hitting my eye," she murmured. "It is something that is occurring all the time now." She was talking about me, of course.

At Kez's house, I made some tea. "Here," I said. She took the tea cup in one hand, the plate piled high with cookies in the other. "Thank you," she whispered, sipping the tea.

I waited. "Aren't you going to have some cookies?"

"No."

"Not even one?"

"I cannot."

"Of course you can!" and I lifted a cookie from her plate and handed it to her. "Just one." She took the cookie and she raised it to her lips. She took a bite. "Come on," I urged.

Tears pooled in her eyes. "I cannot," she whispered.

"One cookie!" I shouted. "Just one cookie!" But she couldn't. I slammed the door behind me as I left.

The next morning I said: "Mercy. How would you like to drive the car?" We were going to Nairobi hospital. Mercy sat motionless in the passenger's seat, her hands folded primly over her handbag. "Mercy," I said again.

She raised a jittery hand: "Anna, you think I can be driving this vehicle?"

"No?"

"You are not getting the seriousness," she said.

I yanked the car into reverse and pushed my foot down on the accelerator. "I guess not."

The hospital was hell: it took me the entire morning and a great deal of shouting to maneuver Mercy to the right spot—twelve bent and speckled metal seats opposite the third floor laboratory. At a quarter to one a nurse holding a chart came out and, rooting into one nostril with one finger, shouted: "Mercy Achungo!" I tried to smile encouragingly but Mercy took no notice of me as she rose unsteadily to her feet. "Mercy Achungo!" the nurse shouted again. Mercy arranged her glasses on her nose and took a step forward. For the third time the nurse shouted her name.

"What's the matter with you?" I yelled, jumping to my feet. "Can't you see she's coming?"

The nurse looked at each of us in turn. Pointing her pen at me she asked Mercy: "Is this lady escorting you?"

"*Ahi*," Mercy sighed tiredly.

"Now what is the problem with her?" the nurse inquired as if I were not there. "She has been shouting. *Ahi!* Shouting and shouting! We have been hearing the noise from far!" Mercy shook her head in a display of impotence and dismay and I watched wordlessly as the nurse came forward and gently wrapped one arm around her. "Let us move away from such noise," she said, casting a dirty backward glance at me. I sat down, tucked my hands between my knees and counted from one to ten.

It got harder. Mercy came out nearly one hour later, her head bent, a hand pressed over her punctured vein. I picked up her bag but just as we were getting ready to leave her name rang out again. "We are needing more blood," the same nurse explained. "More blood for what?" I asked.

Inserting her finger deep into one nostril—clearly a conditioned reflex—the nurse said: "Us, we do what is required to make the patient better." With that, she began to lead Mercy away.

"Sorry," I objected, laying a heavy hand on the nurse's shoulder and turning her around. "My understanding is that once you've inserted a needle correctly in a good vein you can take all the blood you want. Am I wrong?"

"Maybe," the nurse said, her eyes unwavering.

"No, not maybe, certainly. Why do you need to make another hole in her? Can't you see she's sick?"

It was Mercy's turn to step in. "Anna," she pleaded. "They are the ones who are in charge in this place. You leave them, please, to be in charge."

"In charge of what?" I asked, my voice strained from the effort to remain calm. "In charge of making stupid mistakes?"

"*Ahi*!" the nurse exclaimed. "Now this one is harassing us too much! What can we be doing with such a person as this?"

"You can be doing nothing," I said, rage running like raw voltage up my spine. "You can be learning how to do your fucking job, that's what you can be doing!"

Mercy pressed her hands over her ears. "Please Anna," she whimpered. "Please! Let us control ourselves. Let us be like the big people in this world!"

But I couldn't, I couldn't. I grabbed her arm and pulled her—stumbling badly as she tried to keep her glasses on her nose—down the stairs, yelling: "You people don't give a shit! People are sick and you don't give a shit!"

Mercy cried in the car. Her body shook, tears streamed down her cheeks. "For God's sake!" I screamed. "Pull yourself together!" She cried quietly, inaudibly, all the way to Kez's house.

He was there, having arrived unexpectedly from Cairo a half hour earlier. "Jesus fucking Christ," he said when he saw Mercy. And then: "A month of testing? What do you mean a month?"

I gave him a frigid look: "What are you, on Islamic time? Thirty days to a month in this part of the world." He flashed me the finger.

"Mercy is coming home with me," I said.

Kez studied Mercy for a second. "Does she *want* to come home with you?"

I cleared my throat: "I think she feels she has an obligation ..." but Kez silenced me.

"Do you *want* to go home with Anna?"

Mercy hugged her handbag to her chest. Lowering her eyes she said: "Me, I am preferring to be staying here."

10

I CALLED NICK. HIS VOICE was casual, cold. "Sorry, back from where?"

"Nevermind. How are you?"

"Terribly well, terribly well. Yourself?"

"Okay." Then, rubbing my forehead: "Is it too late for an apology?"

"For which of your many acts of clinical insanity, if you don't mind my asking?"

"Zanzibar," I breathed, squeezing my eyes shut.

"Oh *that*. I'd forgotten about that. I was rather hoping you might offer an apology for the time you fell over drunk at Justine's party, shattering her grandmother's crystal. Or the time I found you in the bathroom snorting cocaine with three blokes. Or the time you broke your wristwatch over my head. Or the time you grabbed Andrew Vincour by the ears. Or the time you ..."

"I catch the drift."

"But I don't recall Zanzibar being a problem. No. I had a fantastic time after you left."

"You did."

"Yes. I seem to recall a beautiful Danish chick with great nipples and hair down to her ass."

I hung up the phone, poured myself a tumbler full of gin and went to sit by the pool. There was a strange light in the sky, a dull mantle curving down to the horizon. I wondered between sips whether it would lift or whether it would fracture and come raining down in big jagged pieces, laying bare the nothingness beyond. I drained the last of the gin. As my head began to fall forward, I heard the phone ring. I ran into the house, crashing into couch, table, chair. "Hello?" I said.

"There *was* a Danish chick, and I *did* fuck her but it was out of anger. And, no, I didn't enjoy it." I could hear him moving around.

"What are you doing?" I asked.

"I'm looking for the bloody car keys."

"Where are you going?"

"To the opera."

I waited in the hot silence of the house without moving—half-flesh, half-stone—afraid that a sudden movement might disrupt the magic at work. When the doorbell rang, I closed my eyes. "Thank you," I whispered. "Thank you."

The days and nights that followed were absolute perfection. I'm not saying this lightly: we were, Nick and I, angels. There were no arguments, no plays for power, only the earthly exhilaration of Nick coming home at night to find me busy at the stove. I went back to knives and chopping boards with a slight tremor, burdened by my new understanding of their innate goodness, their enormous power—shifty as hell, too, as if I had unlawfully entered a field of fundamentally balanced forces and risked upsetting it just by being there.

My skill, my dexterity with blades and skillets, my understanding of times and temperatures helped me regain my confidence. I browned and roasted. Cut and seared. I steamed, braised, strained with deepening reverence, between flights of barely controlled emotion. A cubed onion became a marvel to behold, the smoky generosity of stock a gift from the gods.

Nick came home with flowers. We lit a sea of candles and sat down to dinner. In the darkness of the bedroom, night after night, I let my heart rest over his, I let my mouth fall open against his neck as the twin emotions of joy and pain pushed me, silently screaming, back into the world.

11

"IT'S DEAD," FATHER ANSELMO SAID as he raised a worn wristwatch to his ear.

I'd brought him a feast—*prosciutto di parma, cacciatorini toscani, insalata di rucola e parmigiano*, tomatoes with basil and olive oil, fresh mozzarella, and, of course, the usual baguette—but his attention remained focused on the watch. He shook it twice, three times then started banging it on the table. "What are you doing?" I asked.

"Who knows, a good knock might revive it."

"You'll just break it."

"It's already broken. Shame. I've had it since I moved here. The least we can do is give it proper burial. Let us stand."

I rose with a smile as Father Anselmo intoned: "We are gathered here today to pay tribute to a vulgar timepiece worn for over a decade by a priest in a slum. It served its purpose with docility, persistence, and valor inversely proportionate to its price at acquisition. We shall now lay it to rest with the briefest reference to the nature of time."

I stole a glance at him but his face was straight, his eyes set dead ahead. "Time is God and God is time. Few, very few of us are acquainted with this fact. We are constantly propelled toward a *fixed point* in time—the moment in which we'll get our raise, the moment in which we'll get out of traffic, the moment in which the public will notice and praise us, the moment in which our coveted one will suggest dinner in a cozy restaurant. And so we are blind to the very nature of time. If it's any consolation, I've seen monks in the great monasteries of the East sitting in lotus pose for days waiting for enlightenment. Fools, just like us. So. Time is God and God is time: *all* of time, from the beginning of creation to the end to the beginning again. If we could keep our eyes glued to this beautiful, relentless and sometimes unforgiving truth, we would glide through this world free from anxiety and fear—so spare, so true in our form and essence that we could, each of us without exception, slip through the eye of a needle and enter the Kingdom in this lifetime." He tossed the watch in the bin and rubbed his hands. "That was that. Dear Lord, thank you for the food we are about to eat. Is the mozzarella fresh?"

"Not really."

"Better than nothing," and he speared the white globe with a knife, stuffing a whole quarter in his mouth. He ate like the chronically hungry eat, filling his mouth compulsively, pausing only to swallow and to drink.

"Hunger must change you," I noted awkwardly.

He nodded, his eyebrows raised in emphatic confirmation: "Apparently it stays stored in your genes for generations. Thank God I won't reproduce. So. What's going on?"

I shrugged. I hadn't seen Mercy. Nick and I had started fighting, mostly about my drinking but also about what I had christened his "little problem," so I told the priest: "Forget about me. I'm far more interested in this crazy talk of God and time. Why here? Why now?"

"You know, I'm not sure. I've been saying masses for the dead. Twenty-five masses for the dead in the last three days. I suppose I needed a diversion."

"Twenty-five ..."

"Twenty five. And I've got eight more today. It's crazy, it's like watching a wild beast devour itself, I have no other words for it. It's horrific, the sharpest spike in mortality since I've been here and, you know, I can't stop thinking of the Plague, the Black Death, how there really ought to be someone going around every morning with a cart to collect the dead. People *rot* in their homes. The neighbors get them out when they can't bear the smell anymore."

"Jesus."

"Jesus is right," Father Anselmo said. "Is this parmigiano?"

"Yes."

"Where did you find it?" I pushed my plate away. "What's wrong?" the priest asked.

"Mercy."

"Oh for God's sake, stop beating yourself over the head! It's not your fault she's sick!"

"It's not *her* fault either."

"No. Not with that criminal of a husband. Is she on the drugs?"

"I haven't seen her."

The priest stopped eating: "You haven't seen her?" I shook my head. "Why not?"

"Well, I tried to get her to move in with me but she wouldn't."

"Why not?"

Something kicked me under the ribs and I shifted in my chair uncomfortably: "I guess I made her feel vulnerable. And she *was*, you know, vulnerable. When someone is so sick, so weak, you acquire enormous power over them and it *does* something to you." I let a few seconds pass, the priest said nothing so I went on: "When Mercy was well, when she was strong and literally twice my size I would have never dared to say the things I've said to her recently. And then part of you doesn't actually buy it. Part of you thinks, come on, get over yourself, of course you can drive the car! Of course you can walk faster! Of course you can put something under your teeth! Half of you *knows* she's got a foot in the grave, the other half doesn't believe it. Or resents it somehow. I wish I could explain."

Father Anselmo sat back. "Clearly you haven't tried."

I gave him a quick look. "Clearly not."

He picked a speck of food from his teeth. "Mercy was your servant. She served *you*. You did not serve *her* until the moment it was required of you, which was when you found that you couldn't, you did not have it in you. Oh, you had fooled yourself. You had deluded yourself. But that's all it was: a delusion."

I stared at him, at once ashamed and incensed. Leaning over the table, Father Anselmo trapped my hand under his: "We *all* delude ourselves, all of us. This is your opportunity, Anna. Take a long hard look at yourself. Embark on the terrifying project of *seeing*. Nothing, absolutely nothing, will be more rewarding."

Later, as I was leaving, he said: "You know, people love to shit on Saint Paul and I confess that in my younger days I did a fair amount of shitting on him myself. This was until I began to sense the violence in him. Saint Paul hated himself, you see, he loathed himself so I began to love him. I loved him for his flaws, for the antidote he found for them in the Hollywood script he wrote and produced about a man called Jesus. Anyway, I don't judge the beliefs of the church because it's not my place to judge the beliefs of the church. What matters is that Saint Paul built this church and this church has lasted us through the ages. Like the mozzarella you brought, it's better than nothing. The reason I am telling you all this is because this man, this man so full of hatred, left us one of the most beautiful passages ever written on love. It's a trifle, a mere detail, a strange coincidence that crept into my mind as you were talking earlier but perhaps you should know that the noun St. Paul uses in the Greek original can be translated both as 'love' and 'mercy.' A trifle, a mere coincidence but if you're going to *serve* Mercy, if you are going to make so much as a single attempt, I strongly urge you to go home and read it. Corinthians XIII. Do me a favor. Go home. Read it."

At the door I heard him call out after me. "Can you tell the truth?" he asked.

"On the rare occasion."

"Swear."

"I swear."

"Why won't anyone drink my tea?"

"You did not tell him?" Mercy asked in a whisper.

"I did not." She gave me a ghost of a smile then closed her eyes. "How much longer?" I asked.

"For the drugs?"

"Yes."

"Next week," she said. "If they have not put this body in the ground."

The hospital room was cold, the air thick with the rank, sweetish smell of death. Next to Mercy, a woman lay rasping on sheets smattered with excrement. "Can't you do something?" I'd asked the nurse.

"Me?" she'd cried, pointing to herself. "What can I be doing? We are having no sheets in this place."

"Can't you wash them?"

"Ah no! It is for the families to be doing the washing!"

"When will the family come?"

The nurse tossed the woman a long speculative look. "Now this one. . . . This one has been without visitors for some few days. Maybe they shall not be coming very soon."

I'd nodded, sat down on Mercy's bed and taken her long, brittle hand in mine. "No," she gasped as she opened her eyes. "You cannot be seeing me like this."

"I don't care what you look like," I said. But I did, oh I did! It took everything I had for me *not* to turn my face away. Christ, how much deeper would the virus cut? What level of human degradation would it ultimately achieve? Mercy's cheekbones were razor sharp beneath her skin, the corners of her mouth caked with a dense white foam. A mixture of pus and blood oozed from the lower lid of her infected eye halfway down her cheek. "Are they not medicating it?" I asked as she struggled to sit up.

Her hands twitched as she began to pat the bed in small, frantic motions. "Where have I placed my spectacles now?" she muttered. "Are you seeing my spectacles?"

"Forget your glasses. It's so dark in here I can't even see you." A lie, of course, with all the dark, spent energy of lies, but when I covered her fumbling hands with mine she grew rigid for a moment then let herself fall with a sigh against the pillow. "How did you find me?"

"I rang Kez."

"He was promising me not to tell you."

"I know."

Kez was short of breath, running to his gate. "Tell her something, anything. Say the doctor called you, you know, the roly-poly guy, I forget his name."

"Dr. Wasunna," I offered quietly.

It was close to midnight. I was alone: Nick and I had fought, something trivial, of no importance, but he had waited for me to crack open the gin as a cat waits for a mouse to blunder out of its hole. He had not pounced—that was the thing with Nick, he never pounced—he'd just given me his chill stare and settled into a satisfied torpor across the room from me. "I think you ought to go," I'd told him quietly. Without a single word, without a sound, he'd gotten up and left. Now the house was empty and, save for the light of a single bulb in the kitchen, plunged in total darkness. My forehead felt hot and heavy against my palm. "So," I asked Kez, "When did this happen?"

"Three days ago."

"Where?"

"In her bedroom."

"She passed out."

"Cold."

"For how long?"

"Twenty minutes."

"What was she doing?"

"Trying to get out of bed." I felt a stab of anger. "So what the fuck are these geniuses waiting for? Why is she not on the drugs?"

"Don't raise your voice with me, baby, don't raise your voice with me. They need one more lab result before they can go ahead: the lab at Nairobi hospital is backlogged, badly, badly, badly backlogged. Plus no one there gives a shit. I've been every day, every single fucking day. I've bribed everyone along the food chain, from Mwangi at the cash register to the *bwana kubwa*, Richard Ndoto."

"Excellent news," I said, "Now they'll expect me to do the same."

"They most certainly will." I sighed. "Why is she at Mbagathi? Why is she not at Nairobi hospital?"

"Wasunna doesn't work at Nairobi hospital, he works at Mbagathi. And we couldn't afford Nairobi hospital anyway. Even between the two of us we couldn't afford it."

"Mbagathi is a hell-hole."

"Tell me about it."

"Which ward?"

"B, as in boy." I ran a hand through my hair. "I cheated on Michael."

"I know," Kez said.

I felt my face grow hot. "Did Mercy tell you?"

"No."

"Did I?"

"No."

"Then who?"

"You do the math." And the line went dead.

"How did Michael find out?" I asked Mercy at the hospital. She ran a dry tongue over her lips.

"He was coming one night from the airport," she said. "You were leaving in your car so he followed you to the place where Nick stays. He stays in Muthaiga, isn't it?"

"Yes," I whispered.

Mercy nodded, her eyes closed: "That is now how it happened."

The nurse had come back from a leisurely break with a single candle whose stingy, sputtering flame cast the only light in the room. "When?" I asked, not wanting to know the answer.

"Me, I can't be remembering everything but it was soon, very soon. He stayed there inside the car until the morning. Then he came to see me."

"He came to see you?"

"Yes. He was shouting very much. He was accusing me that I was more bad than you because I was his friend and I was deceiving him." She pressed down on her lower lip to conceal the tremor.

"What did you say?" I asked. She lay silent, her jaw clamped, her chest rising and falling rapidly beneath the sheets.

From the corner of one eye I saw the nurse approach with a thermometer. "Not now," I said, but she gave no sign of having heard.

"The time is now finished," she announced.

I turned to Mercy. "What did you say to him?" The nurse poked me in the back: two hard digs directly in my spine.

"The time is now finished."

I shot to my feet and ripped the thermometer out of her hand. "What's this?" I screamed. "You're going to take her temperature? She's got one foot in the grave and you're going to take her fucking temperature? You're going to make sure she doesn't have a *fever*? Why don't you wash those sheets instead? Do something useful for a change?" The nurse jumped back as if bitten. I was about to crush the thermometer under my heel when I heard Mercy murmur: "Anna . . ."

I turned. There was a plea so desperate in Mercy's face that for a second it seemed as if Africa itself—ravaged, ridiculed, spoken for by those who know and care the least—was staring at me through her. I looked at the thermometer. The mercury had risen implausibly past the 106 mark: slowly, carefully, I shook it out and handed it back to the nurse: "Please forgive me," I said.

She raised her chin: "Now, what can you be achieving with such rudeness?"

"Nothing."

Her expression softened: "You have answered the correct way. Five more minutes. Then you go."

Mercy gave me a long look as I sat on the bed. "So," she whispered. "Are you growing to be like the big people in this world?"

"*Sijui*," I said.

She smiled—a warm, soft smile that pierced me like a lance. "You are wanting to know what I said to Michael that time?" she whispered.

"Yes."

"I said me, I work for Anna."

Felicity was in the kitchen when I got back that evening, flour up to her elbows. "What are you doing?" I asked her but she just bit down on her lower lip and went on kneading. "You're making bread?" She shook her head. Then I understood: "Is it *chapatti* for Mercy?"

She nodded, rubbing her chin on one shoulder as tears began to flow freely down her face. "You can bring it to Mbagathi," she sniffled.

"Have you been?" I asked. She nodded, pausing and wiping her eyes with her upper arm. "You have?" Again she nodded. I placed one hand on her shoulder: "Felicity, she's dying! Why didn't you say something?" She began to shake. "Why didn't you say something!"

"Me, I was forbidden!" she yelled. "Forbidden! And I was begging, begging! I was asking her please, please to allow me to tell Anna, but she refused. All the time she refused!"

"Why, Felicity, why?"

Forgetting the flour on her palms, Felicity ran both hands down her tear stained face. Ghost-like, she cried: "Because she is ashamed!"

I went to my study and sat in the dark, recalling with strange satisfaction the moment I'd handed the nurse her little victory on a plate. And Mercy's smile, sweeter than jam. The phone made me jump out of my seat. It was Nick: "I'm being manhandled into a dinner party in Karen. I don't suppose for a minute you want to come."

"I don't suppose for a minute you meant to take me."

"I know how you feel about dinner parties in Karen."

I thought about it for a second. "Actually, I've never been to a dinner party in Karen so, no, I don't feel in any particular way about them."

Nick let a full five seconds tick past. "I see. Well, I'm not entirely sure I can arrange an invitation at such short notice. Would you like me to try?"

"No," I said, and put the phone down.

Mercy kept slipping in and out of consciousness when I went to see her the next morning. "This one is going," the nurse on duty muttered. "Can the relatives be coming for her?"

"Talk to me," I said.

"To you?"

"To me."

"Are you the one who can be taking her?"

"Yes."

"Can you take her today? We have many people waiting for this bed."

"No," I said. "Not today."

I drove to Nairobi hospital and demanded to see the head of the laboratory, Mr. Ndoto himself. "I am a journalist!" I shouted, pounding my fist on the counter. "A woman is dying because you can't produce a test result! It's been three weeks! Three weeks! I will drag you—all of you!—in front of a criminal court for negligence! Negligence!"

In the end, of course, I'd had no choice but to sit down and wait. Hours passed, the traffic of nurses, doctors, and patients slowed and eventually stopped. I sat absolutely alone in the same row of dented metal seats, my arms and legs crossed, my eyes closed. A guard in a dark blue uniform with a sheriff's yellow star stitched over his shirt pocket tapped me gently on the leg. His eyes were shot with blood, a sign of chronic exhaustion from life in the slum. "Madam," he said. "The place is now closing. May you please be collecting your things."

I rubbed my eyes. "Has Mr. Ndoto left?"

The guard raised his hands in the air: "What is the problem now, Madam? Mr. Ndoto is busy. He cannot be seeing you."

"The problem," I said, my voice perfectly calm, "is that a woman is dying. Would you call that a big problem or a small problem?"

The guard gave me a pitying smile: "Madam, there are many people who are dying."

Fighting back tears, I said: "Please, please, may I see Mr. Ndoto?" And, reaching into my bag, I pulled out a one thousand shilling note.

"Ah, no!" the guard protested, taking a step back. "That is not what I am asking."

"For your children," I said, extending the note.

He shook his head. Then, without another word, he strode to the lab door and tapped on it with his baton. There was no answer. He tapped on it again. "Guard on duty!" he hollered.

After a few seconds the door opened. A tired voice asked: "Is there a problem?"

The guard bowed his head deferentially. "How is the evening, Mr. Ndoto?"

"Fine," the voice answered.

"*Sasa bwana*, there is a lady here who has been waiting. Can you be seeing her, please?"

"No!" the voice barked. "I know the lady, she has been very rude! Tell her to go!" And he began to close the door. Deftly, the guard slipped his baton in the crack. "What are you doing?" Mr. Ndoto shouted.

"*Tafadali bwana*," the guard said. "The lady is crying."

Mr. Ndoto eyed me with contempt when I walked in. "What was all that ruckus? All that shouting? 'Me, I am taking you to court! Me, I am doing this! Me, I am doing that!' You think we are not trying? You think we are not trying our level best? Tell me, what time is it?"

I checked my watch. "It's ten o'clock, sir."

"That is what I'm saying! Ten o'clock! The place is empty except for me!"

I put one hand over my heart. "Sir, I was wrong to shout and I'm sorry but there is a woman who is fighting for her life, an extraordinary woman, a wonderful woman ..."

"Is she the only one?" Mr. Ndoto cut in, his eyes flashing, "Tell me: Is she the only one? In this country we are losing seven hundred people a day to this disease! Seven hundred people a day! Now because this woman is your friend, because she is the friend of a *mzungu* I must hurry! And the others? The others standing in line quietly? Must I carry them to their graves? *People are dying!* Are you getting me? They are dying!"

"But this woman could live! This woman will be put on anti-retrovirals the second you give me the test result! How many other people being tested right now have that opportunity?"

"All of them," Mr. Ndoto stated curtly.

My head shot back. "All of them?"

"All of them."

"How many people are we talking about?"

"Between thirty and forty a month."

"You do thirty to forty tests a month?"

"No, we send thirty to forty tests a month to South Africa. We can't perform them here."

"South Africa? Is Mercy's test in South Africa?"

"How can I be knowing such a thing?" Mr. Ndoto snapped. "Am I acquainted with this lady?"

"No, sir, you're not. Her name is Achungo. Mercy Achungo."

"Very fine. You tell your friend Mercy Achungo that we are trying our level best," and, putting a hand on my shoulder, he began nudging me toward the door.

I pushed his hand away. "Mercy Achungo is lying unconscious at Mbagathi District Hospital, so I won't be able to tell her anything."

Mr. Ndoto shook his head: "*Pole sana*," he said, "I am truly sorry."

It was my turn to put a hand on his shoulder. "I don't doubt you're sorry Mr. Ndoto. I do not doubt it for one second. But look at me: I'm here, am I not? I'm standing here in front of you, at ten o'clock on a Thursday night. Where are the relatives of the other forty or fifty people being tested? We don't know. Maybe they're eating dinner, maybe they're sleeping. But *I* am here, I'm standing right here, right now, in front of you, begging you."

The man's eyes became very still. Letting out a long breath he said: "What do you want me to do?"

"Call the lab in South Africa. Get the test result."

"And if they are not ready?"

"I won't trouble you again."

Catch it if you can: the moment a crack appears and lengthens along the crust of a human heart. One second you're looking into eyes made of stone, the next you are watching a small man in a white lab coat screaming into the phone: "Do not be discussing things with me, my friend! It is not your job to be discussing things with me! Your job is to be reaching the place I am telling you to reach! It can be ten or eleven or twelve! It can be three o'clock in the morning!" I stood behind him, my heart leaping in its cage until Mr. Ndoto put the phone down and handed me a scrap of paper with three sets of numbers scrawled on it. "These are the values," he said. "They are bad but not so bad. The doctors at Mbagathi can proceed."

12

WE WITNESSED A MIRACLE, THE raising of Lazarus from the dead. Life seeped painfully back into Mercy's veins, into her sere skin. Her breath lengthened, her mouth moistened, her hands acquired new heft and stillness. Kez and I took turns bringing food, clean sheets, medication for her oozing eye, which the hospital would not supply, and the *Daily Nation*, which she began to read voraciously. "Now, me," she greeted me one morning. "I am seeing trouble *ninghi sana* in the Congo. Is your boss happy for you to be just taking tea in Nairobi?"

That night I told Nick Mercy was coming home from the hospital. "Celebrations are in order," I said, but all I got was a dark look.

"You just want an excuse to drink."

"An excuse? Who needs an excuse?"

"How utterly foolish of me," Nick muttered, picking up the car keys, "Everyone but you."

I let it slide, I don't know why, but I let it slide.

Things had taken a bad turn; Nick seemed to have the world chained to his foot. He hated my drinking, I hated the chill that came over the house the minute he walked through the door. He brought a strange kind of poison with him, a strange kind of frost; I would have given gold for an honest brawl: all I got was a face behind a mask. We gorged ourselves on silence.

I did not know what to do. Quitting drinking in the face of such pressure seemed to me an act of cowardice, of surrender. And I could not do it. The only half-assed attempt I'd made had yielded nothing beyond a simmering resentment. I'd started wishing Nick would keep away so I could crack the goddamn bottle open without him looking magisterially on. We still had some good moments, I suppose—our trips to the bush yielded their magic until the end—but increasingly we found ourselves in opposite corners of the living room, stone-eyed, bone-silent, not a spark between us.

That night, as we drove into town, Nick asked: "Where are you going to put her?"

"Who?"

"Mercy."

"Upstairs."

He nodded: "Don't expect me to come around until you've packed her off. Last bloody thing I'm going to do is tiptoe around some moribund woman just to please you."

I shrugged, but my stomach was burning and half of me was dying to stop the car and get out. The other half clung onto Nick with the fragility of a half-developed organism threatened with extinction. It was, I'd known from the start, an impossible balance: impossible to strike, impossible to hold.

The first thing I saw when we walked into the Muthaiga Club a few minutes later was a woman with flowing hair sitting at the bar. I could not see well without my glasses so it was a minute or two before I was able to establish how beautiful she was. I'd clutched at straws until then, hoping her skin would be pockmarked, her hair died, split at the ends. She was pure perfection; green-eyed, sleek-haired, with a spray of Irish freckles on a delicately sculpted nose. Nick perked up immediately. I ordered a gin and tonic, double.

How would he make contact with her, what route would he take? She wasn't alone; to my immense relief there was a handsome man to the left, an older woman to the right.

Destiny leaves nothing unaccounted for, not the pebble picked up by the current, not the twig coming to rest after a thousand convolutions through the air. Nick knew the older woman. They'd played golf together once. I sipped my gin and tonic rigidly at one end of the bar as Nick held out an eager hand at the other—the young woman took it, the two locked stares, Nick leaned over to say something, the woman bared her throat and laughed. Ten or fifteen minutes passed. I considered going over and asking whether he had lost track of time but my pride would not allow it so I asked for another drink. When it came, I left it sweating on the counter and walked out. I heard my name ring across the parking lot. When Nick caught up with me I tried to slap him but he caught my arm in mid air: "Enough," he said, "I've had enough."

Mercy moved in at noon the next day. The timing seemed to suggest great forces at work. Maybe Nick would call. Maybe we'd run into each other. But he never called and nothing ever happened. In retrospect a sense of whiteness prevails, an absence of color coupled with an absence of sound. I slept and woke and slept again until, on a clear June day, Mercy came roaring back to life.

13

IT WAS JUST BEFORE SIX, the eastern horizon was starting to clear. I'd been awake most of the night, my eyes were raw, my skin felt hot and tight. Battling the urge to weep from exhaustion I had made my way downstairs and found the kitchen light on, the radio blaring. Out of habit, without really looking, I said, "Good morning Felicity," but when the woman standing at the sink spun around and I saw the black patch over one eye, I shrieked: "What are you doing?"

Mercy glared at me. "Are you seeing this sink? Are you seeing the dirt? What has this girl been doing? She cannot be keeping a job when she is leaving things dirty!"

"Who?" I asked.

"That one!" Mercy shouted.

"Felicity?" and from somewhere in the kitchen a small voice said: "Madam ..." I looked and there was poor Felicity, her face a mask of tears. "What happened?" I asked.

Mercy went on as if I had not spoken: "Now I am the one who feeling shame because I am the one who brought her to this house! And look! Look how it has become!"

Felicity began to cry, so I went over and put one arm around her: "It's okay," I crooned. "It's okay ..."

"It's not okay!" roared Mercy. "There is a good way and a bad way! And this . . ." she pointed to the sink, "this is the bad way!" Out of curiosity I went over and took a quick look: the sink gleamed, it positively sparkled.

"What's wrong with the sink?"

Mercy put her hands on her hips: "Me, I have been scrubbing! *Ahi!* I have been scrubbing. But before, it was not okay! It was dirty!" Felicity let out a high, thin wail. "You better shut up," Mercy hissed in Swahili. "I'm trying to keep you from losing your job!"

"But I have no intention of firing Felicity . . ."

Mercy dismissed my statement with a sweep of the arm. "We shall be teaching her how to do her work! We shall be trying very hard to teach her the proper way! Isn't it? Eh? Felicity! Isn't it?" Felicity nodded meekly, hiding her face in the crook of her elbow as I looked helplessly from one woman to the other. "*Kahawa?*" Mercy asked defiantly. I nodded and she began to open the cabinet doors one by one, muttering: "Now where has this foolish girl placed the coffee machine, all the things were in the correct place . . ."

"Mercy," I finally said, "aren't you supposed to be in bed?"

She let out a snort. "Me, I am *through* with staying in bed!"

Time reconstituted itself then, as a bone from a fracture. Felicity scrubbed and cooked and scrubbed some more. I rearranged the furniture in my study and began to plan my first trip since Belgrade. Mercy ate—*kuku, ugali, nyama*, more *kuku*, more *ugali*, more *nyama*—and drove herself to all of

Nairobi's market stalls packed high with second-hand clothes, to find something "nice to wear." In the evening she took a *matatu* to her home in Kawangware to spend time with her children.

Felicity came crying. "Me, I cannot be staying in this house. I am the one who is doing all the work but Mercy is getting all the money! She goes to buy the clothes and she goes to see her children and me, I am just here, doing all the work!"

I soothed her with a negligible raise in pay, privately reflecting that the world was indeed far from fair. Mercy continued to breeze in and out of the house, sitting down only long enough to polish off the meals Felicity cooked for her. "This one has too much onion, " I heard her say once. "Next time don't be putting so much onion." One day Mercy came back from the hairdresser with hair attachments so long and fine that Felicity burst into tears on the spot.

"I don't know where she got the money," I lied shamelessly that night. "She must have had some savings." Felicity buried her face in her hands and wept.

What could I say? How could I explain it? Mercy had come back from the dead with a thirst for life so savage that I was in no position to contain it. "Can you at least do some work?" I whispered one morning before Felicity came in.

Mercy pondered my suggestion from the privileged vantage point of her five-inch heels. "Me, I am driving the car."

"Yeah, to buy clothes and makeup and whatever else you're buying these days. Which reminds me, I've always wanted to ask: why do you do this? Why do you squeeze yourself into these crazy outfits? Why the makeup, the hair, the heels? What's wrong with a nice, comfortable shirt? Nice, comfortable jeans?"

"Why?" she shot back, visibly alarmed. "Am I looking bad?"

I put out a reassuring hand. "No, no, you look fine, but I don't understand why you do it. I never have. I never will."

It took her a while to answer. She got herself a glass, went to the fridge, poured herself some water, and then, with a loud sigh, said: "My husband, he was the one who was preferring me to look like this."

"Your husband? The son of a bitch who gave you the virus?"

"Eh!" she jumped, casting a quick look behind her. "Now let us leave such talk!"

"Leave such talk?" Mercy drained her glass. "Leave such talk? And do what? Gloss over the largely inconsequential fact that that lying sack of shit gave you AIDS? That you're alive by a miracle? That you could have *died* because he couldn't keep his dick in his pants? And since we're at it, let me see if I have this right: you squeeze yourself in these crazy getups on the off-chance you'll run into your husband? Is that what you do? Is that what you do?"

What she did left me speechless. She smashed the glass down on the counter and presented me with a great gleaming shard. "You are finished talking to me in such a way," she growled.

It took me a couple days to digest the incident. Eventually I sent a note through Felicity (whose resistance was so determined I had to produce a bribe) asking for forgiveness. "In this world there are things you cannot be grasping," was Mercy's tense greeting the following day.

"What things?" I asked quietly.

Mercy adjusted her eye-patch with a swift, by now experienced movement. "Me, I was a prostitute. My husband came and married me in front of all the people—my mother, my father, my aunts and uncles—and then he took me away from that place. He was saying to them: 'You see this one here? You see her? She is too good for you!'" Her chin began to tremble and she looked away.

"Then what happened?" I asked.

Mercy picked up a rag, threw it in the sink: "Then I became the woman from River Road and my husband became a drunk."

"Like me."

Mercy's eyes met mine. "Like you," she said.

There are no simple explanations, they don't exist: the minutest crumb of human experience is an aggregate of at least half a dozen elements. In the case of my drinking, which stopped that same day, I had been stung by the exchange. I also happened to be leaving for a particularly inhospitable and undersupplied place: on a whim I decided not to pack a stash. At the airport I had no time, an accident on the Mombasa Road kept me tied in traffic for so long I barely made my flight. The trip lasted nearly three weeks. I returned to Nairobi in a different body, my kidneys and liver fully functional, my memory restored to partial use. When Kez called me, I told him I would not meet him at Ollie's. "What's poor Ollie done to you?"

"I don't want to drink."

"Why not?"

"Because I don't want to drink. Haven't we had this conversation before?"

"Not that I recall."

"My point exactly."

"What point?"

"You're a drunk."

"Me?" Kez sounded genuinely offended.

"You, me. Both."

"So?" he asked.

"So go ahead: sing the unsung virtues of alcoholism to me."

"No, I hear you, I hear you. You were *waaay* out of control in New York."

"Oh yes? I don't recall spending the night in jail."

"Neither do I."

"My point precisely."

"You know, Anna, you get all puritanical from time to time and the next thing I know you start shoveling shit in my face. Leave me out of it, okay? This time I want to be left out of it."

"Fine."

"So you're not coming?"

"No."

He came over instead, and to mark the occasion Mercy sent Felicity home for the night. "Pass by the house," were her curt instructions. "Tell the children I shall be seeing them tomorrow. Make James to be in charge." Watching Felicity sprint for the door, Mercy clacked her tongue. "That girl ... she is bothering me too much these days!" I sputtered into my glass but Mercy went on: "The girl looks like she is being beaten! Like someone is taking a stick and beating her! Now, me, I have been too sick. Too sick!" And with that, Mercy clattered off to the kitchen.

Kez and I looked at each other. "Is she okay?" he whispered. "She eats like a horse," I said. "She goes shopping. She goes to the hairdresser. She treats Felicity like shit. The poor girl, I feel so bad for her."

"Why do you let her?"

"Who?"

"Mercy."

"Well ..." I started, but Kez cut right to the heart of the matter: "You haven't got the balls."

Nothing could have been truer. Mercy looked as if she'd ingested fire. If before her illness she'd commanded respect, even reverence, now she elicited something very close to fear. The butcher, who'd taken pure delight in slighting her in the past, trembled at her approach. "Not for you, Madam," he stammered one day, picking up a leg of lamb and hiding it behind his back, "It's not fresh."

I looked discreetly away as Mercy roared: "Who is talking about fresh? We are just hoping to be having the teeth remain inside the mouth!"

"Naturally, Madam, naturally. May I offer you something from the back of the shop? A tenderloin of beef? Vacuum packed for tenderness?"

"Bring!" Mercy barked. And he brought.

We walked on eggshells. Felicity formed the hysterical habit of curtsying; I kept largely to my study, Kez stopped coming around altogether. I got a note from Mercy's twelve-year-old son, James. On a spectacularly soiled scrap of paper, amidst a million cancellations, I read: "Something bad is happening to our mother, Mercy. She is beating us very badly. Even the little one, Lucy. May you please help."

I thought about it for a minute and then called Father Anselmo. "She's a fury, a harpy."

"Bring her to me. Monday at six."

It wasn't easy. Mercy had things to do, places to go. She was also under no contractual obligation to work after five. "Work? Did you say work?" she snorted.

We got to the church in Kariobangi just as the sun was setting. Mercy slammed the car door and began taking giant strides toward the priest's house. I trotted along, safely if resentfully tucked behind her magnetic field. At the door, she crossed her arms, took a long look around and screwed her mouth into an expression of deep disgust. "Look at these people," she said loudly. "They are living like pigs!" I jumped. "Jesus, Mercy, are you crazy?" but all she did in response was shout: "Pigs! They are living like pigs!" I began banging on the priest's door. Mercy's voice went up. "Imagine now! The way these people can be living!"

"Father Anselmo!" I yelled.

"Pigs!"

"Open the door!"

"Animals!"

"Father Anselmo!" The door opened and I shot inside like a bullet.

"What's all this shouting?" the priest yelled at me, "Have you gone mad?"

"She's calling them pigs! She's standing out there calling everyone a pig!"

Father Anselmo stuck his head out. "Mercy, please come in."

"Pigs!" Mercy thundered as the door closed, "How can they be accepting to be living like this? In the filth, in the dirt ..."

The priest gave her a frigid look: "Not everyone can choose, Mercy." For a second it looked like she might take him down, she swayed from one foot to the other as if about to charge. "Have a seat," he told her and, after a long, simmering moment, she did. "Tea?" Father Anselmo asked.

Mercy narrowed her eyes: "Your tea," she said, "is making people to have very bad diarrhea."

The priest froze. "Diarrhea?"

"*Very bad* diarrhea," Mercy corrected him.

Father Anselmo turned to me in mild shock. I raised both hands: "Leave me out of it."

Mercy shot to her feet: "Anna was the one who was having it! She was the one who was complaining too much!"

"Mercy has gone mad," I informed Father Anselmo. "She's been restored to life but not to sanity. We're not sure what happened."

"Mercy?" the priest asked.

Mercy raised her chin. "Me, I am just okay. It is Anna who is having problems inside her head," and she tapped her forehead. "Mercy's pissed," I said. "She's mad as hell and she's not going to take it anymore."

"Mercy?"

Mercy sat back down, crossing and uncrossing her legs a couple times before standing up and gesturing broadly with one arm: "Have you seen this place?"

I rolled my eyes: "Here we go again ..." but Father Anselmo cut me short: "What about this place?"

Her voice was a razor. "This place is good for animals, not for humans. But us, we are Africans, so it's not so bad. We can be accepting to live like animals. The difference is little."

"Mercy ..." I started, appalled, but the priest raised his hand: "Let her speak."

"Me, I am finished."

"So you're an animal," Father Anselmo said.

"That is correct: me, I am just an animal. They put me in the dirt, I don't complain. My children get sick, I don't complain. My children die, I don't complain. I get sick, I don't complain. I die, I don't complain. I just go quietly in the ground. Me and the rest of Africa."

For a while, Mercy's labored breathing was the only sound in the room. Then Father Anselmo said: "You are alive by the grace of God, how can you possibly judge those who die?"

"I am alive because of drugs!" Mercy exploded. "Drugs I take every day, four times a day! Look at me! I am eating now for three people! Three! My hands are strong, my back is strong, my mind is clear. I was dead! In that dirty bed! In that dirty hospital! Dead!" She took a long shaky breath. "I was counting the ladies who were dying at Mbagathi. Twenty-eight until the day I was released. Twenty-eight. Mothers with children—they are all dead, that is a fact, I am speaking of the children—but me, I survived and sometimes I am saying to myself it can be better to be dead. I am seeing too much of the way we are. We are like animals! If the white man wants to save us by giving us drugs, he can save us. If the white man wants to kill us by keeping the drugs for himself, he can kill us. We don't complain. We just accept. But me, I am different now. I can be taking a gun and shooting. I can be taking a gun and *killing* the person who is keeping such drugs to himself!"

Father Anselmo closed his eyes and touched his chin to his chest. Mercy and I exchanged a long look. "*Twende*, we go now," she said, picking up her handbag—the same bag, I realized with a start, she had clutched so pathetically to her chest when she was sick. I began to clear my throat.

"Wait," the priest said, his head bent, his eyes closed. "Wait one minute." When he finally spoke, his voice was soft, gentle, with none of the spikes and edges I'd come to fear. "So you've killed and gone to jail: what happens then?"

Mercy shrugged. "My children can die just like the other children."

"Good. And what happens to the millions of people who have AIDS in this continent."

"They can also die."

"Good. So if you die and they die, who's going to get the drugs?" Again, Mercy shrugged. The priest put one hand on her shoulder. "You've come back from the dead with your eyes wide open, Mercy. Now it's your turn to open other people's eyes. Because you're right: the cure exists and you have a right to it. But you won't get it with a gun. You'll get it by telling people to wake up. They have the right to these drugs: these drugs exist, they have been made, so why are they not here? Ask them that question. And when they are ready, show them the way to civil disobedience. Do you know what civil disobedience is?"

Mercy freed herself from his hand and leaned into the wall with an alarming mix of indolence and rage. Father Anselmo stood waiting, not a muscle moving. Mercy unpeeled herself from the wall, slung her bag over her shoulder: "The way of Gandhi," she said.

And so my house became Mercy's house. Every day, in ever-increasing numbers, women came to the gate and were admitted. The kitchen became a kind of secretariat, the administrative heart of Mercy's movement. The dining room hosted general meetings and late-night brainstorming. "What's all this noise?" Warren shouted into the phone one day.

"People," I said.

"What people?"

"Mercy's people."

"Who's Mercy?"

"The one who was dying."

"What?"

"The one who had AIDS!"

"Right, right ... I remember ... How is she?"

"Fine."

"What?"

I had the door and window to my study soundproofed. Next, I instituted a curfew: "Not a minute past seven."

"The movement shall suffer," Mercy warned.

"The movement shall be perfectly all right," and in this minor prediction, at least, I was right. It wasn't long before a leadership of five, with Mercy unassailably at the top, set to work. Five committees were formed: one for State House, one for Parliament, one for the Ministry of Public Health, one for the Ministry of Trade and Tourism, and one for the Kenya Wildlife Association. A month later, the first letters were sent. Signed by "The Movement for Life," they predicted the nonviolent disruption of governmental activities unless steps were taken to bring in *affordable* anti-retroviral drugs.

"What's affordable?" Kez asked her over lunch one day, "Five bob? Ten bob a pill?"

Mercy pointed at him with her thumb: "This one is asking too many questions."

"Too many *good* questions," Kez shot back.

Mercy shrugged: "Good? What's good?" but it was clear that his involvement, somewhat obsessive in my opinion, pleased her enormously. Kez had more than joined the movement; he'd embraced it with transport, having glimpsed in it full powers of redemption. He'd shot footage of meetings;

he'd gone to the slums to get images of the dead and the dying, he'd even asked me to arrange an interview with Father Anselmo.

"Be careful," I told him. "He can be distinctly unpleasant," but the two had hit it off famously, with Father Anselmo telling me: "He is one of the strangest people I've ever met. I confess at first I thought he was on drugs. But then we talked about his Muslim faith and he articulated it with such eloquence, such precision, such *clarity* that I just sat there and listened. Wonderful fellow. Absolutely wonderful fellow."

Kez returned the feeling: "The man's got *balls*. Never *seen* such balls in my life."

"The price is a problem," Mercy admitted that day. "We are not reaching an agreement."

"How about a third of a malaria pill?" I suggested.

Mercy nodded. "Me, I am thinking that can be fair but other women are protesting it is too expensive."

"Tell them to shut the fuck up," said Kez. "You're the boss."

"Now you," Mercy warned, raising a finger, "you are using even *more* bad words than before!"

Kez smiled. "Sorry."

"And me, I'm not the boss," but there was no mistaking the pecking order in the movement, though it wasn't so much a question of a pecking order as of Mercy's talent as a leader. She could be soft one moment—listening to lamentations deep into the night—and hard as processed steel the next. She had an unerring intuition of which face to put on for which occasion; maybe it wasn't even a face, it was Mercy rearranging herself at cellular level to meet the moment's demands. There was no shortage of problems, from a chronic lack of punctuality to a generalized inability to focus on the issue at hand. The first Mercy solved by stripping whoever showed up after eight o'clock of membership without the possibility of recourse—sadly we lost some of the best women that way, but Mercy was inflexible—the second by assuming personal control of all general debates. She allotted no more than one minute at any given time, which, given the African tendency to ramble, brought on an initial wave of panic. "But how can I be explaining the problems in just one minute?" a woman had shouted to a chorus of approval.

Mercy had given her a neutral look: "Why? Are you not having the intelligence?"

The woman had looked around her in outrage: "Me?"

"Yes," Mercy said, fixing her with heavy eyes. "You."

The room had gone quiet. The woman had begun to stammer. Mercy had roared: "We are not here to play games! We are here to change the way people live and die in this country! If we are having ladies who cannot be organizing their minds, make them go from this room at once!" No one had moved. Kez, who was filming the meeting, had brought his face slowly away from the camera and turned to look at me across the room.

"She was *born* for this!" he told me later. "It's like she's been waiting her whole life to become this, to *be* this!"

"I know," I said. "I know."

Mercy came out of the kitchen just at that moment and stopped to look at us critically in turn: "You! How are you making yourself useful?" Kez leveled the camera and started shooting. "Enough with this machine!" Mercy shouted, waving him away. "I am having this machine harassing me all day! One cannot be coping with such an harassment!"

Kez lifted his head: "Count your blessings, Mercy," and he was right. When the time came, Kez's footage was like found money.

It was July. The house was an unbelievable mess. Poor Felicity worked around the clock to bring order to a steadily deteriorating situation. "Madam," she whispered one day, "can we be digging an outdoor latrine?" And I understood, without asking, what she was saying: many of the women had full-blown AIDS, which meant chronic diarrhea. We dug three latrines at the bottom of the garden; Kez and I shared the expense, Mercy enforced novel regulation on the use of toilet paper. "This," she announced one day, holding up a piece of toilet paper about a foot long, "is how much of this particular paper we can be using. This paper is costing too much money, with the Chinese now we are having many problems. Also, we cannot be filling the latrines too quickly."

July turned into August. Logistics began to be put in place for a march. None of the letters sent by the movement had been answered, so the question became when to have the march, which government building to target, which route to take to it, and where to stop—whether right in front of it or a few meters away from it to allow full press coverage of the event.

Mercy wanted a march on State House. She felt the element of surprise might help the women get closer to the building than they would in any subsequent march. Others disagreed. They felt an attack, even one as mild as a march, on the head of state would bring out an instinctive violence and possibly cause bloodshed. Parliament, with its ostensibly broader functions of representation, would be a more convenient, less dangerous target. A vote was scheduled, restricted on a first-come, first-served basis to two hundred women. "We cannot be having all of Korogocho in Anna's living room," Mercy explained. The vote was held; Mercy's faction lost by fifteen votes.

And so, on the tenth of September, under a high indigo sky, five thousand women marched peacefully on the House of Parliament. Hundreds were arrested but a small group of about twenty, Mercy at the head, pushed to the building and chained themselves to the gates, swallowing the keys to their padlocks.

I have it on film: Mercy lifting a small key tantalizingly high and dropping it neatly into her mouth. And her eyes: I have her eyes on film. When the first wave of policemen got to the gates they used their batons to try to smash the chains. Mercy, who looked possessed, who looked demented, who looked dangerously close to freeing herself and taking them all down with her, was the only exception. The crowd began to shout. Metal cutters were brought and used instead of sticks. One after the other, the women were lifted by force and thrown in a police truck. All but Mercy, who walked without assistance and without interference to the back of the truck and turned to face the crowd with a raised fist.

Kez was stiff with rage when he showed me the footage later that afternoon. He had a black eye and a swollen lip from a run-in with the police. "Fucking pieces of fucking shit," he croaked. "They better let her go." They did, in matter of hours. Mercy came to the house in a clamor of sirens as thousands stood outside the gate and watched. She shook hands with half a dozen officers, waved to the crowd, strutted in, and ordered dinner on the spot. After the chicken was served on a mountain of *ugali*, Felicity received pardon for her many sins. "She has been a good girl," Mercy said to me with a nod of approval.

Felicity burst into tears: "Me I am happy to be serving you. You are helping the people and, me, I have been so selfish!"

"Felicity!" I snapped. "The last thing you have been is selfish! Stop beating yourself on the head all the time!"

"Yes, madam," she gasped. "Forgive me, madam."

Mercy followed her retreat to the kitchen with a strange look. "Some people can be like that," she said. "They can be allowing themselves to be treated badly until the day they die." She sighed: "What shall we do with such people?"

"The Africans, you mean."

Mercy let her eyes wander: "Not all," she said. "Not all." Then she leaned back in her chair and closed her eyes. A minute passed. "What shall you do, Anna, after we have won the struggle? Will you go back to Italy or to America?"

The question caught me completely off-guard, both for its casual presumption of victory as for the implication that I might one day be separated from her, that I *should*, in fact, one day be separated from her. "America, I think, but let's not put the cart before the horse, it brings bad luck." Mercy pulled the corners of her mouth down and shook her head, as if to say: piece of cake. "We've still got a ways to go," I said.

Again, she shook her head: "This will be over quick: we get the people, we get the drugs."

"Yeah, you get *millions* of people."

"Of course!" she said. "You think I can be wasting my time for some few thousands? We get millions!" I looked at her: there wasn't a trace of doubt in her eyes.

"Fine, you get millions. But Mercy, this is not a democracy. It's on its way to becoming one but don't forget, these so-called democratic institutions are fifty years old. In historical terms, they're in their infancy. They're barely there."

Mercy frowned: "Who is talking about history? Me, I am talking about today."

"Yeah? What if they beat you?"

She turned her head slowly. "They cannot."

"Oh no? They beat hundreds."

"They have assured me that was a mistake."

"Baloney. You caught them by surprise today. It won't happen again."

"Can they dare?"

"I should think so."

She had a sip of water, wiped her mouth. "And the people?"

"Forget the people."

"You are saying the people don't care?"

"I'm saying the people don't *know*. They are not aware of their rights. Not at this stage."

"So?"

"So you slow down. You wait."

But she didn't wait. It's still unclear to me how she did it, how she marshaled the bodies, the souls in so little time. The numbers swelled; the house became so crowded, so chaotic that I turned the keys over to Mercy and moved in with Kez. "Don't get frisky," he warned me, moving to his side of the bed.

In the relative quiet of Kez's apartment I was able to write my first in-depth piece on Mercy and the movement. Warren called: "I was starting to think we had a vacant bureau."

"You liked it?"

"I did. Why don't we do a series?"

I could hardly believe my ears. "A series?"

"Sounds like the woman's onto something," he said.

Kez gave me his blackest look. "That's not fair."

"Tell your editors."

"My editors want me in Monrovia. They're going to fire my ass if I don't go."

"Make a cogent case. Explain the inside access you have."

"Nah. I got a better idea." He walked past me to the bathroom and came back with a mouthful of toothpaste: "Wa-wa-wa-wa-wa," he said.

"What?"

He went to the bathroom again, came back and announced, rather grandly: "I'm going on sabbatical."

"A paid sabbatical, I presume."

"Yeah. By my father," who, it turned out, had not only money, but a fiercely idealistic streak. "He thinks Mercy's onto something."

Mercy came banging at the door a few days later. The women were driving her crazy. "They are like chickens," she said, flapping her arms. "Have you seen chickens, the way they can just *look* stupid?" Kez smiled and, for the millionth time, trained his camera on her. "This one is harassing me too much!" Mercy laughed, trying to push Kez away, but you could tell she had grown used to it, the way a celebrity does. Which is what Mercy had become: a celebrity. Members of parliament jostled daily for a photo-op with her. Local and regional representatives of the world's largest pharmaceutical companies—Pfizer, Glaxo, Merck, Boehringe Ingelheim—all begged for a mere ten minutes of her time. A debate—with a final vote—was scheduled on whether Mercy should meet with them and, at that crucial point, Father Anselmo rode a *matatu* all the way from the slum and pushed through the crowd gathered at the gate. "Mercy!" he shouted. "Anna! Kez! Mercy! For God's sake, *someone* let me in!"

"Sorry, Father," Mercy apologized when he got in. "We were not aware you were coming."

Father Anselmo glared at her. "This is disgraceful! You should have some kind of crowd control beyond this stupid gate!"

Mercy lifted herself on her toes to catch a glimpse of the sea of people gathered at the gate. "They are many," she admitted. "But us, how can we be keeping them away?"

The priest waved her statement aside. "The debate," he asked. "What time is the debate?"

He had read about it in the paper; he felt he had a contribution to make. Mercy took him to the kitchen and personally made him a cup of tea. They sat at the table for a good half hour as Kez and I stood watching. "Leave that fucking thing alone," I said between clenched teeth when Kez tried to take out his camera.

"It's a historic moment!" he whispered.

"Put it away!" I hissed.

Father Anselmo looked up. "Kez, do us a favor."

"You'll regret it . . ." Kez complained, but Mercy brought a finger to her lips. Kez laid his camera soundlessly beside him.

The dining room was packed when we filed in; two hundred women with the power of a vote stood at the front, close to the table, another two hundred or so jostled for space in the back. The air was heavy, rank with sweat. Mercy took the floor. She coughed into her hand a couple times and then began: "Many of you here today do not know who Father Anselmo is. I shall be very brief. Father Anselmo is the man who placed me on this path. He came from Korogocho in a *matatu* this morning because he has something he is feeling very strongly in his heart. Me, I have listened, now it is your turn. The floor shall then be open to debate. Voting shall start exactly at noon."

Father Anselmo stepped forward and he, too, coughed lightly into his fist. Space! I wanted to shout, give him space! Let him breathe! But he didn't seem to mind. He spread his spindly arms and yelled: "The Lord be with you!"

"Also with you!" the women shouted.

"I am here," the priest began, "I am here because of what I have read in the newspapers. I have read that the drug companies want to speak to Mercy. I would, too, if I were them. Mercy is asking for fifteen times *less money per pill* than these companies are willing to settle for today. Fifteen times: that's a lot of money. No corporation can afford to part with that kind of money, and *this*, this is what I want to talk to you about today." Father Anselmo ran his eyes over his audience. "Corporations are machines. They are neither good nor bad, they are just machines. It would be foolish of us to endow them with a heart, to run them through with feeling. They are agglomerations of business interests, by which I mean other people's money. Nothing would be crazier than for us to attempt to bring about a sense of shame. They have no shame, I repeat, not because they are bad, but because they are machines."

He paused, looked around him. Mercy handed him a glass, he drained it in two long gulps. "I come to my point, to the reason I woke early this morning so that I could stand in front of you and shout: Nothing! Do you hear? Nothing other than steadily applied, *overwhelming* pressure can alter the course of a machine and I'm sorry to inform you that we are *not*, individually or collectively, in a position to apply that kind of pressure right now. One day we will, of that I am certain, but even then it will be through international channels like the World Health Organization and the United Nations. Until then, let us not be foolish. Let us not imagine that machines have hearts. Let us not be meeting with the representatives of such machines and imagine we'll gain concessions or watch them squirm. The individual in question may or may not squirm, that hardly concerns us. The machine most certainly will not. So. Let us proceed the way we have been proceeding: quietly, respectfully, with the determination and the strength that *justice* had always lent every human cause." He looked around him once more: "Justice!" he shouted and the room exploded, it exploded; I thought the windows would shatter, the walls crack from the bottom up.

Mercy was hoarse by the time she succeeded in making herself heard. "Silence! Silence! I shall expel all of you!" Father Anselmo stood with his arms crossed, looking down at his feet, beaming.

There was no need for a vote and I took great pleasure in composing the letters we sent to the drug companies that fall. They consisted of a single line: "The Movement for Life sees no reason to meet with a representative of your company at this point."

"You are making a terrible mistake," the Pfizer representative warned me over the phone. "Our position shall only harden."

Machines, I told myself, just machines, but of course when I opened my mouth something entirely different came out: "What did you say?"

"I *said*, our position will only harden."

"You fool," I whispered, my voice shaking. "You fucking fool . . ."

"Anna!" Mercy shouted from across the kitchen.

I put the phone down with a sheepish smile. "Sorry."

November came around; the women voted overwhelmingly for a march on State House. After that, a pall fell over the house as if, having crossed the line between relative and absolute danger, the women were now reevaluating their commitment to the cause. Talk of children and grandchildren filled every spare minute; a terrible premonition of loss lent every word greater weight. The meetings not only took place punctually, they adjourned earlier, so sparse and precise had the women become.

Thinking back, that period marked Mercy's apotheosis: her softness became softer, her hardness harder. I don't know how else to explain it, she pivoted effortlessly from extreme to extreme with the curious result that none of the things she did came across as extreme, only as perfectly calibrated, flawlessly executed responses to the *moment*.

I can't explain it; all I can say is that we changed, all of us, because *she* had changed: we became both lighter and heavier, louder and quieter. Even Felicity experienced a transformation, taking the floor one morning with a scrap of paper quivering in one hand to announce a new set of rules. Cups and dishes had to be washed and put away by whoever used them; the same applied to towels and hand towels; laundry detergent and pegs would be made available outside. The kitchen was out of bounds from eleven in the morning until three in the afternoon, and open again from three to five. There was to be no heating or reheating of food. Access to the second floor was restricted to Mercy and myself; access to the servant's quarters to Mercy and herself. A murmur of protestation ran through the room. Mercy roared with laughter and folded Felicity in a long embrace.

The day of the march came. Mercy stood in the middle of the dining room surrounded by two hundred women as thousands gathered outside.

I'd already taken her to one side. "They will beat you," I'd said.

"Enough with such nonsense!" Mercy had snapped.

"You don't know how these things work! I *do*!"

Her one eye had flashed dangerously: "Anna has become an African now?"

"No," I'd hissed. "I've seen it *done*! In *all* of these supposed democracies! You piss them off, they put you away! You think you're the exception to the rule? You're wrong! There is never an exception!"

"Let them try," Mercy had said, nudging me aside.

I'd been taken aside in turn. "What the *fuck* are you doing?" Kez had hissed, holding my arm in a painful grip.

"She's about to lead a march to State House and you tell her she's going to get *beaten*?"

I'd yanked my arm away. "What do you want me to say? Have a nice *walk*? Enjoy the *weather*?"

"No, you say: I'm with you, Mercy. We're *all* with you. That's what you fucking say!" He'd been spraying me with his spittle so I'd pushed him away.

He had laid his camera down and I can't honestly tell what would have happened had Mercy not come between us.

And maybe I can offer this, this pathetic brawl, this impalpable crumb, as an example of how soft and how hard she could get. First she looked at Kez. In a perfectly level voice she asked: "Were you intending to hit Anna?" Kez looked down at his shoes. "If I see such foolishness again you can be packing your camera and returning to Egypt, am I being clear?" Kez nodded. Then Mercy turned to look at me and there was such *pity* in her face, such *pity*, as if, having leveraged myself with great difficulty to a respectable height, I had fallen once more into the gutter, with the difference that this time I would be unable to pick myself up again. She didn't say a word to me. Not one. She pushed us both into the dining room, where the women were waiting. "Good morning!" she hollered when we got there, the picture of good cheer. "The day has come!"

Her speech was practical, short: how to avoid confrontation with the police, how to keep a steady pace so as not to "arrive at midnight," what to do with raucous or drunken demonstrators who would want to join along the way and, above all, how to hold onto the numbers at State House. Then Mercy let a long silence fall as she looked at each woman in turn. "You are the face and the voice of this disease," she whispered. "You are the face and the voice of Africa." Then, at the top of her voice: "*Twende*!" Let's go!

That day, one million women converged on State House, sending the city of Nairobi into a spasm that took days to subside. As agreed beforehand, the women started to chant. Next they began to clap. They joined hands and cheered. When they ran out of slogans, they switched to Christian hymns. "I have a friend in Jesus," they sang and, when they got to State House and came face to face with a cordon of police ten yards thick, it was the singing and the cheering that prevented a minor massacre from taking place.

Under the puzzled eye of thousands of police and army officers, the women sat in a gigantic circle around State House in what was to be a twenty-two-hour wait. At noon the next day, to thunderous applause, Mercy was escorted into State House for a two-hour meeting with Julius Mena, Kenya's minister of health.

"The man is serious," Mercy told us that night as victorious chanting from outside reached us in the kitchen, "He is someone who is having serious concern for the people. He is saying now that we have the movement the government can be refusing to buy the drugs from the big drug companies."

"Where will they get them from?" I asked.

"From the drug companies," Mercy said, a queer look in her eyes.

I met Mena the next day. He agreed to an interview only after finding out my relationship to Mercy. Tall, tailored, with long smooth hands, the minister waited for me to sit before crossing his legs and pulling out a cigarette. "How did you meet Mercy?" he asked.

"She came looking for a job."

"As a housegirl?" I nodded. The minister shook his head, a small smile tugging at the corners of his mouth. "Us Africans, we know the meaning of the word humility."

I nodded. Turning on my tape recorder I said: "Mercy tells me you're going to stop purchasing patented drugs."

The minister smiled. "We can't afford them. They're beyond our reach. Even if they were to come down eighty, ninety percent in price, we still could not afford them. We don't have the money. But what we do have now, thanks to Mercy, is a grassroots protest, the first in Africa, and that puts us in a different negotiating position."

"You think they'll lower the price?"

"Not really."

"What about generics from India or Brazil? They're a fraction of the cost."

"Aaahh," Mena sighed. "That is a whole other issue we are facing. There are ..." he put his cigarette out, "... obstacles."

"What obstacles?"

"Please turn that off." I leaned over and pressed stop on my recorder. Mena propped his elbows on his knees. "We are being told by the U.S. Department of Trade that if we wish to qualify for tariff reductions on certain goods we must respect intellectual property rights."

"What goods?"

"Cotton for the moment. There will be other offers later, but right now the U.S. is offering to import *all* the cotton we can produce without tariffs. Whatever we give them, they will buy. We are, however, being made to understand that the respect of intellectual property rights is what makes a partner *reliable* in trade."

"Meaning you must not import generic drugs."

"Correct."

"Even if you can't afford the patented drugs."

"Correct."

"That's blackmail."

"Correct."

The minister and I exchanged a long look. "So," I said with a nervous smile, "tell me the good news." Mena brought the tips of his fingers together: "The good news is that we shall have to shape up."

"Who's we?"

"The Africans. Once we obtain the drugs we shall find ourselves in the unenviable position of having to deliver them to non-existent hospitals though non-existent channels. We have a skeleton of a system in place."

"I know."

"That will be our challenge, and we will meet it. But first, the drugs. First, the drugs." He had a strange look, as if he'd been pulled out of a bar by a drunk spoiling for a fight and, having resigned himself to violence, could no longer hide the pleasure the brawl afforded him. "So what's next?"

Mena lit another cigarette: "The part I have been waiting for. Please press play. A statement, in the morning, to the effect that the government of Kenya interrupts all dialogue with the pharmaceutical industry and issues a series of compulsory licenses allowing local manufacturers to copy patented formulas in order to produce anti-retroviral drugs here, in this country, at a fraction of the cost." I thought about it for a second. "You've got the people?" Mena gave me a slow smile. "We've got the people."

I was at the door when Julius Mena said: "You realize the implications."

I swung around. "Sorry?"

"I said, you realize the implications. There will be a shortage. We will be out of anti-retroviral drugs for some time."

"I understand," I said, understanding nothing.

"There will be a countrywide shortage."

"I get it."

"How will Mercy live?"

Our eyes locked. "I'll go to Uganda or something."

"Will Mercy let you?" Julius Mena asked.

And I knew then that she would not.

14

I REMEMBER ONCE, COMING HOME from an assignment. Mercy had been around for two, maybe three months. I was desperate for a glass of wine but all I found were cheap plastic cups and no sign of the fine crystal I'd hand-carried all the way from Rome. "What's this shit?" I'd asked Mercy, lifting a plastic cup.

"*Ahi!* Why you are always using bad words?"

"Where are the other glasses?"

"I have removed them."

"Why?"

"You are breaking them too much! You come from these bad places and things are always falling from your hands. Now me, I can see these things are expensive. Let us wait a few days."

"For what?"

"For your hands to be still."

And so that day, after leaving Mena's office, Mercy knew immediately something was wrong because I picked up a glass and watched it slip from my hand in slow motion. I watched it fall. I watched it hit the ground. I watched it shatter into a million peaces. "Felicity!" Mercy barked. "Remove the glasses! Bring the plastic cups!" Turning to me she said: "Where are you coming from?"

I left her standing in the kitchen. I climbed the stairs, closed the door to my room and sat on the bed. She would let herself die. A month, maybe two, and she'd be one more body in the ground.

Grief works like a knife, it slices past intellect, past reason. But first it stuns you, it makes you hollow, stuffs you with nothing. I had to lie down, so strong was the feeling of weightlessness, so hard and deep the impression of buoyancy. I'd levitate in defiance of gravity; not even the ceiling would keep me from slipping out of orbit.

I did not hear her come in, I did not hear a sound. I felt her weight on the bed and then a sharp release of breath. "That bastard," I said.

"Mena?"

"He'll watch you die without moving a muscle. Tomorrow he puts out a statement boycotting the pharmaceutical industry. You know what that means?"

Mercy smiled—a small indulgent smile. "That is now what I was trying to explain: we shall be having no drugs."

"In Kenya, Mercy. In Kenya. But I can go to Uganda. Or Tanzania. Or Switzerland. Or the North Pole." She began to shake her head. "Listen to me, Mercy. I beg you to listen to me. Mena is a politician. He doesn't care, that's the way politicians are. You must not let him. What do you think will happen when you're dead? You think the movement will survive? You think they'll go on without you? Forget it. You said it yourself: they're like chickens. Think about it, Mercy!

Who will replace you? Give me one name! Emily? She's half-dead. Christine? She talks, nobody listens. Meredith? Meredith is good with details but the big picture is totally beyond her. Agatha? You may as well put Felicity in charge. Think, Mercy, think! They haven't got the balls! They haven't got the spine! You're the spine! You're the brain! Don't let this happen. Please don't let this happen."

Mercy let a few seconds pass. Softly she said: "You know what I am hearing? I am hearing, 'Mercy, please don't leave me alone.'" I grabbed my head with both hands but she reached and pulled one hand away so that I could watch her say: "I am hearing a child speaking from the fear inside. A child. And me, I was telling everyone Anna had become like the big people in this world."

"Mercy, I beg you. I beg you with everything I have. Don't do this."

Again she smiled. "'People shall laugh at me! I shall laugh at myself!'"

I yanked my hand away. "Okay, go then! Go! But if you go, if you die, I don't want to be around for any of it anymore. I'm going too, man. I'm not sticking around for this shit!"

"*Ahi*!" Mercy cried. "Now that is blackmail!"

"Yeah," I snapped. "It's blackmail: what are you going to do about it?"

"I think," she said, "we shall be calling Father Anselmo."

He came the next day and I could have murdered him, standing there with his sharp eyes. "There is no kindness in you!" I screamed. "You *talk* of love but there's no love in you! You're like a knife, you cut through human emotions as if they were nothing. Nothing!"

"Are you finished?"

"No, I'm not. You're like that piece of shit Mena. Neither of you will *blink* when Mercy gets put into the ground. The *mission*, you say, the mission! What mission? It's all going to hell after she dies!"

"Are you finished?"

"Fuck you," I said, and left.

I called Kez from the car. "Meet me at Ollie's."

He was sitting at the bar when I walked in—his face horribly cut up. "Jesus, what happened?"

"I got into a fight."

"Who with?"

"A truck disguised as a Texan. Sit down."

I pulled out a stool. "I need a drink."

"I thought you stopped."

"Not today. Today I drink until I don't know who I am or where I came from."

"Good. What can I get you?"

"Aaaahhh, " I started to say but my eyes filled with tears. "Mercy is going to die," I said.

"It's what I hear," Kez said.

I turned: "You talked to her?"

"Mena put out a statement."

"Right. Of course. This morning at nine."

"We got it yesterday, embargoed to today."

I looked at his cuts. "So you went out last night and picked a fight."

"You could say that."

"Oh, Kez. How?"

"I went up to the biggest motherfucker at the bar, grabbed his glass, and spat in his beer."

"You did not."

"I'm afraid I did."

We looked at each other and I don't know what it was in those long Mediterranean eyes that nailed me to the truth of things. Maybe the acceptance I saw; more likely it was the sadness, something trembling wildly below the fixity. I'd seen it there after Michael's death, after that initial sting of madness in New York. There he was again, staring down the same hole, but for some reason calm. "Why are you so calm?"

"I know her," he said. "I can jump and scream all I want, it's not going to make her change her mind. It's only going to make things harder for her."

For a second I saw nothing. Then I touched my forehead to the counter and let out a low moan. "Oh Jesus."

"What?"

"Oh God."

"What?"

"I have to go."

They were both by the pool. Father Anselmo had uncharacteristically, and disturbingly for someone so thin, stripped to his undershirt. He lay in lizard lounge mode with his eyes closed, legs crossed, one arm folded under his head. Mercy was sitting close by, her back straight, her arms folded, her legs up on her chair. She watched me approach, Sphinx-like once more. I lowered myself into the seat next to her; Father Anselmo did not stir. "I'm sorry," I said.

She tilted her head. "You shall not be killing yourself?"

"I shall be doing whatever you want me to do."

She gave me a deep nod. Looking into the distance she said: "Me, I am troubled for my children. Can you be looking after them?"

"Yes."

"Maybe we can be arranging some ... *nini* ... some schooling in America for the oldest one."

"James?"

"James," nodded Mercy. "He is the one who is sharp."

"*Sawa*," I said.

"*Sawa*," she said, closing her eyes: "Now me, I can just relax."

Father Anselmo sprang up, a Jack-in-the-box. Rubbing his hands he said: "I think it's time for lunch."

Mercy touched my arm. "Tell Felicity to prepare."

I stood up. The priest was looking at me with glittering eyes. "I'm sorry," I whispered, "I did not mean to insult you."

He slapped his thighs: "No apologies needed! I never take things personally."

"Still."

"Still nothing. It's over and done with. We've got a few hard weeks ahead of us, Anna. I've decided to move in, to make sure this doesn't *desinit in piscem*."

"What?" I asked weakly.

Father Anselmo pulled his shirt over his neck. "You know Latin, don't you?"

"No."

His face fell: "You don't? Good God! What are they teaching in Italian schools these days? *Desinit in Piscem*! *Piscem*! For something to end inconclusively, amorphously. Latin." He looked at me, a gleam of hope in his eyes.

"Not a word," I said and he sat down.

I looked over at Mercy but her eyes were still shut.

15

THE MOVEMENT REACTED LIKE I did; after the initial shock came a deeply irrational response, a collective descent into pure emotion. First, the committee leaders threatened Mercy with their resignation; she talked to them privately over the course of five days, devoting one day to each, until, at the end of the week they were able to come together and announce to the assembly that they would do nothing to compromise the momentum of the movement.

Next, the assembly came together and voted unanimously to dissolve as a body unless Mercy could prove, beyond reasonable doubt, that she was taking her medicines. "We shall not be satisfied until we can be seeing the swallowing of pills," a representative of the assembly read from her notes. "We can be gathering for the purpose of watching the swallowing of pills in this very room at six and eleven in the morning, and at three and seven in the afternoon. Nothing else, we repeat, nothing else shall be considered satisfactory by this assembly." The room erupted into applause as Mercy looked sadly on. She had already stopped. She had given me her month's supply and asked me to keep it for when the battle was won and Kenya awash with affordable drugs. "Choose a child," she had said. "A girl. Sharp. Like me. She can be getting started on these."

That day, in front of the assembly, Mercy rose slowly from her seat—the virus had already gained ground—and asked for a glass of water. She drank from it in small sips, catching her breath between each one. Someone started sobbing. Mercy handed me the glass. "No," she said. "This is not the way. This movement shall be finished if we cannot be keeping the strength inside of us." She looked around her. "Who will forgive us then? Will our children forgive us after we have left them there to die? Will our grandchildren, the few who will be left, when they find what we have wasted, what we have thrown out like dirty water?" A hush came over the room. "No one will forgive us. No one. Even me, I will not forgive us. Please, Anna," she said, "help me with a chair." I brought a chair over. Mercy sat down. "Now," she said, "We know each other. We have been spending time together. We have had disagreements but together we have marched on Parliament *and* State House! Us! The women of Korogocho and Kibera! The women of Mathare, Kawangware, and Kamakunji! The women of the slums! The women of this place they called Kenya. All of us! Together!" Applause broke out.

"Now, me, I have a story to tell. Me and Anna, we have been staying together longer." I grew stiff in my corner but Mercy turned and gave me one of her new smiles: slow to start and slow to end. "Anna and me, we had a friend. His name was Michael. He was a journalist, like

Anna. He was killed in the war in Sierra Leone. The day Michael died, Anna told me he was dead because the African tribes were having no respect. And so, me, I feared for our movement because I knew she was right." She held out her hand. I took it briefly, tears streaming freely down my face.

"Now us, we have come together and there have been no tribes. No tribes, no sub-tribes, no sub-sub-tribes. Nothing. There have been women with children. *Bas*. Women with children. We have left the men standing outside because the time is little." Laughter rippled from the back to the front of the room. Mercy looked around her and shouted: "The time is little! You think you can be letting the movement collapse and something new can be coming to replace it? Nothing shall come to replace what we have built! Nothing! There shall be tribes and there shall be problems, and my life, *my life*," Mercy raised her palms, "my life will come to nothing. Thrown out. Like dirty water."

Silence fell until Felicity, who had been crouching in a corner, stood up and said: "Please, Mercy, we are still not getting why you cannot be taking the drugs."

"Yes!" someone shouted. "Felicity is right!"

Mercy laughed. "Felicity! Come here!" Felicity inched bashfully closer. "It is simple: If seven hundred people can be dying in this country every day because there are no drugs, how can I be the only one living? If Julius Mena can be telling the drug companies that they are *killing us* with their prices, how can I be going outside our country and paying the price that is killing us just because *you* cannot be taking control of the movement?" Mercy shook her head. "Me, I cannot be doing such a thing. I can be doing many other things, but not this one. Not this one. You can be getting used to this fact, all of you."

Felicity brought a quivering hand to her mouth. In the front row, a woman broke into such violent sobbing that Mercy ordered her out of the room. "I shall be expelling people who cannot be keeping quiet!" she thundered. "I shall be expelling them not from the room, I shall be expelling them from the movement!"

It took days. Days. Every morning Mercy took her seat by the door and waited for the women to start talking. They talked, and though Mercy did little more than listen, a sense began to emerge of future possibilities, something in its infancy which might one day be able to stand on its own.

We all met in the kitchen for lunch, Mercy, Father Anselmo, Kez, and I then one day Mercy asked me to help her up the stairs. "You're not having lunch?" I asked.

She shook her head. "Help me with the bedcovers," she whispered, and from that moment on, she never went downstairs again.

James came to the house with Lucy, who sat on Felicity's lap and gorged herself on *chapatti* as the two of us climbed the stairs to the second floor. "Come," Mercy told her son, and he went to her stiffly, his hands folded awkwardly before him. "You are going to America with Anna," Mercy said. The boy gave an obedient nod. "You will be getting your degree and helping your family with the money you will be earning there." Again, he nodded and Mercy's eyes filled with tears. "My son," she whispered.

She died so quickly after that. The weaker she got, the calmer, the more composed her face became. Just before she died, one or two days before, her skin acquired a strange luminosity, as if dipped in gold. Several of the women asked if they could see it for themselves. Father Anselmo told them they could, and so word of Mercy's transfiguration spread like fire, spilling out of the house and down the city's streets, into the farthest corners of the slums.

At noon on the first day of the New Year, Father Anselmo made a sign for me to go upstairs. Together we slipped quietly into Mercy's room. "God be with you," the priest said.

"Also with you," Mercy whispered, struggling to sit up. Father Anselmo took out his breviary. Chest heaving, muscles tensed, Mercy leaned her head against the wall and closed her eyes.

"I am the Lord of the oceans," the priest read, "I am the dust beneath your feet ..."

I don't know who noticed it first, him or me. All I remember is Father Anselmo letting go of his breviary and burying his face in his hands. And this, I remember this: Mercy's face composing itself into a vision of such peace, such beauty that my hands flew to my mouth and I began to cry.

People came and went.

Three days later, the red earth received her.

"Though I have mastered the tongues of men and angels, and have not mercy, I am like sounding brass or clashing cymbal. And though I have the gift of prophecy and understand all mysteries, and possess all knowledge, and have faith enough to move mountains, and have not mercy, I am nothing. And though I give all my goods to feed the poor and give my body to be burned, and have not mercy, I am nothing."

Corinthians XIII

Acknowledgments

For the character of Father Anselmo I am indebted in equal measure to the writings of Fr. Anthony De Mello and to the mission of Fr. Alex Zanutelli, who served the poor in a slum for more than ten years. For the description of evil as "aporia," roadlessness, I am indebted to Elaine Pagels and her "Gnostic Gospels."

Special thanks to my agent, Elaine Markson, and to my editor Rosemary Ahern. Thanks also to Susan Linnee, Allegra Huston, and Jacqueline Richard.